The Rupa Book of
Great Suspense Stories

Other books by Ruskin Bond:

Ghost Stories from the Raj
The Rupa Book of Great Animal Stories
The Rupa Book of True Tales of Mystery and Adventure
The Rupa Book of Ruskin Bond's Himalayan Tales
Ruskin Bond's Children's Omnibus
Angry River
Hanuman to the Rescue
A Long Walk for Bina
The Blue Umbrella
Strange Men, Strange Places
The Road to the Bazaar

The Rupa Book of
Great Suspense Stories

Edited by
Ruskin Bond

Rupa & Co

Published by

Rupa & Co

7/16, Ansari Road, Daryaganj,
New Delhi 110 002

Sales Centres:

Allahabad Bangalore Chandigarh Chennai
Hyderabad Jaipur Kathmandu
Kolkata Mumbai Pune

Typeset in 11 pts. Classical Garamond by
Nikita Overseas Pvt Ltd.
1410 Chiranjiv Tower
43 Nehru Place
New Delhi 110 019

Printed in India by
Rekha Printers Pvt Ltd.
A-102/1 Okhla Industrial Area, Phase-II
New Delhi-110 020

Contents

Introduction

*I*n one of the stories in this collection, *The Road to the Shore*, the narrator remarks: "...the unseen danger is the father and mother of suspense, and suspense is a dangerous emotion." This is as good a definition as any of the best kind of suspense story, in which unseen dangers lie ahead for the protagonists in the story as well as for the emotions of the reader.

A good suspense story does not date. This is because, to be successful, to really grip the attention of the reader, it stretches the story-teller's skills to the limit. It *has* to be a good story, well-told, different, carrying the reader forward with every sentence, every tick of the clock.

If you look at any anthology of great "thrillers", you will find the work of the old masters well represented. Dickens, Marryat, Wilkie Collins, Nathaniel Hawthorne, Poe, M.R. James, H.G. Wells....the list is endless. And many of these writers are better known today for their short tales of mystery and suspense than they are for more scholarly or ambitious works. I have not met anyone who has read F. Marion Crawford's novels (if, indeed, they can be located), but no anthology is complete without his story *The Upper Berth*. H.G. Wells and Conan Doyle wrote many voluminous novels, but today we read Wells for his tales of fantasy and science fiction and Doyle for his detective stories. W.W. Jacobs wrote hundreds of humorous sea stories, seldom read now; his few tales of terror continue to enthral.

A good suspense story is not necessarily a crime or horror story. In his account of a duel, Wilkie Collins builds up the suspense without any seeming effort. A.A. Beldon, in his sea story, creates suspense out of an unlucky ship that proves difficult to handle. And Alice Perrin creates a tale of horror out of a woman's obsessive fear of snakes. The natural world poses a very real threat in the story by Carl Stephenson, a German who for many years made a living from driving a taxi before his stories brought him fame.

This anthology opens with one of my favourite stories of suspense, *The Lodger,* by Marie Belloc Lowndes (the sister of the poet and essayist, Hilaire Belloc). It takes me back to the fog-bound London I knew in the early 1950s, when as a young man I tramped all over the East End in search of colour, incident and the exotic; for I had grown up on Dickens, W.W. Jacobs, Edgar Wallace and other writers who found mystery and adventure in the old dockland. *The Lodger*, of course, belongs to turn-of-century London, to those foggy, gas-lit streets where Jack the Ripper pursued his victims. In her story, Mrs. Lowndes builds up the suspense in the lives of a humdrum East End couple who let out rooms to an eccentric stranger. Gradually it dawns on them that he might be the homicidal maniac who is stalking the streets of Whitechapel. The suspense is created through suggestion and a growing sense of disquiet. The story caught the attention of the young Alfred Hitchcock, whose very first film, a silent made in 1926, was based on it. It was remade as a talkie in 1932 and again in 1944. This last version I saw as a schoolboy, and it turned me into a fan of the suspense story, both on and off the screen.

Foggy, gas-lit London of the early 1900s was the perfect setting for tales of mystery and suspense. *The Ivory God* and *The Beast With Five Fingers* are two stories from that period. The sea, the Borneo jungle, the Indian sub-continent, and the Brazilian wilderness, provide the background for some of the other stories. And who says suspense and humour don't mix? In *Miss Bracegirdle Does Her Duty,* the charming and witty Stacy Aumonier entertains us with his account of the terrible experience of a maiden lady on her first trip abroad—and the sensational scandal she only just avoided.

Ruskin Bond
March, 2003

The Lodger

"There he is at last, and I'm glad of it, Ellen. 'Tain't a night you would wish a dog to be out in."

Mr. Bunting's voice was full of unmistakable relief. He was close to the fire, sitting back in a deep leather armchair—a clean-shaven, dapper man, still in outward appearance what he had been so long, and now no longer was—a self-respecting butler.

"You needn't feel so nervous about him; Mr. Sleuth can look out for himself, all right." Mrs. Bunting spoke in a dry, rather tart tone. She was less emotional, better balanced, than was her husband. On her the marks of past servitude were less apparent, but they were there all the same—especially in her neat black stuff dress and scrupulously clean, plain collar and cuffs. Mrs. Bunting, as a single woman, had been for long years what is known as a useful maid.

"I can't think why he wants to go out in such weather. He did it in last week's fog, too," Bunting went on complaining.

"Well, it's none of your business—now, is it?"

"No; that's true enough. Still, 'twould be a very bad thing for us if anything happened to him. This lodger's the first bit of luck we've had for a very long time."

Mrs. Bunting made no answer to this remark. It was too obviously true to be worth answering. Also she was listening—following in imagination her lodger's quick, singularly quiet—"stealthy," she called it to herself—progress through the dark, fog-filled hall and up the staircase.

"It isn't safe for decent folk to be out in such weather—not unless they have something to do that won't wait till tomorrow." Bunting had at last turned round. He was now looking straight into his wife's narrow, colorless face; he was an obstinate man, and liked to prove himself right. "I read you out the accidents in *Lloyd's* yesterday—shocking, they were, and all brought about by the fog! And then, that 'orrid monster at his work again—"

"Monster?" repeated Mrs. Bunting absently. She was trying to hear the lodger's footsteps overhead; but her husband went on as if there had been no interruption:

"It wouldn't be very pleasant to run up against such a party as that in the fog, eh?"

"What stuff you do talk!" she said sharply; and then she got up suddenly. Her husband's remark had disturbed her. She hated to think of such things as the terrible series of murders that were just then horrifying and exciting the nether world of London. Though she enjoyed pathos and sentiment—Mrs. Bunting would listen with mild amusement to the details of a breach-of-promise action, —she shrank from stories of either immorality or physical violence.

Mrs. Bunting got up from the straight-backed chair on which she had been sitting. It would soon be time for supper.

She moved about the sitting-room, flecking off an imperceptible touch of dust here, straightening a piece of furniture there.

Bunting looked around once or twice. He would have liked to ask Ellen to leave off fidgeting, but he was mild and fond of peace, so he refrained. However, she soon gave over what irritated him of her own accord.

But even then Mrs. Bunting did not at once go down to the cold kitchen, where everything was in readiness for her simple cooking. Instead, she opened the door leading into the bedroom behind, and there, closing the door quietly, stepped back into the darkness and stood motionless, listening.

At first she heard nothing, but gradually there came the sound of some one moving about in the room just overhead; try as she might, however, it was impossible for her to guess what her lodger was doing. At last she heard him open the door leading out on the landing. That meant that he would spend the rest of the evening in the rather cheerless room above the drawing-room floor—oddly enough, he liked sitting there best, though the only warmth obtainable was from a gas-stove fed by a shilling-in-the-slot arrangement.

It was indeed true that Mr. Sleuth had brought the Buntings luck, for at the time he had taken their rooms it had been touch and go with them.

After having each separately led the sheltered, impersonal, and, above all, the financially easy existence that is the compensation life offers to those men and women who deliberately take upon themselves the yoke of domestic service, these two, butler and useful maid, had suddenly, in middle age, determined to join their fortunes and savings.

Bunting was a widower; he had one pretty daughter, a girl of seventeen, who now lived, as had been the case ever since the death of her mother, with a prosperous aunt. His second wife had been reared in the Foundling Hospital, but she had gradually worked her way up into the higher ranks of the servant class and as useful maid she had saved quite a tidy sum of money.

Unluckily, misfortune had dogged Mr. and Mrs. Bunting from the very first. The seaside place where they had begun by taking a lodging-house became the scene of an epidemic. Then had followed a business experiment which had proved disastrous. But before going back into service, either together or separately, they had made up their minds to make one last effort, and, with the little money that remained to them, they had taken over the lease of a small house in the Marylebone Road.

Bunting, whose appearance was very good, had retained a connection with old employers and their friends, so he occasionally got a good job as waiter. During this last month his jobs had perceptibly increased in number and in profit; Mrs. Bunting was not superstitious, but it seemed that in this matter, as in everything else, Mr. Sleuth, their new lodger, had brought them luck.

As she stood there, still listening intently in the darkness of the bedroom, she told herself, not for the first time, what Mr. Sleuth's departure would mean to her and Bunting. It would almost certainly mean ruin.

Luckily, the lodger seemed entirely pleased both with the rooms and with his landlady. There was really no reason why he should ever leave such nice lodgings. Mrs. Bunting shook off her vague sense of apprehension and unease. She turned round, took a step forward, and, feeling for the handle of the door giving into the passage, she opened it, and went down with light, firm steps into the kitchen.

She lit the gas and put a frying-pan on the stove, and then once more her mind reverted, as if in spite of herself, to her lodger, and there came back to Mrs. Bunting, very vividly, the memory of all that had happened the day Mr. Sleuth had taken her rooms.

The date of this excellent lodger's coming had been the twenty-ninth of December, and the time late afternoon. She and Bunting had been sitting, gloomily enough over their small banked-up fire. They had dined in the middle of the day—he on a couple of sausages, she on a little cold ham. They were utterly out of heart, each trying to pluck up courage to tell the other that it was no use trying any more. The two had also had a little tiff on that dreary afternoon. A newspaper-seller had come yelling down the Marylebone Road, shouting out, "'Orrible murder in Whitechapel!" and just because Bunting had an old uncle living in the East End he had gone and bought a paper, and at a time, too, when every penny, nay, every half-penny, had its full value! Mrs. Bunting remembered the circumstances because that murder in Whitechapel had been the first of these terrible crimes—there had been four since—which she would never allow Bunting to discuss in her presence, and yet which had of late begun to interest curiously, uncomfortably, ever her refined mind.

But, to return to the lodger. It was then, on that dreary afternoon, that suddenly there had come to the front door a tremulous, uncertain double knock.

Bunting ought to have got up, but he had gone on reading the paper and so Mrs. Bunting, with the woman's greater courage, had gone out into the passage, turned up the gas, and opened the door to see who it could be. She remembered, as if it were yesterday instead of nigh on a month ago, Mr. Sleuth's peculiar appearance. Tall, dark, lanky, an old-fashioned top hat concealing his high bald forehead, he had stood there, an odd figure of a man, blinking at her.

"I believe—is it not a fact that you let lodgings?" he had asked in a hesitating, whistling voice, a voice that she had known in a moment to be that of an educated man—of a gentleman. As he had stepped into the hall, she had noticed that in his right hand he held a narrow bag—a quite new bag of strong brown leather.

Everything had been settled in less than a quarter of an hour. Mr. Sleuth had at once "taken" to the drawing-room floor, and then, as Mrs. Bunting eagerly lit the gas in the front room above, he had looked around him and said, rubbing his hands with a nervous movement, "Capital—capital! This is just what I've been looking for!"

The sink had specially pleased him—the sink and the gas-stove. "This is quite first-rate!" he had exclaimed, "for I make all sorts of experiments. I am, you must understand, Mrs. —er—Bunting, a man of science." Then he had sat down—suddenly. "I'm very tired," he had said in a low tone, "very tired indeed! I have been walking about all day."

From the very first the lodger's manner had been odd, sometimes distant and abrupt, and then, for no reason at all that she could see, confidential and plaintively confiding. But Mrs. Bunting was aware that eccentricity has always been a perquisite, as it were the special luxury, of the well born and well educated. Scholars and such-like are never quite like other people.

And then, this particular gentleman had proved himself so eminently satisfactory as to the one thing that really matters to those who let lodgings. "My name is Sleuth," he said, "S-l-e-u-t-h. Think of a hound, Mrs. Bunting, and you'll never forget my name. I could give you references," he had added, giving her, as she now remembered, a funny sidewise look, "but I prefer to dispense with them. How much did you say? Twenty-three shillings a week, with attendance? Yes, that will suit me perfectly; and I'll begin by paying my first month's rent in advance. Now, four times twenty-three shillings is" —he looked at Mrs. Bunting, and for the first time he smiled, a queer, wry smile—"ninety-two shillings."

He had taken a handful of sovereigns out of his pocket and put them down on the table. "Look here," he had said, "there's five pounds; and you can keep the change, for I shall want you to do a little shopping for me tomorrow."

After he had been in the house about an hour, the bell had rung, and the new lodger had asked Mrs. Bunting if she could oblige him with the loan of a Bible. She brought up to him her best Bible, the one that had been given to her as a wedding present by a lady with whose mother she had lived for several years. This Bible and one other book, of which the odd name was Cruden's Concordance, formed Mr. Sleuth's only reading: he spent hours each day poring over the Old Testament and over the volume which Mrs. Bunting had at last decided to be a queer kind of index to the Book.

However, to return to the lodger's first arrival. He had had no luggage with him, barring the small brown bag, but very soon parcels had begun to arrive addressed to Mr. Sleuth, and it was then that Mrs. Bunting first became curious. These parcels were full of clothes; but it was quite clear to the landlady's feminine eye that none of these clothes had been made for Mr. Sleuth. They were, in fact, second-hand clothes, bought at good second-hand places, each marked, when marked at all, with a different name. And the really extraordinary thing was that occasionally a complete suit disappeared—became, as it were, obliterated from the lodger's wardrobe.

As for the bag he had brought with him, Mrs. Bunting had never caught sight of it again. And this also was certainly very strange.

Mrs. Bunting thought a great deal about that bag. She often wondered what had been in it; not a nightshirt and comb and brush, as she had at first supposed, for Mr. Sleuth had asked her to go out and buy him a brush and comb and tooth-brush the morning after his arrival. That fact was specially impressed on her memory, for at the little shop, a barber's, where she had purchased the brush and comb, the foreigner who had served her had insisted on telling her some of the horrible details of the murder that had taken place the day before in Whitechapel, and it had upset her very much.

As to where the bag was now, it was probably locked up in the lower part of a chiffonnier in the front sitting-room. Mr. Sleuth evidently always carried the key of the little cupboard on his person, for Mrs. Bunting, though she looked well for it, had never been able to find it.

And yet, never was there a more confiding or trusting gentleman. The first four days that he had been with them he had allowed his money—the considerable sum of one hundred and eighty-four pounds in gold—to lie about wrapped up in pieces of paper on his dressing-table. This was a very foolish, indeed a wrong thing to do, as she had allowed herself respectfully to point out to him; but as only answer he had laughed, a loud, discordant shout of laughter.

Mr. Sleuth had many other odd ways; but Mrs. Bunting, a true woman in spite of her prim manner and love of order, had an infinite patience with masculine vagaries.

On the first morning of Mr. Sleuth's stay in the Buntings' house, while Mrs. Bunting was out buying things for him, the new lodger had turned most of the pictures and photographs hanging in his sitting-room with their faces to the wall! But this queer action on Mr. Sleuth's part had not surprised Mrs. Bunting as much as it might have done; it recalled an incident of her long-past youth—something that had happened a matter of twenty years ago, at a time when Mrs. Bunting, then the still youthful Ellen Cottrell, had been maid to an old lady. The old lady had a favorite nephew, a bright, jolly young gentleman who had been learning to paint animals in Paris; and it was he who had had the impudence, early one summer morning, to turn to the wall six beautiful engravings of paintings done by the famous Mr. Landseer! The old lady thought the world of those pictures, but her nephew, as only excuse for the extraordinary thing he had done, had observed that "they put his eye out."

Mr. Sleuth's excuse had been much the same; for, when Mrs. Bunting had come into his sitting-room and found all her pictures, or at any rate all those of her pictures that happened to be portraits of ladies, with their faces to the wall, he had offered as only explanation, "Those women's eyes follow me about."

Mrs. Bunting had gradually become aware that Mr. Sleuth had a fear and dislike of women. When she was "doing" the staircase and landing, she often heard him reading bits of the Bible aloud to himself, and in the majority of instances the texts he chose contained uncomplimentary reference to her own sex. Only to-day she had stopped and listened while he uttered threateningly the awful words, "A strange woman is a narrow pit. She also lieth in wait as for a prey, and increaseth the transgressors among men." There had been a pause, and then had come, in a high singsong, "Her house is the way to hell, going down to the chambers of death." It had made Mrs. Bunting feel quite queer.

The lodger's daily habits were also peculiar. He stayed in bed all the morning, and sometimes part of the afternoon, and he never went out before the street lamps were alight. Then, there was his dislike of an open fire; he generally sat in the top front room, and while there he always used the large gas-stove, not only for his experiments, which he carried on at night, but also in the daytime, for warmth.

But there! Where was the use of worrying about the lodger's funny ways? Of course, Mr. Sleuth was eccentric; if he hadn't been "just a leetle 'touched' upstairs"—as Bunting had once described it—he wouldn't be their lodger now; he would be living in a quite different sort of way with some of his relations, or with a friend of his own class.

Mrs. Bunting, while these thoughts galloped disconnectedly through her brain, went on with her cooking, doing everything with a certain delicate and cleanly precision.

While in the middle of making the toast on which was to be poured some melted cheese, she suddenly heard a noise, or rather a series of noises. Shuffling, hesitating steps were creaking down the house above. She looked up and listened. Surely Mr. Sleuth was not going out again into the cold, foggy night? But no; for the sounds did not continue down the passage leading to the front door.

The heavy steps were coming slowly down the kitchen stairs. Nearer and nearer came the thudding sounds, and Mrs. Bunting's heart began to beat as if in response. She put out the gas-stove, unheedful of the fact that the cheese would stiffen and spoil in the cold air; and then she turned and faced the door. There was a fumbling at the handle, and a moment later the door opened and revealed, as she had known it would, her lodger.

Mr. Sleuth was clad in a plaid dressing-gown, and in his hand was a candle. When he saw the lit-up kitchen, and the woman standing in it, he looked inexplicably taken aback, almost aghast.

"Yes, sir? What can I do for you, sir? I hope you didn't ring, sir?" Mrs. Bunting did not come forward to meet her lodger;

instead, she held her ground in front of the stove. Mr. Sleuth had no business to come down like this into her kitchen.

"No, I—I didn't ring," he stammered; "I didn't know you were down here, Mrs. Bunting. Please excuse my costume. The truth is, my gas-stove has gone wrong, or, rather, that shilling-in-the-slot arrangement has done so. I came down to see if *you* had a gas-stove. I am going to ask leave to use it to-night for an experiment I want to make."

Mrs. Bunting felt troubled—oddly, unnaturally troubled. Why couldn't the lodger's experiment wait till to-morrow? "Oh, certainly, sir; but you will find it very cold down here." She looked round her dubiously.

"It seems most pleasantly warm," he observed, "warm and cozy after my cold room upstairs."

"Won't you let me make you a fire?" Mrs. Bunting's housewifely instincts were roused. "Do let me make you a fire in your bedroom, sir; I'm sure you ought to have one there these cold nights."

"By no means—I mean, I would prefer not. I do not like an open fire, Mrs. Bunting." He frowned, and still stood, a strange-looking figure, just inside the kitchen door.

"Do you want to use this stove now, sir? Is there anything I can do to help you?"

"No, not now—thank you all the same, Mrs. Bunting. I shall come down later, altogether later—probably after you and your husband have gone to bed. But I should be much obliged if you would see that the gas people come tomorrow and put my stove in order."

"Perhaps Bunting could put it right for you, sir. I'll ask him to go up."

"No, no—I don't want anything of that sort done to-night. Besides, he couldn't put it right. The cause of the trouble is quite simple. The machine is choked up with shillings: a foolish plan, so I have always felt it to be."

Mr. Sleuth spoke very pettishly, with far more heat than he was wont to speak; but Mrs. Bunting sympathized with him. She had always suspected those slot-machines to be as dishonest as if they were human. It was dreadful, the way they swallowed up the shillings!

As if he were divining her thoughts, Mr. Sleuth, walking forward, stared up at the kitchen slot-machine. "Is it nearly full?" he asked abruptly. "I expect my experiment will take some time, Mrs. Bunting."

"Oh, no, sir; there's plenty of room for shillings there still. We don't use our stove as much as you do yours, sir. I'm never in the kitchen a minute longer than I can help this cold weather."

And then, with him preceding her, Mrs. Bunting and her lodger made a slow progress to the ground floor. There Mr. Sleuth courteously bade his landlady good night, and proceeded upstairs to his own apartments.

Mrs. Bunting again went down into her kitchen, again she lit the stove, and again she cooked the toasted cheese. But she felt unnerved, afraid of she knew not what. The place seemed to her alive with alien presences, and once she caught herself listening, which was absurd, for of course she could not hope to hear what her lodger was doing two, if not three, flights upstairs. She had never been able to discover what Mr. Sleuth's experiments really were; all she knew was that they required a very high degree of heat.

The Buntings went to bed early that night. But Mrs. Bunting intended to stay awake. She wanted to know at what hour of the night her lodger would come down into the kitchen, and, above all, she was anxious as to how long he would stay there. But she had had a long day, and presently she fell asleep.

The church clock hard by struck two in the morning, and suddenly Mrs. Bunting awoke. She felt sharply annoyed with herself. How could she have dropped off like that? Mr. Sleuth must have been down and up again hours ago.

Then, gradually, she became aware of a faint acrid odor; elusive, almost intangible, it yet seemed to encompass her and the snoring man by her side almost as a vapor might have done.

Mrs. Bunting sat up in bed and sniffed; and then, in spite of the cold, she quietly crept out of the nice, warm bedclothes and crawled along to the bottom of the bed. There Mr. Sleuth's landlady did a very curious thing; she leaned over the brass rail and put her face close to the hinge of the door. Yes, it was from there that this strange, horrible odor was coming; the smell must be very strong in the passage. Mrs. Bunting thought she knew now what became of those suits of clothes of Mr. Sleuth's that disappeared.

As she crept back, shivering, under the bedclothes, she longed to give her sleeping husband a good shake, and in fancy she heard herself saying: "Bunting, get up! There is something strange going on downstairs that we ought to know about."

But Mr. Sleuth's landlady, as she lay by her husband's side, listening with painful intentness, knew very well that she would do nothing of the sort. The lodger had a right to destroy his clothes by burning if the fancy took him. What if he did make a certain amount of mess, a certain amount of smell, in her nice kitchen? Was he not—was he not such a good lodger! If they did anything to upset him, where could they ever hope to get another like him?

Three o'clock struck before Mrs. Bunting heard slow, heavy steps creaking up her kitchen stairs. But Mr. Sleuth did not go straight up to his own quarters, as she expected him to do. Instead, he went to the front door, and, opening it, put it on the chain. At the end of ten minutes or so he closed the front door, and by that time Mrs. Bunting had divined why the lodger had behaved in this strange fashion—it must have been to get the strong acrid smell of burning wool out of the passage. But Mrs. Bunting felt as if she herself would never get rid of the horrible odor. She felt herself to be all smell.

At last the unhappy woman fell into a deep, troubled sleep; and then she dreamed a most terrible and unnatural dream; hoarse voices seemed to be shouting in her ear, " 'Orrible murder off the Edgeware Road!" Then three words, indistinctly uttered, followed by "—at his work again! Awful details!"

Even in her dream Mrs. Bunting felt angered and impatient; she knew so well why she was being disturbed by this horrid nightmare. It was because of Bunting—Bunting, who insisted on talking to her of those frightful murders, in which only morbid, vulgar-minded people took any interest. Why, even now, in her dream, she could hear her husband speaking to her about it.

"Ellen,"—so she heard Bunting say in her ear,—"Ellen, my dear, I am just going to get up to get a paper. It's after seven o'clock."

Mrs. Bunting sat up in bed. The shouting, nay, worse, the sound of tramping, hurrying feet smote on her ears. It had been no nightmare, then, but something infinitely worse—reality. Why couldn't Bunting have lain quietly in bed awhile longer, and let his poor wife go on dreaming? The most awful dream would have been easier to bear than this awakening.

She heard her husband go to the front door, and, as he bought the paper, exchange a few excited words with the newspaper boy. Then he came back and began silently moving about the room.

"Well!" she cried. "Why don't you tell me about it?"

"I thought you'd rather not hear."

"Of course I like to know what happens close to our own front door!" she snapped out.

And then he read out a piece of the newspaper—only a few lines, after all—telling in brief, unemotional language that the body of a woman, apparently done to death in a peculiarly atrocious fashion some hours before, had been found in a passage leading to a disused warehouse off the Marylebone Road.

"It serves that sort of hussy right!" was Mrs. Bunting's only comment.

When Mrs. Bunting went down into the kitchen, everything there looked just as she had left it, and there was no trace of the acrid smell she had expected to find there. Instead, the cavernous whitewashed room was full of fog, and she noticed that, though the shutters were bolted and barred as she had left them, the windows behind them had been widely opened to the air. She, of course, had left them shut.

She stooped and flung open the oven door of her gas-stove. Yes, it was as she had expected; a fierce heat had been generated there since she had last used the oven, and a mass of black, gluey soot had fallen through to the stone floor below.

Mrs. Bunting took the ham and eggs that she had bought the previous day for her own and Bunting's breakfast, and broiled them over the gas-ring in their sitting-room. Her husband watched her in surprised silence. She had never done such a thing before.

"I couldn't stay down there," she said, "it was so cold and foggy. I thought I'd make breakfast up here, just for to-day."

"Yes," he said kindly; "that's quite right, Ellen. I think you've done quite right, my dear."

But, when it came to the point, his wife could not eat any of the nice breakfast she had got ready; she only had another cup of tea.

"Are you ill?" Bunting asked solicitously.

"No," she said shortly; "of course I'm not ill. Don't be silly! The thought of that horrible thing happening so close by has upset me. Just hark to them, now!"

Through their closed windows penetrated the sound of scurrying feet and loud, ribald laughter. A crowd, nay, a mob, hastened to and from the scene of the murder.

Mrs. Bunting made her husband lock the front gate. "I don't want any of those ghouls in here!" she exclaimed angrily. And then, "What a lot of idle people there must be in the world," she said.

The coming and going went on all day. Mrs. Bunting stayed indoors; Bunting went out. After all, the ex-butler was human— it was natural that he should feel thrilled and excited. All their neighbors were the same. His wife wasn't reasonable about such things. She quarreled with him when he didn't tell her anything, and yet he was sure she would have been angry with him if he had said very much about it.

The lodger's bell rang about two o'clock, and Mrs. Bunting prepared the simple luncheon that was also his breakfast. As she rested the tray a minute on the drawing-room floor landing, she heard Mr. Sleuth's high, quavering voice reading aloud the words:

"She saith to him, Stolen waters are sweet, and bread eaten in secret is pleasant. But he knoweth not that the dead are there; and that her guests are in the depths of hell."

The landlady turned the handle of the door and walked in

with the tray. Mr. Sleuth was sitting close by the window, and Mrs. Bunting's Bible lay open before him. As she came in he hastily closed the Bible and looked down at the crowd walking along the Marylebone Road.

"There seem a great many people out to-day," he observed, without looking round.

"Yes, sir, there do." Mrs. Bunting said nothing more, and offered no other explanation; and the lodger, as he at last turned to his landlady, smiled pleasantly. He had acquired a great liking and respect for this well-behaved, taciturn woman; she was the first person for whom he had felt any such feeling for many years past.

He took a half sovereign out of his waistcoat pocket; Mrs. Bunting noticed that it was not the same waistcoat Mr. Sleuth had been wearing the day before. "Will you please accept this half sovereign for the use of your kitchen last night?" he said. "I made as little mess as I could, but I was carrying on a rather elaborate experiment."

She held out her hand, hesitated, and then took the coin. As she walked down the stairs, the winter sun, a yellow ball hanging in the smoky sky, glinted in on Mrs. Bunting, and lent blood-red gleams, or so it seemed to her, to the piece of gold she was holding in her hand.

It was a very cold night—so cold, so windy, so snow-laden the atmosphere, that every one who could do so stayed indoors. Bunting, however, was on his way home from what had proved a very pleasant job; he had been acting as waiter at a young lady's birthday party, and a remarkable piece of luck had come his way. The young lady had come into a fortune that day, and she had had the gracious, the surprising thought of presenting each of the hired waiters with a sovereign.

This birthday treat had put him in mind of another birthday. His daughter Daisy would be eighteen the following Saturday. Why shouldn't he send her a postal order for half a sovereign, so that she might come up and spend her birthday in London?

Having Daisy for three or four days would cheer up Ellen. Mr. Bunting, slackening his footsteps, began to think with puzzled concern of how queer his wife had seemed lately. She had become so nervous, so "jumpy," that he didn't know what to make of her sometimes. She had never been a really good-tempered woman,— your capable, self-respecting woman seldom is,—but she had never been like what she was now. Of late she sometimes got quite hysterical; he had let fall a sharp word to her the other day, and she had sat down on a chair, thrown her black apron over her face, and burst out sobbing violently.

During the last ten days Ellen had taken to talking in her sleep. "No, no, no!" she had cried out, only the night before. "It isn't true! I won't have it said! It's a lie!" And there had been a wail of horrible fear and revolt in her unusually quiet, mincing voice. Yes, it would certainly be a good thing for her to have Daisy's company for a bit. Whew! It *was* cold; and Bunting had stupidly forgotten his gloves. He put his hands in his pockets to keep them warm.

Suddenly he became aware that Mr. Sleuth, the lodger who seemed to have "turned their luck," as it were, was walking along on the opposite side of the solitary street.

Mr. Sleuth's tall, thin figure was rather bowed, his head bent toward the ground. His right arm was thrust into his long Inverness cape; the other occasionally sawed the air, doubtless in order to help him keep warm. He was walking rather quickly. It was clear that he had not yet become aware of the proximity of his landlord.

Bunting felt pleased to see his lodger; it increased his feeling of general satisfaction. Strange, was it not, that that odd, peculiar-looking figure should have made all the difference to his (Bunting's) and Mrs. Bunting's happiness and comfort in life?

Naturally, Bunting saw far less of the lodger than did Mrs. Bunting. Their gentleman had made it very clear that he did not like either the husband or wife to come up to his rooms without being definitely asked to do so, and Bunting had been up there only once since Mr. Sleuth's arrival five weeks before. This seemed to be a good opportunity for a little genial conversation.

Bunting, still an active man for his years, crossed the road, and, stepping briskly forward, tried to overtake Mr. Sleuth; but the more he hurried, the more the other hastened, and that without even turning to see whose steps he heard echoing behind him on the now freezing pavement.

Mr. Sleuth's own footsteps were quite inaudible—an odd circumstance, when you came to think of it, as Bunting did think of it later, lying awake by Ellen's side in the pitch-darkness. What it meant was, of course, that the lodger had rubber soles on his shoes.

The two men, the pursued and the pursuer, at last turned into the Marylebone Road. They were now within a hundred yards of home; and so, plucking up courage, Bunting called out, his voice echoing freshly on the still air:

"Mr. Sleuth, sir! Mr. Sleuth!"

The lodger stopped and turned round. He had been walking so quickly, and he was in so poor a physical condition, that the sweat was pouring down his face.

"Ah! So it's you, Mr. Bunting? I heard footsteps behind me, and I hurried on. I wish I'd known that it was only you; there are so many queer characters about at night in London."

"Not on a night like this, sir. Only honest folk who have business out of doors would be out such a night as this. It *is* cold, sir!" And then into Bunting's slow and honest mind there suddenly crept the query as to what Mr. Sleuth's own business out could be on this cold, bitter night.

"Cold?" the lodger repeated. "I can't say that I find it cold, Mr. Bunting. When the snow falls the air always becomes milder."

"Yes, sir; but to-night there's such a sharp east wind. Why, it freezes the very marrow in one's bones!"

Bunting noticed that Mr. Sleuth kept his distance in a rather strange way: he walked at the edge of the pavement, leaving the rest of it, on the wall side, to his landlord.

"I lost my way," he said abruptly. "I've been over Primrose Hill to see a friend of mine, and then, coming back, I lost my way."

Bunting could well believe that, for when he had first noticed Mr. Sleuth he was coming from the east, and not, as he should have done if walking home from Primrose Hill, from the north.

They had now reached the little gate that gave on to the shabby, paved court in front of the house. Mr. Sleuth was walking up the flagged path, when, with a "By your leave, sir," the ex-butler, stepping aside, slipped in front of his lodger, in order to open the front door for him.

As he passed by Mr. Sleuth, the back of Bunting's bare left hand brushed lightly against the long Inverness cape the other man was wearing, and, to his surprise, the stretch of cloth against which his hand lay for a moment was not only damp, damp from the flakes of snow that had settled upon it, but wet—wet and gluey. Bunting thrust his left hand into his pocket; it was with the other that he placed the key in the lock of the door.

The two men passed into the hall together. The house seemed blackly dark in comparison with the lighted up road outside; and then, quite suddenly, there came over Bunting a feeling of mortal terror, an instinctive knowledge that some terrible and immediate danger was near him. A voice—the voice of his first wife, the long-dead girl to whom his mind so seldom reverted nowadays—uttered in his ear the words, "Take care!"

"I'm afraid, Mr. Bunting, that you must have felt something dirty, foul, on my coat? It's too long a story to tell you now, but I brushed up against a dead animal—a dead rabbit lying across a bench on Primrose Hill."

Mr. Sleuth spoke in a very quiet voice, almost in a whisper.

"No, sir; no, I didn't notice nothing. I scarcely touched you, Sir," It seemed as if a power outside himself compelled Bunting to utter these lying words. "And now, sir, I'll be saying good night to you," he added.

He waited until the lodger had gone upstairs, and then he turned into his own sitting-room. There he sat down, for he felt very queer. He did not draw his left hand out of his pocket till he heard the other man moving about in the room above. Then he lit the gas and held up his left hand; he put it close to his face. It was flecked, streaked with blood.

He took off his boots, and then, very quietly, he went into the room where his wife lay asleep. Stealthily he walked across to the toilet-table, and dipped his hand into the water-jug.

The next morning Mr. Sleuth's landlord awoke with a start; he felt curiously heavy about the limbs and tired about the eyes.

Drawing his watch from under his pillow, he saw that it was nearly nine o'clock. He and Ellen had overslept. Without waking her, he got out of bed and pulled up the blind. It was snowing heavily, and, as is the way when it snows, even in London, it was strangely, curiously still.

After he had dressed he went out into the passage. A newspaper and a letter were lying on the mat. Fancy having slept through the postman's knock! He picked them both up and went into the sitting-room; then he carefully shut the door behind him, and, tossing the letter aside, spread the newspaper wide open on the table and bent over it.

As Bunting at last looked up and straightened himself, a look of inexpressible relief shone upon his stolid face. The item of news he had felt certain would be there, printed in big type on the middle sheet, was not there.

He folded the paper and laid it on a chair, and then eagerly took up his letter.

Dear Father [it ran]: I hope this finds you as well as it leaves me. Mrs. Puddle's youngest child has got scarlet fever, and aunt thinks I had better come away at once, just to stay with you for a few days. Please tell Ellen I won't give her no trouble.

Your loving daughter,
Daisy.

Bunting felt amazingly light-hearted; and, as he walked into the next room, he smiled broadly.

"Ellen," he cried out, "here's news! Daisy's coming today. There's scarlet fever in their house, and Martha thinks she had better come away for a few days. She'll be here for her birthday!"

Mrs. Bunting listened in silence; she did not even open her eyes. "I can't have the girl here just now," she said shortly; "I've got just as much as I can manage to do."

But Bunting felt pugnacious, and so cheerful as to be almost light-headed. Deep down in his heart he looked back to last night with a feeling of shame and self-rebuke. Whatever had made such horrible thoughts and suspicions come into his head?

"Of course Daisy will come here," he said shortly. "If it comes to that, she'll be able to help you with the work, and she'll brisk us both up a bit."

Rather to his surprise, Mrs. Bunting said nothing in answer to this, and he changed the subject abruptly. "The lodger and me came in together last night," he observed. "He's certainly a funny kind of gentleman. It wasn't the sort of night one would choose to go for a walk over Primrose Hill, and yet that was what he had been doing—so he said."

It stopped snowing about ten o'clock, and the morning wore itself away.

Just as twelve was striking, a four-wheeler drew up to the gate. It was Daisy—pink-cheeked, excited, laughing-eyed Daisy, a sight to gladden any father's heart. "Aunt said I was to have a cab if the weather was bad," she said.

There was a bit of a wrangle over the fare. King's Cross, as all the world knows, is nothing like two miles from the Marylebone Road, but the man clamored for one-and-six-pence, and hinted darkly that he had done the young lady a favour in bringing her at all.

While he and Bunting were having words, Daisy, leaving them to it, walked up the path to the door where her stepmother was awaiting her.

Suddenly there fell loud shouts on the still air. They sounded strangely eerie, breaking sharply across the muffled, snowy air.

"What's that?" said Bunting, with a look of startled fear. "Why, whatever's that?"

The cabman lowered his voice: "Them are crying out that 'orrible affair at King's Cross. He's done for two of 'em this time!

That's what I meant when I said I might have got a better fare; I wouldn't say anything before Missy there, but folk 'ave been coming from all over London—like a fire; plenty of toffs, too. But there—there's nothing to see now!"

"What! Another woman murdered last night?" Bunting felt and looked convulsed with horror.

The cabman stared at him, surprised. "Two of 'em, I tell yer—within a few yards of one another. He 'ave got a nerve—"

"Have they caught him?" asked Bunting perfunctorily.

"Lord, no! They'll never catch 'im! It must 'ave happened hours and hours ago—they was both stone-cold. One each end of an archway. That's why they didn't see 'em before."

The hoarse cries were coming nearer and nearer—two news-venders trying to outshout each other.

" 'Orrible discovery near King's Cross!" they yelled exultantly. And as Bunting, with his daughter's bag in his hand, hurried up the path and passed through his front door, the words pursued him like a dreadful threat.

Angrily he shut out the hoarse, insistent cries. No, he had no wish to buy a paper. That kind of crime wasn't fit reading for a young girl, such a girl as was his Daisy, brought up as carefully as if she had been a young lady by her strict Methody aunt.

As he stood in his little hall, trying to feel "all right" again, he could hear Daisy's voice—high, voluble, excited—giving her stepmother a long account of the scarlet-fever case to which she owed her presence in London. But, as Bunting pushed open the door of the sitting-room there came a note of sharp alarm in his daughter's voice, and he heard her say: "Why, Ellen! Whatever is the matter? You do look bad!" and his wife's muffled answer: "Open the window—do."

Rushing across the room, Bunting pushed up the sash. The newspaper-sellers were now just outside the house. "Horrible discovery near King's Cross—a clue to the murderer!" they yelled. And then, helplessly, Mrs. Bunting began to laugh. She laughed and laughed and laughed, rocking herself to and fro as if in an ecstasy of mirth.

"Why, father, whatever's the matter with her?" Daisy looked quite scared.

"She's in 'sterics—that's what it is," he said shortly. "I'll just get the water-jug. Wait a minute."

Bunting felt very put out, and yet glad, too, for this queer seizure of Ellen's almost made him forget the sick terror with which he had been possessed a moment before. That he and his wife should be obsessed by the same fear, the same terror, never crossed his simple, slow-working mind.

The lodger's bell rang. That, or the threat of the water-jug, had a magical effect on Mrs. Bunting. She rose to her feet, still trembling, but composed.

As Mrs. Bunting went upstairs she felt her legs trembling under her, and put out a shaking hand to clutch at the bannister for support. She waited a few minutes on the landing, and then knocked at the door of her lodger's parlor.

But Mr. Sleuth's voice answered her from the bedroom. "I'm, not well," he called out querulously; "I think I caught a chill going out to see a friend last night. I'd be obliged if you'll bring me up a cup of tea and put it outside my door, Mrs. Bunting."

"Very well, sir."

Mrs. Bunting went downstairs and made her lodger a cup of tea over the gas-ring, Bunting watching her the while in heavy silence.

During their midday dinner the husband and wife had a little discussion as to where Daisy should sleep. It had already been settled that a bed should be made up for her in the sitting-room, but Bunting saw reason to change this plan. As the two women were clearing away the dishes, he looked up and said shortly: "I think 'twould be better if Daisy were to sleep with you, Ellen, and I were to sleep in the sitting room."

Ellen acquiesced quietly.

Daisy was a good-natured girl; she liked London, and wanted to make herself useful to her stepmother. "I'll wash up; don't you bother to come downstairs," she said.

Bunting began to walk up and down the room. His wife gave him a furtive glance; she wondered what he was thinking about.

"Didn't you get a paper?" she said at last.

"There's the paper," he said crossly, "the paper we always do take in, the *Telegraph*." His look challenged her to a further question.

"I thought they was shouting something in the street—I mean just before I was took bad."

But he made no answer; instead, he went to the top of the staircase and called out sharply: "Daisy! Daisy, child, are you there?"

"Yes, father," she answered from below.

"Better come upstairs out of that cold kitchen."

He came back into the sitting-room again.

"Ellen, is the lodger in? I haven't heard him moving about. I don't want Daisy to be mixed up with him."

"Mr. Sleuth is not well to-day," his wife answered; "he is remaining in bed a bit. Daisy needn't have anything to do with him. She'll have her work cut out looking after things down here. That's where I want her to help me."

"Agreed," he said.

When it grew dark, Bunting went out and bought an evening paper. He read it out of doors in the biting cold, standing beneath a street lamp. He wanted to see what was the clue to the murderer.

The clue proved to be a very slender one—merely the imprint in the snowy slush of a half-worn rubber sole; and it was, of course, by no means certain that the sole belonged to the boot or shoe of the murderer of the two doomed women who had met so swift and awful a death in the arch near King's Cross station. The paper's special investigator pointed out that there were thousands of such soles being worn in London. Bunting found comfort in that obvious fact. He felt grateful to the special investigator for having stated it so clearly.

As he approached his house, he heard curious sounds coming from the inner side of the low wall that shut off the courtyard from the pavement. Under ordinary circumstances Bunting would have gone at once to drive whoever was there out into the roadway. Now he stayed outside, sick with suspense and anxiety. Was it possible that their place was being watched—already?

But it was only Mr. Sleuth. To Bunting's astonishment, the lodger suddenly stepped forward from behind the wall on to the flagged path. He was carrying a brown-paper parcel, and, as he walked along, the new boots he was wearing creaked and the tap-tap of wooden heels rang out on the stones.

Bunting, still hidden outside the gate, suddenly understood what his lodger had been doing the other side of the wall. Mr. Sleuth had been out to buy himself a pair of boots, and had gone inside the gate to put them on, placing his old footgear in the paper in which the new boots had been wrapped.

Bunting waited until Mr. Sleuth had let himself into the house; then he also walked up the flagged pathway, and put his latch-key in the door.

In the next three days each of Bunting's waking hours held its meed of aching fear and suspense. From his point of view, almost any alternative would be preferable to that which to most people would have seemed the only one open to him. He told himself that it would be ruin for him and for his Ellen to be mixed up publicly in such a terrible affair. It would track them to their dying day.

Bunting was also always debating within himself as to whether he should tell Ellen of his frightful suspicion. He could not believe that what had become so plain to himself could long be concealed from all the world, and yet he did not credit his wife with the same intelligence. He did not even notice that, although she waited on Mr. Sleuth as assiduously as ever, Mrs. Bunting never mentioned the lodger.

Mr. Sleuth, meanwhile, kept upstairs, he had given up going out altogether. He still felt, so he assured his landlady, far from well.

Daisy was another complication, the more so that the girl, whom her father longed to send away and whom he would hardly let out of his sight, showed herself inconveniently inquisitive concerning the lodger.

"Whatever does he do with himself all day?" she asked her stepmother.

"Well, just now he's reading the Bible," Mrs. Bunting had answered, very shortly and dryly.

"Well, I never! That's a funny thing for a gentleman to do!" Such had been Daisy's pert remark, and her stepmother had snubbed her well for it.

Daisy's eighteenth birthday dawned uneventfully. Her father gave her what he had always promised she should have on her eighteenth birthday—a watch. It was a pretty little silver watch, which Bunting had bought second-hand on the last day he had been happy; it seemed a long time ago now.

Mrs. Bunting thought a silver watch a very extravagant present, but she had always had the good sense not to interfere between her husband and his child. Besides, her mind was now full of other things. She was beginning to fear that Bunting suspected something, and she was filled with watchful anxiety and unease. What if he were to do anything silly—mix them up with the police, for instance? It certainly would be ruination to them both. But there—one never knew, with men! Her husband, however, kept his own counsel absolutely.

Daisy's birthday was a Saturday. In the middle of the morning Ellen and Daisy went down into the kitchen. Bunting didn't like the feeling that there was only one flight of stairs between Mr. Sleuth and himself, so he quietly slipped out of the house and went to buy himself an ounce of tobacco.

In the last four days Bunting had avoided his usual haunts. But to-day the unfortunate man had a curious longing for human companionship—companionship, that is, other than that of Ellen and Daisy. This feeling led him into a small, populous thoroughfare hard by the Edgeware Road. There were more people there than usual, for the housewives of the neighborhood were doing their marketing for Sunday.

Bunting passed the time of day with the tobacconist, and the two fell into desultory talk. To the ex-butler's surprise, the man said nothing at all to him on the subject of which all the neighborhood must still be talking.

And then, quite suddenly, while still standing by the counter, and before he had paid for the packet of tobacco he held in his hand, Bunting, through the open door, saw, with horrified surprise, that his wife was standing outside a green-grocer's shop just opposite. Muttering a word of apology, he rushed out of the shop and across the road.

"Ellen!" he gasped hoarsely. "You've never gone and left my little girl alone in the house?"

Mrs. Bunting's face went chalky white. "I thought you were indoors," she said. "You *were* indoors. Whatever made you come out for, without first making sure I was there?"

Bunting made no answer; but, as they stared at each other in exasperated silence, *each knew that the other knew.*

They turned and scurried down the street.

"Don't run," he said suddenly; "we shall get there just as quickly if we walk fast. People are noticing you, Ellen. Don't run."

He spoke breathlessly, but it was breathlessness induced by fear and excitement, not by the quick pace at which they were walking.

At last they reached their own gate. Bunting pushed past in front of his wife. After all, Daisy was his child—Ellen couldn't know how he was feeling. He made the path almost in one leap, and fumbled for a moment with his latch-key. The door opened.

"Daisy!" he called out in a wailing voice. "Daisy, my dear, where are you?"

"Here I am, father; what is it?"

"She's all right!" Bunting turned his gray face to his wife. "She's all right, Ellen!" Then he waited a moment, leaning against the wall of the passage. "It did give me a turn," he said; and then, warningly, "Don't frighten the girl, Ellen."

Daisy was standing before the fire in the sitting-room, admiring herself in the glass. "Oh, father," she said, without turning round, "I've seen the lodger! He's quite a nice gentleman—though, to be sure, he does look a cure! He came down to ask Ellen for something, and we had quite a nice little chat. I told him it was my birthday, and he asked me to go to Madame Tussaud's with him this afternoon." She laughed a little self-consciously. "Of course I could see he was 'centric, and then at first he spoke so funnily. 'And who be you?' he says, threatening-like. And I says to him, 'I'm Mr. Bunting's daughter, sir.' 'Then you're a very fortunate girl'—that's what he said, Ellen—'to 'ave such a nice stepmother as you've got. That's why,' he says, 'you look such a good, innocent girl.' And then he quoted a bit of the prayer-book at me. 'Keep innocency,' he says, wagging his head at me. Lor'! It made me feel as if I was with aunt again."

"I won't have you going out with the lodger—that's flat." He was wiping his forehead with one hand, while with the other he mechanically squeezed the little packet of tobacco, for which, as he now remembered, he had forgotten to pay.

Daisy pouted. "Oh, father, I think you might let me have a treat on my birthday! I told him Saturday wasn't a very good day—at least, so I'd heard—for Madame Tussaud's. Then he said we could go early, while the fine folk are still having their dinners. He wants you to come, too." She turned to her stepmother, then giggled happily. "The lodger has a wonderful fancy for you, Ellen; if I was father, I'd feel quite jealous!"

Her last words were cut across by a loud knock on the door. Bunting and his wife looked at each other apprehensively.

Both felt a curious thrill of relief when they saw that it was only Mr. Sleuth—Mr. Sleuth dressed to go out: the tall hat he had worn when he first came to them was in his hand, and he was wearing a heavy overcoat.

"I saw you had come in,"—he addressed Mrs. Bunting in his high, whistling, hesitating voice,—"and so I've come down to ask if you and Miss Bunting will come to Madame Tussaud's now. I have never seen these famous waxworks, though I've heard of the place all my life."

As Bunting forced himself to look fixedly at his lodger, a sudden doubt, bringing with it a sense of immeasurable relief, came to him. Surely it was inconceivable that this gentle, mild-mannered gentleman could be the monster of cruelty and cunning that Bunting had but a moment ago believed him to be!

"You're very kind, sir, I'm sure." He tried to catch his wife's eye, but Mrs. Bunting was looking away, staring into vacancy. She still, of course, wore the bonnet and cloak in which she had just been out to do her marketing. Daisy was already putting on her hat and coat.

Madame Tussaud's had hitherto held pleasant memories for Mrs. Bunting. In the days when she and Bunting were courting they often spent part of their "afternoon out" there. The butler had an acquaintance, a man named Hopkins, who was one of the waxworks' staff, and this man had sometimes given him passes for "self and lady." But this was the first time Mrs. Bunting had been inside the place since she had come to live almost next door, as it were, to the big building.

The ill-sorted trio walked up the great staircase and into the first gallery; and there Mr. Sleuth suddenly stopped short. The presence of those curious, still figures, suggesting death in life, seemed to surprise and affright him.

Daisy took quick advantage of the lodger's hesitation and unease.

"Oh, Ellen," she cried, "do let us begin by going into the Chamber of Horrors! I've never been in there. Aunt made father promise he wouldn't take me, the only time I've ever been here. But now that I'm eighteen I can do just as I like; besides, aunt will never know!"

Mr. Sleuth looked down at her.

"Yes," he said, "let us go into the Chamber of Horrors; that's a good idea, Miss Bunting."

They turned into the great room in which the Napoleonic relics are kept, and which leads into the curious, vaultlike chamber where waxen effigies of dead criminals stand grouped in wooden docks. Mrs. Bunting was at once disturbed and relieved to see her husband's old acquaintance, Mr. Hopkins, in charge of the turnstile admitting the public to the Chamber of Horrors.

"Well, you *are* a stranger," the man observed genially. "I do believe this is the very first time I've seen you in here, Mrs. Bunting, since you married!"

"Yes," she said; "that is so. And this is my husband's daughter, Daisy; I expect you've heard of her, Mr. Hopkins. And this"— she hesitated a moment—"is our lodger, Mr. Sleuth."

But Mr. Sleuth frowned and shuffled away. Daisy, leaving her stepmother's side, joined him.

Mrs. Bunting put down three sixpences.

"Wait a minute," said Hopkins; "you can't go into the Chamber of Horrors just yet. But you won't have to wait more than four or five minutes, Mrs. Bunting. It's this way, you see; our boss is in there, showing a party round." He lowered his voice. "It's Sir John Burney—I suppose you know who Sir John Burney is?"

"No," she answered indifferently; "I don't know that I ever heard of him." She felt slightly—oh, very slightly—uneasy about Daisy. She would like her stepdaughter to keep well within sight and sound. Mr. Sleuth was taking the girl to the other end of the room.

"Well, I hope you never *will* know him—not in any personal sense, Mrs. Bunting." The man chuckled. "He's the Head Commissioner of Police—that's what Sir John Burney is. One of the gentlemen he's showing round our place is the Paris Prefect of Police, whose job is on all fours, so to speak, with Sir John's. The Frenchy has brought his daughter with him, and there are several other ladies. Ladies always like 'orrors, Mrs. Bunting; that's our experience here. 'Oh, take me to the Chamber of 'Orrors!'—that's what they say the minute they gets into the building."

A group of people, all talking and laughing together, were advancing from within toward the turnstile.

Mrs. Bunting stared at them nervously. She wondered which of them was the gentleman with whom Mr. Hopkins had hoped she would never be brought into personal contact. She quickly picked him out. He was a tall, powerful, nice-looking gentleman with a commanding manner. Just now he was smiling down into the face of a young lady. "Monsieur Barberoux is quite right," he was saying; "the English law is too kind to the criminal, especially to the murderer. If we conducted our trials in the French fashion, the place we have just left would be very much fuller than it is to-day! A man of whose guilt we are absolutely assured is oftener than not acquitted, and then the public taunt us with 'another undiscovered crime'!"

"D'you mean, Sir John, that murderers sometimes escape scot-free? Take the man who has been committing all those awful murders this last month. Of course, I don't know much about it, for father won't let me read about it, but I can't help being interested!" Her girlish voice rang out, and Mrs. Bunting heard every word distinctly.

The party gathered round, listening eagerly to hear what the Head Commissioner would say next.

"Yes." He spoke very deliberately. "I think we may say—now, don't give me away to a newspaper fellow, Miss Rose—that we do know perfectly well who the murderer in question is—"

Several of those standing near by uttered expressions of surprise and incredulity.

"Then why don't you catch him?" cried the girl indignantly.

"I didn't say we know *where* he is; I only said we know *who* he is; or, rather, perhaps I ought to say that we have a very strong suspicion of his identity."

Sir John's French colleague looked up quickly. "The Hamburg and Liverpool man?" he said interrogatively.

The other nodded. "Yes; I suppose you've had the case turned up?"

Then, speaking very quickly, as if he wished to dismiss the subject from his own mind and from that of his auditors, he went on:

"Two murders of the kind were committed eight years ago— one in Hamburg, the other just afterward in Liverpool, and there were certain peculiarities connected with the crimes which made it clear they were committed by the same hand. The perpetrator was caught, fortunately for us red-handed, just as he was leaving the house of his victim, for in Liverpool the murder was committed in a house. I myself saw the unhappy man—I say unhappy, for there is no doubt at all that he was mad,"—he hesitated, and added in a lower tone—"suffering from an acute form of religious mania. I myself saw him, at some length. But now comes the really interesting point. Just a month ago this criminal lunatic, as we must regard him, made his escape from the asylum where he was confined. He arranged the whole thing with extraordinary cunning and intelligence, and we should probably have caught him long ago were it not that he managed, when on his way out of the place, to annex a considerable sum of money in gold with which the wages of the staff were about to be paid."

The Frenchman again spoke. "Why have you not circulated a description?" he asked.

"We did that at once,"—She John Burney smiled a little grimly,—"but only among our own people. We dare not circulate the man's description among the general public. You see, we may be mistaken, after all."

"That is not very probable!" The Frenchman smiled a satirical little smile.

A moment later the party were walking in Indian file through the turnstile, Sir John Burney leading the way.

Mrs. Bunting looked straight before her. Even had she wished to do so, she had neither time nor power to warn her lodger of his danger.

Daisy and her companion were now coming down the room, bearing straight for the Head Commissioner of Police. In another moment Mr. Sleuth and Sir John Burney would be face to face.

Suddenly Mr. Sleuth swerved to one side. A terrible change came over his pale, narrow face; it became discomposed, livid with rage and terror.

But, to Mrs. Bunting's relief,—yes, to her inexpressible relief,—Sir John Burney and his friends swept on. They passed by Mr. Sleuth unconcernedly, unaware, or so it seemed to her, that there was any one else in the room but themselves.

"Hurry up, Mrs. Bunting," said the turnstile-keeper; "you and your friends will have the place all to yourselves." From an official he had become a man, and it was the man in Mr. Hopkins that gallantly addressed pretty Daisy Bunting. "It seems strange that a young lady like you should want to go in and see all those 'orrible frights," he said jestingly.

"Mrs. Bunting, may I trouble you to come over here for a moment?" The words were hissed rather than spoken by Mr. Sleuth's lips.

His landlady took a doubtful step forward.

"A last word with you, Mrs. Bunting." The lodger's face was still distorted with fear and passion. "Do you think to escape the consequences of your hideous treachery? I trusted you, Mrs. Bunting, and you betrayed me! But I am protected by a higher power, for I still have work to do. Your end will be bitter as wormwood and sharp as a two-edged sword. Your feet shall go down to death, and your steps take hold on hell." Even while Mr. Sleuth was uttering these strange, dreadful words, he was looking around, his eyes glancing this way and that, seeking a way of escape.

At last his eyes become fixed on a small placard placed about a curtain. "Emergency Exit" was written there. Leaving his landlady's side, he walked over to the turnstile. He fumbled in his pocket for a moment, and then touched the man on the arm. "I feel ill," he said, speaking very rapidly; "very ill indeed! It's the atmosphere of this place. I want you to let me out by the quickest way. It would be a pity for me to faint here—especially with ladies about." His left hand shot out and placed what he had been fumbling for in his pocket on the other's bare palm. "I see there's an emergency exit over there. Would it be possible for me to get out that way?"

"Well, yes, sir; I think so." The man hesitated; he felt a slight, a very slight, feeling of misgiving. He looked at Daisy, flushed and smiling, happy and unconcerned, and then at Mrs. Bunting. She was very pale; but surely her lodger's sudden seizure was enough to make her feel worried. Hopkins felt the half sovereign pleasantly tickling his palm. The Prefect of Police had given him only half a crown—mean, shabby foreigner!

"Yes, I can let you out that way," he said at last, "and perhaps when you're standing out in the air on the iron balcony you'll feel better. But then you know, sir, you'll have to come round to the front if you want to come in again, for those emergency doors only open outward."

"Yes, yes," said Mr. Sleuth hurriedly; "I quite understand! If I feel better I'll come in by the front way, and pay another shilling—that's only fair."

"You needn't do that if you'll just explain what happened here."

The man went and pulled the curtain aside, and put his shoulder against the door. It burst open, and the light for a moment blinded Mr. Sleuth. He passed his hand over his eyes.

"Thank you," he said; "thank you. I shall get all right here."

Five days later Bunting identified the body of a man found drowned in the Regent's Canal as that of his late lodger; and, the morning following, a gardener working in the Regent's Park found a newspaper in which were wrapped, together with a half-worn pair of rubber-soled shoes, two surgical knives. This fact was not chronicled in any newspaper; but a very pretty and picturesque paragraph went the round of the press, about the same time, concerning a small box filled with sovereigns which had been forwarded anonymously to the Governor of the Foundling Hospital.

Mr. and Mrs. Bunting are now in the service of an old lady, by whom they are feared as well as respected, and whom they make very comfortable.

MARIE BELLOC LOWNDES

The Upper Berth

I

*S*omebody asked for the cigars. We had talked long, and the conversation was beginning to languish; the tobacco smoke had got into the heavy curtains, the wine had got into those brains which were liable to become heavy, and it was already perfectly evident that, unless somebody did something to rouse our oppressed spirits, the meeting would soon come to its natural conclusion, and we, the guests, would speedily go home to bed, and most certainly to sleep. No one had said anything very remarkable; it may be that no one had anything very remarkable to say. Jones had given us every particular of his last hunting adventure in Yorkshire. Mr. Tompkins, of Boston, had explained at elaborate length those working principles, by the due and careful maintenance of which the Atchison, Topeka, and Santa

Fé Railroad not only extended its territory, increased its departmental influence, and transported live stock without starving them to death before the day of actual delivery, but, also, had for years succeeded in deceiving those passengers who bought its tickets into the fallacious belief that the corporation aforesaid was really able to transport human life without destroying it. Signor Tombola had endeavoured to persuade us, by arguments which we took no trouble to oppose, that the unity of this country in no way resembled the average modern torpedo, carefully planned, constructed with all the skill of the greatest European arsenals, but, when constructed, destined to be directed by feeble hands into a region where it must undoubtedly explode, unseen, unfeared, and unheard, into the illimitable wastes of political chaos.

It is unnecessary to go into further details. The conversation had assumed proportions which would have bored Prometheus on his rock, which would have driven Tantalus to distraction, and which would have impelled Ixion to seek relaxation in the simple but instructive dialogues of Herr Ollendorff, rather than submit to the greater evil of listening to our talks. We had sat at table for hours; we were bored, we were tired, and nobody showed signs of moving.

Somebody called for cigars. We all instinctively looked towards the speaker. Brisbane was a man of five-and-thirty years of age, and remarkable for those gifts which chiefly attract the attention of men. He was a strong man. The external proportions of his figure presented nothing extraordinary to the common eye, though his size was above the average. He was a little over six feet in height, and moderately broad in the shoulder; he did not appear to be stout, but, on the other hand, he was certainly not thin; his small head was supported by a strong and sinewy neck; his broad, muscular hands appeared to possess a peculiar skill in breaking walnuts without the assistance of the ordinary cracker, and, seeing him in profile, one could not help remarking the extraordinary breadth of his sleeves, and the unusual thickness of his chest. He was one of those men who are commonly spoken of among men as deceptive; that is to say, that though he looked exceedingly strong he was in reality very much stronger than he looked. Of his features I need say little. His head is small, his hair is thin, his eyes are blue, his nose is large, he has a small moustache, and a square jaw. Everybody knows Brisbane, and when he asked for a cigar everybody looked at him.

"It is a very singular thing," said Brisbane. Everybody stopped talking. Brisbane's voice was not loud, but possessed a peculiar quality of penetrating general conversation, and cutting it like a knife. Everybody listened. Brisbane, perceiving that he had attracted their general attention, lit his cigar with great equanimity.

"It is very singular," he continued, "that thing about ghosts. People are always asking whether anybody has seen a ghost. I have."

"Bosh! What, you? You don't mean to say so, Brisbane? Well, for a man of his intelligence!"

A chorus of exclamations greeted Brisbane's remarkable statement. Everybody called for cigars, and Stubbs, the butler, suddenly appeared from the depths of nowhere with a fresh bottle of dry champagne. The situation was saved; Brisbane was going to tell a story.

I am an old sailor, said Brisbane, and as I have to cross the Atlantic pretty often, I have my favourites. Most men have their favourites. I have seen a man wait in a Broadway bar for three-quarters of an hour for a particular car which he liked. I believe the bar-keeper made at least one-third of his living by that man's preference. I have a habit of waiting for certain ships when I am obliged to cross that duck-pond. It may be a prejudice, but I was never cheated out of a good passage but once in my life. I remember it very well; it was a warm morning in June, and the Custom House officials, who were hanging about waiting for a steamer already on her way up from the Quarantine, presented a peculiarly hazy and thoughtful appearance. I had not much luggage—I never have. I mingled with the crowd of passengers, porters, and officious individuals in blue coats and brass buttons, who seemed to spring up like mushrooms from the deck of a moored steamer to obtrude their unnecessary services upon the independent passenger. I have often noticed with a certain interest the spontaneous evolution of these fellows. They are not there when you arrive; five minutes after the pilot has called "Go ahead!" they, or at least their blue coats and brass buttons, have disappeared from deck and gangway as completely as though they had been consigned to that locker which tradition unanimously ascribes to Davy Jones. But, at the moment of starting, they are there, clean shaved, blue coated, and ravenous for fees. I hastened on board. The *Kamtschatka* was one of my favourite ships. I say was, because she emphatically no longer is. I cannot conceive of any inducement which could entice me to make another voyage in her. Yes, I know what you are going to say. She is uncommonly clean in the run aft', she has enough bluffing off in the bows to keep her dry, and the lower berths are most of them double. She has a lot of advantages, but I won't cross in her again. Excuse the digression. I got on board. I hailed a steward, whose red nose and redder whiskers were equally familiar to me.

"One hundred and five, lower berth," said I, in the business-like tone peculiar to men who think no more of crossing the Atlantic than taking a whisky cocktail at downtown Delmonico's.

The steward took my portmanteau, great-coat, and rug. I shall never forget the expression of his face. Not that he turned pale. It is maintained by the most eminent divines that even miracles cannot change the course of nature. I have no hesitation in saying that he did not turn pale; but, from his expression, I judged that he was either about to shed tears, to sneeze, or to drop my portmanteau. As the latter contained two bottles of particularly fine old sherry presented to me for my voyage by my old friend Snigginson van Pickyns, I felt extremely nervous. But the steward did none of these things.

"Well, I'm d——d!" said he in a low voice, and led the way.

I supposed my Hermes, as he led me to the lower regions, had had a little grog, but I said nothing, and followed him. 105 was on the port side, well aft. There was nothing remarkable about the state-room. The lower berth, like most of those upon the *Kamtschatka*, was double. There was plenty of room; there was the usual washing apparatus calculated to convey an idea of luxury to the mind of a North American Indian; there were the usual inefficient racks of brown wood, in which it is more easy to hang a large-sized umbrella than the common tooth-brush of commerce. Upon the uninviting mattresses were carefully folded together those blankets which a great modern humorist has aptly compared to cold buck-wheat cakes. The question of towels was left entirely to the imagination. The glass decanters were filled with a transparent liquid faintly tinged with brown, but from which an odour less faint, but not more pleasing, ascended to the nostrils like a far-off sea-sick reminiscence of oily machinery. Sad-coloured curtains half closed the upper berth. The hazy June daylight shed a faint illumination upon the desolate little scene. Ugh! how I hate that state-room!

The steward deposited my traps and looked at me, as though he wanted to get away—probably in search of more passengers and more fees. It is always a good plan to start in favour with those functionaries, and I accordingly gave him certain coins there and then..

"I'll try and make yer comfortable all I can," he remarked, as he put the coins in his pocket. Nevertheless, there was a doubtful intonation in his voice which surprised me. Possibly his scale of fees had gone up, and he was not satisfied; but on the whole I was inclined to think that, as he himself would have expressed it, he was "the better for a glass." I was wrong, however, and did the man injustice.

II

*N*othing especially worthy of mention occurred during that day. We left the pier punctually, and it was very pleasant to be fairly under way, for the weather was warm and sultry, and the motion of the steamer produced a refreshing breeze. Everybody knows what the first day at sea is like. People pace the decks and stare at each other, and occasionally meet acquaintances whom they did not know to be on board. There is the usual uncertainty as to whether the food will be good, bad, or indifferent, until the first two meals have put the matter beyond a doubt; there is the usual uncertainty about the weather, until the ship is fairly off Fire Island. The tables are crowded at first, and then suddenly thinned. Pale-faced people spring from their seats and precipitate themselves towards the door, and each old sailor breathes more freely as his sea-sick neighbour rushes from his side, leaving him plenty of elbow-room and an unlimited command over the mustard.

One passage across the Atlantic is very much like another, and we who cross very often do not make the voyage for the sake of novelty. Whales and icebergs are indeed always objects of interest, but, after all, one whale is very much like another whale, and one rarely sees an iceberg at close quarters. To the majority of us the most delightful moment of the day on board an ocean steamer is when we have taken our last turn on deck, have smoked our last cigar, and having succeeded in tiring ourselves, feel at liberty to turn in with a clear conscience. On that first night of the voyage I felt particularly lazy, and went to bed in 105 rather earlier than I usually do. As I turned in, I was amazed to see that I was to have a companion. A portmanteau, very like my own, lay in the opposite corner, and in the upper berth had been deposited a neatly-folded rug, with a stick and umbrella. I had hoped to be alone, and I was disappointed; but I wondered who my room-mate was to be, and I determined to have a look at him.

Before I had been long in bed he entered. He was, as far as I could see, a very tall man, very thin, very pale, with sandy hair and whiskers and colourless grey eyes. He had about him, I thought, an air of rather dubious fashion; the sort of man you might see in Wall Street, without being able precisely to say what he was doing there—the sort of man who frequents the Café Anglais, who always seems to be alone, and who drinks champagne; you might meet him on a race-course, but he would never appear to be doing anything there either. A little over-dressed—a little odd. There are three or four of his kind on every ocean steamer. I made up my mind that I did not care to make his acquaintance, and I went to sleep saying to myself that I would study his habits in order to avoid him. If he rose early, I would rise late; if he went to bed late, I would go to bed early. I did not care to know him. If you once know people of that kind they are always turning up. Poor fellow! I need not have taken the trouble to come to so many decisions about him, for I never saw him again after that first night in 105.

I was sleeping soundly when I was suddenly waked by a loud noise. To judge from the sound, my room-mate must have sprung with a single leap from the upper berth to the floor. I heard him fumbling with the latch and bolt of the door, which opened almost immediately, and then I heard his footsteps as he ran at full speed down the passage, leaving the door open behind him. The ship was rolling a little, and I expected to hear him stumble or fall, but he ran as though he were running for his life. The door swung on its hinges with the motion of the vessel, and the sound annoyed me. I got up and shut it, and groped my way back to my berth in the darkness. I went to sleep again; but I have no idea how long I slept.

When I awoke it was still quite dark, but I felt a disagreeable sensation of cold, and it seemed to me that the air was damp. You know the peculiar smell of a cabin which has been wet with sea-water. I covered myself up as well as I could and dozed off again, framing complaints to be made the next day, and selecting the most powerful epithets in the language. I could hear my room-mate turn over in the upper berth. He had probably returned while I was asleep. Once I thought I heard him groan, and I argued that he was sea-sick. That is particularly unpleasant when one is below. Nevertheless I dozed off and slept till early daylight.

The ship was rolling heavily, much more than on the previous evening, and the grey light which came in through the porthole changed in tint with every movement according as the angle of the vessel's side turned the glass seawards or skywards. It was very cold—unaccountably so for the month of June. I turned my head and looked at the porthole, and saw to my surprise that it was wide open and hooked back. I believe I swore audibly. Then I got up and shut it. As I turned back I glanced at the upper berth. The curtains were drawn close together; my companion had probably felt cold as well as I. It struck me that I had slept enough. The state-room was uncomfortable, though, strange to say, I could not smell the dampness which had annoyed me in the night. My room-mate was still asleep—excellent opportunity for avoiding him, so I dressed at once and went on deck. The day was warm and cloudy, with an oily smell on the water. It was seven o'clock as I came out—much later than I had imagined. I came across the doctor, who was taking his first sniff of the morning air. He was a young man from the West of Ireland—a tremendous fellow, with black hair and blue eyes, already inclined to be stout; he had a happy-go-lucky, healthy look about him which was rather attractive.

"Fine morning," I remarked, by way of introduction.

"Well," said he, eyeing me with an air of ready interest, "it's a fine morning and it's not a fine morning. I don't think it's much of a morning."

"Well, no—it is not so very fine," said I.

"It's just what I call fuggly weather," replied the doctor.

"It was very cold last night, I thought," I remarked. "However, when I looked about, I found that the porthole was wide open. I had not noticed it when I went to bed. And the state-room was damp, too."

"Damp!" said he. "Whereabouts are you?"

"One hundred and five——"

To my surprise the doctor started visibly, and stared at me.

"What is the matter?" I asked.

"Oh—nothing," he answered; "only everybody has complained of that state-room for the last three trips."

"I shall complain too," I said. "It has certainly not been properly aired. It is a shame!"

"I don't believe it can be helped," answered the doctor. "I believe there is something—well, it is not my business to frighten passengers."

"You need not be afraid of frightening me," I replied. "I can stand any amount of damp. If I should get a bad cold I will come to you."

I offered the doctor a cigar, which he took and examined very critically.

"It is not so much the damp," he remarked. "However, I dare say you will get on very well. Have you a roommate?"

"Yes; a deuce of a fellow, who bolts out in the middle of the night, and leaves the door open."

Again the doctor glanced curiously at me. Then he lit the cigar and looked grave.

"Did he come back?" he asked presently.

"Yes. I was asleep, but I waked up, and heard him moving. Then I felt cold and went to sleep again. This morning I found the porthole open."

"Look here," said the doctor quietly, "I don't care much for this ship. I don't care a rap for her reputation. I tell you what I will do. I have a good-sized place up here. I will share it with you, though I don't know you from Adam."

I was very much surprised at the proposition. I could not imagine why he should take such a sudden interest in my welfare. However, his manner, as he spoke of the ship, was peculiar.

"You are very good, doctor," I said. "But, really, I believe even now the cabin could be aired, or cleaned out, or something. Why do you not care for the ship?"

"We are not superstitious in our profession, sir," replied the doctor, "but the sea makes people so. I don't want to prejudice you, and I don't want to frighten you, but if you will take my advice you will move in here. I would as soon see you overboard," he added earnestly, "as know that you or any other man was to sleep in 105."

"Good gracious! Why?" I asked.

"Just because on the last three trips the people who have slept there actually have gone overboard," he answered gravely.

The intelligence was startling and exceedingly unpleasant, I confess. I looked hard at the doctor to see whether he was making game of me, but he looked perfectly serious. I thanked him warmly for his offer, but told him I intended to be the exception to the rule by which every one who slept in that particular state-room went overboard. He did not say much, but looked as grave as ever, and hinted that, before we got across, I should probably reconsider his proposal. In the course of time we went to breakfast, at which only an inconsiderable number of passengers assembled. I noticed that one or two of the officers who breakfasted with us looked grave. After breakfast I went into my state-room in order to get a book. The curtains of the upper berth were still closely drawn. Not a word was to be heard. My room-mate was probably still asleep.

As I came out I met the steward whose business it was to look after me. He whispered that the captain wanted to see me, and then scuttled away down the passage as if very anxious to avoid any questions. I went towards the captain's cabin, and found him waiting for me.

"Sir," said he, "I want to ask a favour of you."

I answered that I would do anything to oblige him.

"Your room-mate has disappeared," he said. "He is known to have turned in early last night. Did you notice anything extraordinary in his manner?"

The question coming, as it did, in exact confirmation of the fears the doctor had expressed half an hour earlier, staggered me.

"You don't mean to say he has gone overboard?" I asked.

"I fear he has," answered the captain.

"This is the most extraordinary thing——" I began.

"Why?" he asked.

"He is the fourth, then?" I explained. In answer to another question from the captain, I explained, without mentioning the doctor, that I had heard the story concerning 105. He seemed very much annoyed at hearing that I knew of it. I told him what had occurred in the night.

"What you say," he replied, "coincides almost exactly with what was told me by the room-mates of two of the other three. They bolt out of bed and run down the passage. Two of them were seen to go overboard by the watch; we stopped and lowered boats, but they were not found. Nobody, however, saw or heard the man who was lost last night—if he is really lost. The steward, who is a superstitious fellow, perhaps, and expected something to go wrong, went to look for him this morning, and found his berth empty, but his clothes lying about, just as he had left them. The steward was the only man on board who knew him by sight, and he has been searching everywhere for him. He has disappeared! Now, sir, I want to beg you not mention the circumstance to any of the passengers; I don't want the ship to get a bad name, and nothing hangs about an ocean-goer like stories of suicides. You shall have your choice of any one of the officers' cabins you like, including my own, for the rest of the passage. Is that a fair bargain?"

"Very," said I; "and I am much obliged to you. But since I am alone, and have the state-room to myself, I would rather not move. If the steward will take out that unfortunate man's things, I would as lief stay where I am, I will not say anything about the matter, and I think I can promise you that I will not follow my room-mate."

The captain tried to dissuade me from my intention, but I preferred having a state-room alone to being the chum of any officer on board. I do not know whether I acted foolishly, but if I had taken his advice I should have had nothing more to tell. There would have remained the disagreeable coincidence of several suicides occurring among men who had slept in the same cabin, but that would have been all.

That was not the end of the matter, however, by any means. I obstinately made up my mind that I would not be disturbed by such tales, and I even went so far as to argue the question with the captain. There was something wrong about the state-room, I said. It was rather damp. The porthole had been left open last night. My room-mate might have been ill when he came on board, and he might have become delirious after he went to bed. He might even now be hiding somewhere on board, and might be found later. The place ought to be aired and the fastening of the port looked to. If the captain would give me leave, I would see what I thought necessary were done immediately.

"Of course you have a right to stay where you are if you please," he replied, rather petulantly; "but I wish you would turn out and let me lock the place up, and be done with it."

I did not see it in the same light, and left the captain, after promising to be silent concerning the disappearance of my companion. The latter had had no acquaintances on board, and was not missed in the course of the day. Towards evening I met the doctor again, and he asked me whether I had changed my mind. I told him I had not.

"Then you will before long," he said, very gravely.

III

$\mathcal{W}$e played whist in the evening, and I went to bed late. I will confess now that I felt a disagreeable sensation when I entered my state-room. I could not help thinking of the tall man I had seen on the previous night, who was now dead, drowned, tossing about in the long swell, two or three hundred miles astern. His face rose very distinctly before me as I undressed, and I even went so far as to draw back the curtains of the upper berth, as though to persuade myself that he was actually gone. I also bolted the door of the state-room. Suddenly I became aware that the porthole was open, and fastened back. This was more than I could stand. I hastily threw on my dressing-gown and went in search of Robert, the steward of my passage. I was very angry, I remember, and when I found him I dragged him roughly to the door of 105, and pushed him towards the open porthole.

"What the deuce do you mean, you scoundrel, by leaving that port open every night? Don't you know it is against the regulations? Don't you know that if the ship heeled and the water began to come in, ten men could not shut it? I will report you to the captain, you blackguard, for endangering the ship!"

I was exceedingly wroth. The man trembled and turned pale, and then began to shut the round glass plate with the heavy brass fittings.

"Why don't you answer me?" I said roughly.

"If you please, sir," faltered Robert, "there's nobody on board as can keep this 'ere port shut at night. You can try it yourself, sir. I ain't a-going to stop any longer on board o' this vessel, sir; I ain't, indeed. But if I was you, sir, I'd just clear out and go to sleep with the surgeon, or something, I would. Look 'ere, sir, is that fastened what you may call securely, or not, sir! Try it, sir, see if it will move a hinch."

I tried the port, and found it perfectly tight.

"Well, sir," continued Robert triumphantly, "I wager my reputation as a A1 steward that in 'arf an hour it will be open again; fastened back, too, sir, that's the horful thing—fastened back!"

I examined the great screw and the looped nut that ran on it.

"If I find it open in the night, Robert, I will give you a sovereign. It is not possible. You may go."

"Soverin' did you say, sir? Very good, sir. Thank ye, sir. Good night, sir. Pleasant reepose, sir, and all manner of hinchantin' dreams, sir."

Robert scuttled away, delighted at being released. Of course I thought he was trying to account for his negligence by a silly story, intended to frighten me, and I disbelieved him. The consequence was that he got his sovereign, and I spent a very peculiarly unpleasant night.

I went to bed, and five minutes after I had rolled myself up in my blankets the inexorable Robert extinguished the light that burned steadily behind the ground-glass pane near the door. I lay quite still in the dark trying to go to sleep, but I soon found that impossible. It had been some satisfaction to be angry with the steward, and the diversion had banished that unpleasant sensation I had at first experienced when I thought of the drowned man who had been my chum; but I was no longer sleepy, and I lay awake for some time, occasionally glancing at the porthole, which I could just see from where I lay, and which, in the darkness, looked like a faintly-luminous soup-plate suspended in blackness. I believe I must have lain there for an hour, and, as I remember, I was just dozing into sleep when I was roused by a draught of cold air, and by distinctly feeling the spray of the sea blown upon my face. I started to my feet, and not having allowed in the dark for the motion of the ship, I was instantly thrown violently across the state-room upon the couch which was placed beneath the porthole. I recovered myself immediately, however, and climbed upon my knees. The porthole was again wide open and fastened back!

Now these things are facts. I was wide awake when I got up, and I should certainly have been waked by the fall had I still been dozing. Moreover, I bruised my elbows and knees badly, and the bruises were there on the following morning to testify to the fact, if I myself had doubted it. The porthole was wide open and fastened back—a thing so unaccountable that I remember very well feeling astonishment rather than fear when I discovered it. I at once closed the plate again, and screwed down the loop nut with all my strength. It was very dark in the state-room. I reflected that the port had certainly been opened within an hour after Robert had at first shut it in my presence, and I determined to watch it, and see whether it would open again. Those brass fittings are very heavy and by no means easy to move; I could not believe that the clump had been turned by the shaking of the screw. I stood peering out through the thick glass at the alternate white and grey streaks of the sea that foamed beneath the ship's side. I must have remained there a quarter of an hour.

Suddenly, as I stood, I distinctly heard something moving behind me in one of the berths, and a moment afterwards, just as I turned instinctively to look—though I could, of course, see nothing in the darkness—I heard a very faint groan. I sprang across the state-room, and tore the curtains of the upper berth aside, thrusting in my hands to discover if there were any one there. There was some one.

I remember that the sensation as I put my hands forward was as though I were plunging them into the air of a damp cellar, and from behind the curtains came a gust of wind that smelled horribly of stagnant sea-water. I laid hold of something that had the shape of a man's arm, but was smooth, and wet, and icy cold. But suddenly, as I pulled, the creature sprang violently forward against me, a clammy, oozy mass, as it seemed to me, heavy and wet, yet endowed with a sort of supernatural strength. I reeled across the state-room, and in an instant the door opened and the thing rushed out. I had not had time to be frightened, and quickly recovering myself, I sprang through the door and gave chase at the top of my speed, but I was too late. Ten yards before me I could see—I am sure I saw it—a dark shadow moving in the dimly lighted passage, quickly as the shadow of a fast horse thrown before a dog-cart by the lamp on a dark night. But in a moment it had disappeared, and I found myself holding on to the polished rail that ran along the bulkhead where the passage turned towards the companion. My hair stood on end, and the cold perspiration rolled down my face. I am not ashamed of it in the least: I was very badly frightened.

Still I doubted my senses, and pulled myself together. It was absurd, I thought. The Welsh rare-bit I had eaten had disagreed with me. I had been in a nightmare. I made my way back to my state-room, and entered it with an effort. The whole place smelled of stagnant sea-water, as it had when I had waked on the previous evening. It required my utmost strength to go in, and grope among my things for a box of wax lights. As I lighted a railway reading-lantern which I always carry in case I want to read after the lamps are out, I perceived that the porthole was again open, and a sort of creeping horror began to take possession of me which I never felt before, nor wish to feel again. But I got a light and proceeded to examine the upper berth, expecting to find it drenched with sea-water.

But I was disappointed. The bed had been slept in, and the smell of the sea was strong; but the bedding was as dry as a bone. I fancied that Robert had not had the courage to take the bed after the accident of the previous night—it had all been a hideous dream. I drew the curtains back as far as I could and examined the place very carefully. It was perfectly dry. But the porthole was open again. With a sort of dull bewilderment of horror I closed it and screwed it down, and thrusting my heavy stick through the brass loop, wrenched it with all my might, till the thick metal began to bend under the pressure. Then I hooked my reading-lantern into the red velvet at the head of the couch, and sat down to recover my senses if I could. I sat there all night, unable to think of rest—hardly able to think at all. But the porthole remained closed, and I did not believe it would now open again without the application of a considerable force.

The morning dawned at last, and I dressed myself slowly, thinking over all that had happened in the night. It was a beautiful day and I went on deck, glad to get out into the early, pure sunshine, and to smell the breeze from the blue water, so different from the noisome, stagnant odour of my state-room. Instinctively I turned aft, towards the surgeon's cabin. There he stood, with a pipe in his mouth, taking his morning airing precisely as on the preceding day.

"Good morning," said he quietly, but looking at me with evident curiosity.

"Doctor, you were quite right," said I. "There is something wrong about that place."

"I thought you would change your mind," he answered, rather triumphantly. "You have had a bad night, eh? Shall I make you a pick-me-up? I have a capital recipe."

"No, thanks," I cried. "But I would like to tell you what happened."

I then tried to explain as clearly as possible precisely what had occurred, not omitting to state that I had been scared as I had never been scared in my whole life before. I dwelt particularly on the phenomenon of the porthole, which was a fact to which I could testify, even if the rest had been an illusion. I had closed it twice in the night, and the second time I had actually bent the brass in wrenching it with my stick. I believe I insisted a good deal on this point.

"You seem to think I am likely to doubt the story," said the doctor, smiling at the detailed account of the state of the porthole. "I do not doubt it in the least. I renew my invitation to you. Bring your traps here, and take half my cabin."

"Come and take half of mine for one night," I said. "Help me to get at the bottom of this thing."

"You will get to the bottom of something else if you try," answered the doctor.

"What?" I asked.

"The bottom of the sea. I am going to leave this ship. It is not canny."

"Then you will not help me to find out——"

"Not I," said the doctor quickly. "It is my business to keep my wits about me—not to go fiddling about with ghosts and things."

"Do you really believe it is a ghost?" I enquired, rather contemptuously. But as I spoke I remembered very well the horrible sensation of the supernatural which had got possession of me during the night. The doctor turned sharply on me.

"Have you any reasonable explanation of these things to offer?" he asked. "No; you have not. Well, you say you will find an explanation. I say that you won't, sir, simply because there is not any."

"But, my dear sir," I retorted, "do you, a man of science, mean to tell me that such things cannot be explained?"

"I do," he answered stoutly. "And, if they could I would not be concerned in the explanation."

I did not care to spend another night alone in the state-room, and yet I was obstinately determined to get at the root of the disturbances. I do not believe there are many men who would have slept there alone, after passing two such nights. But I made up my mind to try it, if I could not get any one to share a watch with me. The doctor was evidently not inclined for such an experiment. He said he was a surgeon, and that in case any accident occurred on board he must be always in readiness. He could not afford to have his nerves unsettled. Perhaps he was quite right, but I am inclined to think that his precaution was prompted by his inclination. On enquiry, he informed me that there was no one on board who would be likely to join me in my investigations, and after a little more conversation I left him. A little later I met the captain, and told him my story. I said that, if no one would spend the night with me, I would ask leave to have the light burning all night, and would try it alone.

"Look here," said he, "I will tell you what I will do. I will share your watch myself, and we will see what happens. It is my belief that we can find out between us. There may be some fellow skulking on board, who steals a passage by frightening the passengers. It is just possible that there may be something queer in the carpentering of that berth."

I suggested taking the ship's carpenter below and examining the place; but I was overjoyed at the captain's offer to spend the night with me. He accordingly sent for the workman and ordered him to do anything I required. We went below at once. I had all the bedding cleared out of the upper berth, and we examined the place thoroughly to see if there was a board loose anywhere, or a panel which could be opened or pushed aside. We tried the planks everywhere, tapped the flooring, unscrewed the fittings of the lower berth and took it to pieces—in short, there was not a square inch of the state-room which was not searched and tested. Everything was in perfect order, and we put everything back in its place. As we were finishing our work, Robert came to the door and looked in.

"Well, sir—find anything, sir?" he asked, with a ghastly grin.

"You were right about the porthole, Robert," I said, and I gave him the promised sovereign. The carpenter did his work silently and skilfully, following my directions. When he had done he spoke.

"I'm a plain man, sir," he said. "But it's my belief you had better just turn out your things, and let me run half a dozen four-inch screws through the door of this cabin. There's no good never came o' this cabin yet, sir, and that's all about it. There's been four lives lost out o' here to my own remembrance, and that in four trips. Better give it up, sir—better give it up!"

"I will try it for one night more," I said.

"Better give it up, sir—better give it up! It's a precious bad job," repeated the workman, putting his tools in his bag and leaving the cabin.

But my spirits had risen considerably at the prospect of having the captain's company, and I made up my mind not to be prevented from going to the end of the strange business. I abstained from Welsh rare-bits and grog that evening, and did not even join in the customary game of whist. I wanted to be quite sure of my nerves, and my vanity made me anxious to make a good figure in the captain's eyes.

IV

*T*he captain was one of those splendidly tough and cheerful specimens of seafaring humanity whose combined courage, hardihood, and calmness in difficulty leads them naturally into high positions of trust. He was not the man to be led away by an idle tale, and the mere fact that he was willing to join me in the investigation was proof that he thought there was something seriously wrong, which could not be accounted for on ordinary theories, nor laughed down as a common superstition. To some extent, too, his reputation was at stake, as well as the reputation of the ship. It is no light thing to lose passengers overboard, and he knew it.

About ten o'clock that evening, as I was smoking a last cigar, he came up to me, and drew me aside from the beat of the other passengers who were patrolling the deck in the warm darkness.

"This is a serious matter, Mr. Brisbane," he said. "We must make up our minds either way—to be disappointed or to have a pretty rough time of it. You see I cannot afford to laugh at the affair, and I will ask you to sign your name to a statement of whatever occurs. If nothing happens tonight we will try it again to-morrow and next day. Are you ready?"

So we went below, and entered the state-room. As we went in I could see Robert the steward, who stood a little farther down the passage, watching us, with his usual grin, as though certain that something dreadful was about to happen. The captain closed the door behind us and bolted it.

"Supposing we put your portmanteau before the door," he suggested. "One of us can sit on it. Nothing can get out then. Is the port screwed down?"

I found it as I had left it in the morning. Indeed, without using a lever, as I had done, no one could have opened it. I drew back the curtains of the upper berth so that I could see well into it. By the captain's advice I lighted my reading-lantern, and placed it so that it shone upon the white sheets above. He insisted upon sitting on the portmanteau, declaring that he wished to be able to swear that he had sat before the door.

Then he requested me to search the state-room thoroughly, an operation very soon accomplished, as it consisted merely in looking beneath the lower berth and under the couch below the porthole. The spaces were quite empty.

"It is impossible for any human being to get in," I said, "or for any human being to open the port."

"Very good," said the captain calmly. "If we see anything now, it must be either imagination or something supernatural."

I sat down on the edge of the lower berth.

"The first time it happened," said the captain, crossing his legs and leaning back against the door, "was in March. The passenger who slept here, in the upper berth, turned out to have been a lunatic—at all events, he was known to have been a little touched, and he had taken his passage without the knowledge of his friends. He rushed out in the middle of the night, and threw himself overboard, before the officer who had the watch could stop him. We stopped and lowered a boat; it was a quiet night, just before that heavy weather came on; but we could not find him. Of course his suicide was afterwards accounted for on the ground of his insanity."

"I suppose that often happens?" I remarked, rather absently.

"Not often—no," said the captain; "never before in my experience, though I have heard of it happening on board of other ships. Well, as I was saying, that occurred in March. On the very next trip——What are you looking at?" he asked, stopping suddenly in his narration.

I believe I gave no answer. My eyes were riveted upon the porthole. It seemed to me that the brass loop-nut was beginning to turn very slowly upon the screw—so slowly, however, that I was not sure it moved at all. I watched it intently, fixing its position in my mind, and trying to ascertain whether it changed. Seeing where I was looking, the captain looked, too.

"It moves!" he exclaimed, in a tone of conviction. "No, it does not," he added, after a minute.

"If it were the jarring of the screw," said I, "it would have opened during the day; but I found it this evening jammed tight as I left it this morning."

I rose and tried the nut. It was certainly loosened, for by an effort I could move it with my hands.

"The queer thing," said the captain, "is that the second man who was lost is supposed to have got through that very port. We had a terrible time over it. It was in the middle of the night, and the weather was very heavy; there was an alarm that one of the ports was open and the sea running in. I came below and found everything flooded, the water pouring in every time she rolled, and the whole port swinging from the top bolts—the porthole in the middle. Well, we managed to shut it, but the water did some damage. Ever since that the place smells of sea-water from time to time. We supposed the passenger had thrown himself out, though the Lord only knows how he did it. The steward kept telling me that he cannot keep anything shut here. Upon my word—I can smell it now, cannot you?" he enquired, sniffing the air suspiciously.

"Yes—distinctly," I said, and I shuddered as that same odour of stagnant sea-water grew stronger in the cabin. "Now, to smell like this, the place must be damp," I continued, "and yet when I examined it with the carpenter this morning everything was perfectly dry. It is most extraordinary—hallo!"

My reading-lantern, which had been placed in the upper berth, was suddenly extinguished. There was still a good deal of light from the pane of ground glass near the door, behind which loomed the regulation lamp. The ship rolled heavily, and the curtain of the upper berth swung far out into the state-room and back again. I rose quickly from my seat on the edge of the bed, and the captain at the same moment started to his feet with a loud cry of surprise. I had turned with the intention of taking down the lantern to examine it, when I heard his exclamation, and immediately afterwards his call for help. I sprang towards him. He was wrestling with all his might with the brass loop of the port. It seemed to turn against his hands in spite of all his efforts. I caught up my cane, a heavy oak stick I always used to carry, and thrust it through the ring and bore on it with all my strength. But the strong wood snapped suddenly and I fell upon the couch. When I rose again the port was wide open, and the captain was standing with his back against the door, pale to the lips.

"There is something in that berth!" he cried, in a strange voice, his eyes almost starting from his head. "Hold the door, while I look—it shall not escape us, whatever it is!"

But instead of taking his place, I sprang upon the lower bed, and seized something which lay in the upper berth.

It was something ghostly, horrible beyond words, and it moved in my grip. It was like the body of a man long drowned, and yet it moved, and had the strength of ten men living; but I gripped it with all my might—the slippery, oozy, horrible thing—the dead white eyes seemed to stare at me out of the dusk; the putrid odour of rank sea-water was about it, and its shiny hair hung in foul wet curls over its dead face. I wrestled with the dead thing; it thrust itself upon me and forced me back and nearly broke my arms; it wound its corpse's arms about my neck, the living death, and overpowered me, so that I, at last, cried aloud and fell, and left my hold.

As I fell the thing sprang across me, and seemed to throw itself upon the captain. When I last saw him on his feet his face was white and his lips set. It seemed to me that he struck a violent blow at the dead being, and then he, too, fell forward upon his face, with an inarticulate cry of horror.

The thing paused an instant, seeming to hover over his prostrate body, and I could have screamed again for very fright, but I had no voice left. The thing vanished suddenly, and it seemed to my disturbed senses that it made its exit through the open port, though how that was possible, considering the smallness of the aperture, is more than any one can tell. I lay a long time upon the floor, and the captain lay beside me. At last I partially recovered my senses and moved, and instantly I knew that my arm was broken—the small bone of the left forearm near the wrist.

I got upon my feet somehow, and with my remaining hand I tried to raise the captain. He groaned and moved, and at last came to himself. He was not hurt, but he seemed badly stunned.

Well, do you want to hear any more? There is nothing more. That is the end of my story. The carpenter carried out his scheme of running half a dozen four-inch screws through the door of 105; and if ever you take a passage in the *Kamtschatka,* you may ask for a berth in that state-room. You will be told that it is engaged—yes—it is engaged by that dead thing.

I finished the trip in the surgeon's cabin. He doctored my broken arm, and advised me not to "fiddle about with ghosts and things" any more. The captain was very silent, and never sailed again in that ship, though it is still running. And I will not sail in her either. It was a very disagreeable experience, and I was very badly frightened, which is a thing I do not like. That is all. That is how I saw a ghost—if it was a ghost. It was dead, anyhow.

F. MARION CRAWFORD

The Biscobra

*T*hey were truly a dismal-looking group when they got out of the train, and stood shivering and sleepy on the dusty platform of the little railway station one raw, cold-weather's morning—young Krey, his still younger wife, and a few draggled servants in dirty white clothing and tumbled puggaries.

Young Krey had landed in India three months before, a newly-fledged Bengal civilian, with narrow, stooping shoulders, deep-set, intelligent eyes shining through powerful spectacles, a bald, bumpy forehead—and a wife!

Now, for a youngster to commence his official existence as a married man is an unpardonable piece of stupidity in the eyes of the Indian authorities. To marry at the outset of his career is to write himself down an ass, and he usually suffers accordingly for his folly. A bachelor can always be taken in at once by his superior official, housed, fed, schooled in the manners and customs of the country, pitied for his homesickness by the female members of his host's family, and often has an uncommonly good time of it during the first few months of his service. But when there is a wife to be considered the aspect of affairs changes entirely. Married couples cannot always be 'put up' at a moment's notice; the lady may have an inconsiderate habit of falling ill in other people's houses, or a tendency to stay in them longer than she is wanted, she may be exasperatingly helpless, or hopelessly bumptious, and also, a man alone is seldom any trouble, whereas a lady has more or less to be 'entertained.'

So the Kreys, on their arrival at headquarters, found themselves pondering vaguely over all they had heard concerning the proverbial hospitality of Anglo-Indians, in a dirty, ill-kept hotel, the horrors of which they patiently endured for the space of ten days. Then came the taking of a huge barrack of a house at a fabulous rent, and impossible to make comfortable, but the only dwelling available at the time, and after being cheated right and left over the matting, floor-cloth and furniture, having unpacked their wedding presents, cut the curtains to fit the doors, and more or less settled down, there came orders for a transfer to a small station—the outcome of which was the afore-mentioned doleful group on the platform of the bare little railway station.

The Kreys had arrived at their new destination cold, tired and miserable, and the drive that followed to the dâk bungalow in a shaky hired vehicle was not calculated to raise the spirits of the young couple. First they passed an evil-smelling village tank, almost covered with thick, green slime, in which buffaloes wallowed and dirty clothes were being soused. Then came the post-office, an ugly little red brick edifice with iron bars in front of the windows, and the postmaster seated outside on a string bedstead, wrapped in a quilt of many colours, warming himself in the misty morning sunshine. Then a bare length of road devoid of trees, bounded by crops on either side, and dotted with cattle being driven to the jungle to graze. Then, rising conspicuously from the surrounding flatness, a large fig tree with thick, whispering leaves which shaded a tiny temple containing a strange, many-limbed idol smeared with red paint, that made Mrs. Krey think of blood, and the Mutiny, and hideous tales of human sacrifice.

A few European dwellings followed, and at last came the dâk bungalow, a severe little blue-washed building standing in a dusty area of bare ground, with the usual accessories of long-legged fowls, expectant crows, bearded khansamah, uncompromising furniture, and stuffy rooms filled with mosquitoes.

'I'm afraid we *must* stay here till we've got a house.' said young Krey, peering through his spectacles at the uninviting surroundings, 'but it's beastly uncomfortable. I'm so sorry, Nell!'

'What does it matter?' answered Mrs. Krey cheerfully, diving into her travelling bag. 'I shall be all right. Don't get depressed, Frank.'

Nevertheless, though she spoke brightly enough, she was feeling very low and weary. She was not in the best possible health, and had been packing hard for the last week, but she was a brave little person in spite of her fragile appearance and pathetic blue eyes, and her very pluck and patience often caused Krey to blame himself bitterly for having brought her with him to a country where discomfort was rife for the uninitiated, and the so-called luxuries no more than mere necessities.

Just now she longed to indulge in a good cry, but she refrained heroically because she would bear anything rather than call up that look of remorse and self-condemnation in her husband's boyish face. All she wanted, she said, was *rest*. So Frank helped her to take off her things, and tenderly drew the dusty shoes from the aching little feet, while he tried to speak in hopeful accents of the station. He felt sure his father had been judge there in bygone days, for he recollected hearing the governor speak of the place. If so, it would be a link, and perhaps some of the locals might remember, which would be a good beginning. He arranged the bed for her, brought her a cup of tea, and then left her to enjoy the rest she needed so badly.

She felt much more cheerful a few days later, when they had taken the only suitable house in the station, though it was an old bungalow and had not been occupied very lately. The thatched roof needed renewing, the walls seemed to be composed of mud and white ants, and nails driven into them disappeared and were no more seen. Wasps made their dwellings in corners, and sparrows had built in the fireplaces, owls of all sizes lived in a state of sleepy serenity along the beams of the verandah, and mysterious creatures ran to and fro with sharp, pattering feet over the loose, discoloured ceiling cloths.

All this was a trial to Mrs. Krey, but it gave her plenty to do and think of, and she waged untiring war against these unwelcome occupants of her house, for she dreaded and hated animals, as she called owls, ants, rats, spiders, snakes, or anything else she was afraid of. She always looked under her chair before she sat down, peered with a lamp into every nook and corner before she got into bed, and was continually on the watch for insect, reptile, bird or beast.

However, better times were not long in coming. The Kreys soon settled down, and were exceedingly happy in their rather dilapidated abode. He had enough work to keep him busy, but not too much to prevent his being home from office every evening in time to take his wife for a drive and a visit to the dingy little club. There were two other ladies in the station, who were kind to Mrs. Krey, gave her good advice, and helped to make the time pass pleasantly. Everybody liked her and admired her delicate, girlish face and gentle manner, even including the crusty bachelor Collector, who quite fell in love with her, and poured the whole of his family history into her sympathetic ears.

But in spite of all her popularity there was no one in the place who was so absolutely devoted to Mrs. Krey as old Beni, the aged Hindu bearer. He was the real ruler of the Krey household, for he had been bearer to young Krey's father before him. He journeyed many miles from the village of his ancestors to discover whether this new sahib was the son of his old master, and having satisfied himself that such was the case, he had calmly attached himself to the young couple, and taken them under his special protection.

The morning that Beni first put in an appearance was one to be remembered. He arrived on a diminutive chestnut pony with a foal running at its heels, and his bedding tied across its back, on the summit of which Beni balanced himself, holding a stick threateningly aloft with one hand, and clinging to the bundle of quilts with the other.

He demanded audience of the sahib, obtained an interview, explained his errand, and displayed a testimonial of his merits as a bearer written by young Krey's father, together with a faded photograph of the judge's wife in a crinoline, with a child on her knee, who, Beni asserted, was Frank himself!

Krey sought his wife's room to tell her the news.

'Such a queer old beggar, Nell,' he concluded. 'He must be at least a hundred. Do come and see him. He says I shall never do such good work as my father, but that all the same he means to stay with us. He looks much too old for work, but, I suppose, we can't refuse to keep him.'

Mrs. Krey's politeness was somewhat severely tried when she saw the old man. He looked like a mummified monkey, with his wrinkled brown skin, sunken black eyes and wizened features. He gazed at her intently, and then, to her infinite embarrassment, stopped and touched the toe of her little shoe, calling loudly on his gods to bless her and the unborn grandchild of his old master.

'Frank, he is dreadful; we can't keep him!' she said when this trying interview was over. Nevertheless, the Kreys did keep the old bearer, for he absolutely refused to go, and at once constituted himself the 'mem-sahib's' guide, philosopher and friend. He initiated her into the mysteries of the true bazaar prices, took possession of the key of the store-room, because she left it lying about and there was no knowing who might not profit by such carelessness; he saw the horses groomed and fed, kept an eye on the fowls and took care that none of the eggs were stolen, rated the other servants when necessary, and was the terror of the compound. On the other hand, he was a god-send to Mrs. Krey, as she was soon obliged to admit.

'I can't think what I should do without him,' she confessed to her husband a month later. 'He's wonderfully good, and I have learnt no end of Hindustani from him. But sometimes he's very trying, Frank! He seems to think I'm a perfect child, and hardly ever leaves me by myself. All the time you are at office he sits just outside the drawing-room door, and comes in now and then to see if I am all right. It's really very humiliating, and then' (with a pink blush rising in her cheeks) 'he does say such awful things. He asked me only this morning if I had ordered a cot yet! What *would* mother say if she knew? I call this a shameless country!'

Frank said the old man meant well, and she must remember the natives were not distinguished for delicacy of feeling. Gradually Mrs. Krey became accustomed to Beni's plain speaking, and often found his advice more useful than she would own even to herself. He purchased an excellent cow on her behalf, and was a dragon over its food and management. He wrote to a friend in Madras and secured a first-rate ayah, who was well-mannered and experienced, and saved her new mistress much trouble and fatigue. For, as time went on and the weather grew hot, Mrs. Krey became more easily tired and less inclined to exert herself. She had never been very strong, her nerves were shaky, she was unconsciously home-sick, and also frightened at the thought of the new experience that was to come to her in less than a couple of months.

And just then, to crown it all, the Collector suddenly sent for her husband to join him in camp for a week, and the night before he was to leave she was feeling more foolish and nervous than ever as they sat outside in the garden after dinner—she on a low couch, with a soft shawl over her shoulders and the bright moonlight sharpening her delicate features till her face looked almost ethereal.

'I *wish you* hadn't to go, Frank,' she sighed.

'So do I, Nell,' he answered fervently, 'and I'm afraid this is only the forerunner of other separations. You will have to go to the hills this year, I expect—at any-rate, for the rains.'

Krey was young, and it did not occur to him that in giving utterance to his own forebodings he was causing his wife's spirits to sink lower still.

'No, no,' she said harshly, 'don't talk about it. I couldn't go away alone. What should I do without you? What would you do without me?'

She put out a white slender hand towards him, and he clasped it in both of his, shivering slightly.

'The evenings are still chilly,' he said, glancing uneasily round. 'Are you cold, darling?'

'No, not cold,' in a weary, depressed voice, 'only miserable. I can't bear the thought of your going tomorrow. I feel as if something dreadful were going to happen. Frank, tell me, do you ever realise that some day a time will come when one of us will be left alone? When either you or I will have to face life with nothing in the way of comfort, but just recollections. Oh, Frank,' clinging to his hand, with a stifled sob, 'which of us will it be?'

'Hush, Nell, hush, my dearest,' stroking her soft hair with anxious tenderness, 'don't go on like this. For God's sake, don't, darling, you'll make yourself ill. Do promise not to fret while I'm away. The time will soon pass.'

He sat puzzled and wretched, for Nell was crying hysterically, and he was at his wits' end to know how to comfort her.

Then, seeing the gloomy, despondent look on his face, she choked back her tears and smiled at him.

'I'm all right now,' she said tremulously. 'I don't know what was the matter with me.'

She raised herself from the couch, put her arms round his neck, and they kissed each other passionately.

There was a short silence, broken by a noise in the verandah.

'What in the world is Beni doing?' ejaculated Krey, in astonishment.

The old bearer was mounted on an inverted packing case, poking violently up into the thatch with a long bamboo, while another servant brandished a lantern tied to the end of a stick.

'What is it, Beni?' shouted Krey.

'Sahib, it is a biscobra,' with another lunge into the thatch. 'It is an evil beast, and it's sting is more deadly than even the bite of the karait or cobra.'

"Oh! *What* is a biscobra?' cried Mrs. Krey, half rising, and turning pale with horror. Here was a new 'animal' that she had never even heard of, and in her own verandah roof, too!

'They are only big lizards,' said her husband, reassuringly. 'I read a description of them somewhere the other day. Natives are awfully afraid of them because they are so uncanny-looking, and have a head like a snake's but I believe they are perfectly harmless. Leave it alone, Beni,' he called 'you can't get at it to-night.'

Beni reluctantly scrambled from his rickety perch, and approached his master and mistress describing the evil qualities of a biscobra with so much vehemence that Mrs. Krey refused to go to bed till it was killed.

'But it's only a lizard, and quite harmless. We can't kill it to-night, Nell, dear; we should never see it.'

So she unwillingly agreed to leave the creature in peace for the night, but would not cross the verandah till the lantern was held before her to guide her over the dark shadows.

'It might have fallen down,' she said, advancing with cautious steps and peering nervously about.

The light of the lantern flickered up into the rafters, disturbing a family of bats that swooped down and out into the darkness, while some little owls chattered and objected and cuddled together indignantly on their beam.

'What was that noise?' whispered Mrs. Krey, clutching her husband's arm.

There was a slight scratching sound directly overhead, as of claws clinging to woodwork, a faint hiss, and the next moment flapping and turning in the air, the green scaly body of a large biscobra fell heavily on to Mrs. Krey's shoulder, where it hung for one hideous second, and then dropped with a thud on to the stone verandah floor.

That night death came to the little thatched bungalow and carried away the happiness of young Krey's life, leaving him only a wailing scrap of humanity that he turned from with loathing when it was brought to him. The time had come only too swiftly and surely when one of them was left alone; when one of them was forced to face life with nothing but memories for comfort.

People in the station were very kind to him. The motherly-hearted doctor's wife forced him to eat and drink, wrote letters home for him, and put away his wife's clothes that the sight of them might not harrow him at every turn. She also took charge of the weakly little baby, doing all that her experience knew to keep the faint flame of life alight. And Beni did everything in his power to help her, poor old Beni, who was in despair over the 'mem-sahib's' death, but who found consolation in the child. Then, when the feeble, premature little life died out, his grief was pitiable to see. He closely followed the tiny coffin to the grave in which the young mother had been laid but a few days previously; he stayed in the cemetery for hours, and finally sought out his master, and proffered a piteous, humble bequest.

'Sahib,' he wailed, 'I cannot leave the mem-sahib and the babba. I am an old man, my time is short, and I would stay with them while I am on earth. Speak to the Collector sahib and get me made caretaker of the cemetery. I do not want wages. I only wish to be with them.'

So when Krey left the station, transferred by his own desire to the other end of the province, old Beni remained behind and tended the little cemetery. Every morning he laid scented jessamine or sacred marigolds on the newly-made mound, and every evening he sat beside it and talked, or crooned songs, to the beloved 'mem-sahib' and 'babba' that lay beneath.

Shortly afterwards a marble cross arrived, which, under Beni's supervision, was erected at once. It did not occur to anyone to interfere, and Beni did not know that it was put up too soon, and that, when the ground became sodden and loose with the rains, it would lean over to one side, or perhaps fall down altogether.

However, for the present, it reared itself in all its white purity amongst the stained and time-worn tombstones, and was kept fresh and clean by the old bearer's tender, untiring care.

On the anniversary of his wife's death Krey came once more to the station. At first glance it would have been hard to recognise him as the same man, for his health had broken down, his nerves were shattered, and he looked ten years older than his age. Sleep was now a rare visitor to him, and his eyes held a strange, restless gleam. He had just been ordered home on medical certificate, but Krey could not leave the country without saying good-bye to Nell and the baby; so, telling no one of his intention, he arrived at the dâk bungalow late one close, stuffy evening. The atmosphere of the little building was terribly oppressive. The narrow ill-ventilated rooms were crowded with bitter memories. Sleep, he well knew, was not to be expected, and so, instead of waiting till the following morning, he started on his solitary walk to the cemetery in the vivid moonlight shortly after midnight.

The air was warm and heavy as he entered the gates of the graveyard, the silence being broken only now and again by the cries of the jackals or the shrill scream of a cricket in one of the mango trees. He walked up the dry, dusty path and then stopped, searching for the cross he had chosen. The moonlight sharpened the edges of the irregular groups of stones and monuments, some of which were crumbling away into mere ruins, and deepened the shadows of the trees and shrubs that bordered the path. He spied a corner of the white cross, and strode rapidly towards it, picking his way amongst the quiet graves.

On reaching the spot he saw that the cross was leaning down to one side, and that a gaping hole had formed in the ground at its base. A sudden rage seized him. Where was Beni, who had pretended to be so faithful and who had promised to tend the grave? What had the Collector and the doctor's wife been about to allow this to happen? He made his way swiftly towards a grass hut at the further end of the cemetery, but as he came alongside the miserable little dwelling, a sound of moaning from within made him pause to listen.

He stooped and looked into the shed, which held a low bedstead, a guttering oil lamp, a few cooking vessels and a hookah. On the bed, beneath a coarse brown blanket, lay Beni, shaking and groaning in the last stage of fever. His bloodshot eyes were vacant and staring, but as they fell on his master recognition flashed into them, and he struggled to raise himself.

'Sahib,' he whispered, 'now have my prayers been answered, for thou hast come, now I can speak and tell thee what I feared I should say to no man, for I am going quickly.'

'Beni, why did you not let me know you were ill?' cried Krey, in sore distress, his anger gone as he saw the old man's moments were numbered.

'How could I, sahib? Sickness came upon me, and none visit the cemetery save when a sahib dies. So I have lain and waited, for surely I knew that I could not die without seeing thy face once more——' He ceased abruptly, and his head sank.

'Beni?' said Krey.

He thought the end had come, but presently the bleared old eyes opened again.

'The babba,' came in a faint whisper; 'who will feed her?'

'Yes, yes, it will be all right,' said Krey, thinking his mind was wandering.

'She was not fed last night, nor the night before. I could not go to her. She will be watching for me. Sahib, go and feed her.

The goat is tethered to a tree outside, and the vessel for the milk lies on the floor.' Beni paused for a moment to get his breath, then he said impatiently, 'Go sahib, go quickly.'

'Yes,' answered Krey again.

'Thou thinkest I lie?' cried the old man, with sudden energy. 'I speak but the truth. Every night has the babba left the grave and I have fed her with goat's milk. I bought the goat with my own savings. Thou believest me not!' he continued with angry despair. 'Come, then, and I will show thee! Nay, I *will* rise. I have enough life left to go forth once more and feed the babba, but it will be for the last time.'

Krey could not prevent his carrying out his purpose, and the old man rose slowly from the bed, tottering and shaking. Together they unfastened the goat, and with Krey carrying the brass 'lota' for the milk, they slowly wended their way towards the marble cross, Beni hanging helplessly on to the arm of the young man, while the goat followed bleating anxiously.

When they reached the grave Beni sat down on the ground exhausted. Krey stood by him in silence. He felt as if he were dreaming, and a vague horror oppressed him. Gradually the old man revived, and with an almost superhuman effort called the goat to him and milked her into the 'lota.' Then he crawled to the gap under the cross, set the vessel down at the edge of the fissure, and made a chirruping sound with his lips.

'Now, sahib,' he said, turning to Krey.

Two or three seconds passed. The moon glittered on brilliantly, a fox barked in a neighbouring field, an owl hooted and flew from one tree to another with a melancholy flap of its wings—and then came a scrambling inside the hole. Krey leant forward and held his breath, and saw a large biscobra slowly emerge from the crack in the ground and begin to lap the milk.

A cry of horror, rage and madness escaped his dry lips. He made a dash at the creature's snake-like head with his stick, and beat it to a pulp with all his strength.

Another cry arose on the night air.

'Sahib! Sahib! What hast thou done? Thou hast slain the soul of the child—thou hast——' A rattle in the old man's throat choked his utterance, and he fell forward on his face.

The next morning a half-caste clerk and his wife came to lay a painted metal wreath on the grave of a relative, and they found Beni's lifeless body lying by the crooked white cross. Near at hand was an overturned brass vessel and a dead biscobra with its head beaten off, and wandering about the cemetery was an Englishman, who laughed and danced foolishly when they spoke to him, and from whose eyes the light of understanding had gone for ever.

ALICE PERRIN

The Avu Observatory

The observatory at Avu, in Borneo, stands on the spur of the mountain. To the north rises the old crater, black as night against the unfathomable blue of the sky. From the little circular building, with its mushroom dome, the slopes plunge steeply downward into the black mysteries of the tropical forest beneath. The little house in which the observer and his assistant live is about fifty yards from the observatory, and beyond this are the huts of their native attendants.

Thaddy, the chief observer, was down with a slight fever. His assistant, Woodhouse, paused for a moment in silent contemplation of the tropical night before commencing his solitary vigil. The night was very still. Now and then voices and laughter came from the native huts, or the cry of some strange animal was heard from the midst of the mystery of the forest. Nocturnal insects appeared in ghostly fashion out of the darkness and fluttered round his light. He thought, perhaps, of all the possibilities of discovery that still lay in the black tangle beneath him; for to the naturalist the virgin forests of Borneo are still a wonderland full of strange questions and half-suspected discoveries. Woodhouse carried a small lantern in his hand, and its yellow glow contrasted vividly with the infinite series of tints between lavender-blue and black in which the landscape was painted. His hands and face were smeared with ointment against the attacks of the mosquitoes.

Even in these days of celestial photography, work done in a purely temporary erection, and with only the most primitive appliances in addition to the telescope, still involves a very large amount of cramped and motionless watching. He sighed as he thought of the physical fatigues before him, stretched himself, and entered the observatory.

The reader is probably familiar with the structure of an ordinary astronomical observatory. The building is usually cylindrical in shape, with a very light hemispherical roof capable of being turned round from the interior. The telescope is supported upon a stone pillar in the centre, and a clockwork arrangement compensates for the earth's rotation, and allows a star once found to be continuously observed. Besides this, there is a compact tracery of wheels and screws about its point of support, by which the astronomer adjusts it. There is, of course, a slit in the movable roof which follows the eye of the telescope in its survey of the heavens. The observer sits or lies on a sloping wooden arrangement, which he can wheel to any part of the observatory as the position of the telescope may require. Within it is advisable to have things as dark as possible, in order to enhance the brilliance of the stars observed.

The lantern flared as Woodhouse entered his circular den, and the general darkness fled into black shadows behind the big machine, from which it presently seemed to creep back over the whole place again as the light waned. The slit was a profound transparent blue, in which six stars shone with tropical brilliance, and their light lay, a pallid gleam, along the black tube of the instrument. Woodhouse shifted the roof, and then proceeding to the telescope, turned first one wheel and then another, the great cylinder slowly swinging into a new position. Then he glanced through the finder, the little companion telescope, moved the roof a little more, made some further adjustments, and set the clockwork in motion. He took off his jacket, for the night was very hot, and pushed into position the uncomfortable seat to which he was condemned for the next four hours. Then with a sigh he resigned himself to his watch upon the mysteries of space.

There was no sound now in the observatory, and the lantern waned steadily. Outside there was the occasional cry of some animal in alarm or pain, or calling to its mate, and the intermittent sounds of the Malay and Dyak servants. Presently one of the men began a queer chanting song, in which the others joined at intervals. After this it would seem that they turned in for the night, for no further sound came from their direction, and the whispering stillness became more and more profound.

The clockwork ticked steadily. The shrill hum of a mosquito explored the place and grew shriller in indignation at Woodhouse's ointment. Then the lantern went out and all the observatory was black.

Woodhouse shifted his position presently, when the slow movement of the telescope had carried it beyond the limits of his comfort.

He was watching a little group of stars in the Milky Way, in one of which his chief had seen or fancied a remarkable colour variability. It was not a part of the regular work for which the establishment existed and for that reason perhaps Woodhouse was deeply interested. He must have forgotten things terrestrial.

All his attention was concentrated upon the great blue circle of the telescope field—a circle powdered, so it seemed, with an innumerable multitude of stars, and all luminous against the blackness of its setting. As he watched he seemed to himself to become incorporeal, as if he too were floating in the ether of space. Infinitely remote was the faint red spot he was observing.

Suddenly the stars were blotted out. A flash of blackness passed, and they were visible again.

"Queer," said Woodhouse. "Must have been a bird."

The thing happened again, and immediately after the great tube shivered as though it had been struck. Then the dome of the observatory resounded with a series of thundering blows. The stars seemed to sweep aside as the telescope—which had been unclamped—swung round and away from the slit in the roof.

"Great Scott!" cried Woodhouse. "What's this?"

Some huge vague black shape, with a flapping something like a wing, seemed to be struggling in the aperture of the roof. In another moment the slit was clear again, and the luminous haze of the Milky Way shone warm and bright.

The interior of the roof was perfectly black, and only a scraping sound marked the whereabouts of the unknown creature.

Woodhouse had scrambled from the seat to his feet. He was trembling violently and in perspiration with the suddenness of the occurrence. Was the thing, whatever it was, inside or out? It was big, whatever else it might be. Something shot across the skylight, and the telescope swayed. He started violently and put his arm up. It was in the observatory, then, with him. It was clinging to the roof apparently. What the devil was it? Could it see him?

He stood for perhaps a minute in a state of stupefaction. The beast, whatever it was, clawed at the interior of the dome, and then something flapped almost into his face, and he saw the momentary gleam of starlight on a skin like oiled leather. His water-bottle was knocked off his little table with a smash.

The sense of some strange bird-creature hovering a few yards from his face in the darkness was indescribably unpleasant to Woodhouse. As his thought returned he concluded that it must be some night-bird or large bat. At any risk he would see what it was, and pulling a match from his pocket, he tried to strike it on the telescope seat. There was a smoking streak of phosphorescent light, the match flared for a moment, and he saw a vast wing sweeping towards him, a gleam of grey-brown fur, and then he was struck in the face and the match knocked out of his hand. The blow was aimed at his temple, and a claw tore sideways down to his cheek. He reeled and fell, and he heard the extinguished lantern smash. Another blow followed as he fell. He was partly stunned, he felt his own warm blood stream out upon his face. Instinctively he felt his eyes had been struck at, and turning over on his face to save them, tried to crawl under the protection of the telescope.

He was struck again upon the back, and he heard his jacket rip, and then the thing hit the roof of the observatory. He edged as far as he could between the wooden seat and the eyepiece of the instrument, and turned his body round so that it was chiefly his feet that were exposed. With these he could at least kick. He was still in a mystified state. The strange beast banged about in the darkness, and presently clung to the telescope, making it sway and the gear rattle. Once it flapped near him, and he kicked out madly and felt a soft body with his feet. He was horribly scared now. It must be a big thing to swing the telescope like that. He saw for a moment the outline of a head black against the starlight, with sharply-pointed upstanding ears and a crest between them. It seemed to him to be as big as a mastiff's. Then he began to bawl out as loudly as he could for help.

At that the thing came down upon him again. As it did so his hand touched something beside him on the floor. He kicked out, and the next moment his ankle was gripped and held by a row of keen teeth. He yelled again, and tried to free his leg by kicking with the other. Then he realised he had the broken water-bottle at his hand, and snatching it, he struggled into a sitting posture, and feeling in the darkness towards his foot, gripped a velvety ear, like the ear of a big cat. He had seized the water-bottle by its neck and brought it down with a shivering crash upon the head of the strange beast. He repeated the blow, and then stabbed and jabbed with the jagged end of it, in the darkness, where he judged the face might be.

The small teeth relaxed their hold, and at once Woodhouse pulled his leg free and kicked hard. He felt the sickening feel of fur and bone giving under his boot. There was a tearing bite at his arm, and he struck over it at the face, as he judged, and hit damp fur.

There was a pause; then he heard the sound of claws and the dragging of a heavy body away from him over the observatory floor. Then there was silence, broken only by his own sobbing, breathing, and a sound like licking. Everything was black except the parallelogram of the blue skylight with the luminous dust of stars, against which the end of the telescope now appeared in silhouette. He waited, as it seemed, an interminable time.

Was the thing coming on again? He felt in his trouser-pocket for some matches, and found one remaining. He tried to strike this, but the floor was wet, and it spat and went out. He cursed. He could not see where the door was situated. In his struggle he had quite lost his bearings. The strange beast, disturbed by the splutter of the match, began to move again. "Time!" called Woodhouse, with a sudden gleam of mirth, but the thing was not coming at him again. He must have hurt it, he thought, with the broken bottle. He felt a dull pain in his ankle. Probably he was bleeding there. He wondered if it would support him if he tried to stand up. The night outside was very still. There was no sound of anyone moving. The sleepy fools had not heard those wings battering upon the dome, nor his shouts. It was no good wasting strength in shouting. The monster flapped its wings and startled him into a defensive attitude. He hit his elbow against the seat, and it fell over with a crash. He cursed this, and then he cursed the darkness.

Suddenly the oblong patch of starlight seemed to sway to and fro. Was he going to faint? It would never do to faint. He clenched his fists and set his teeth to hold himself together. Where had the door got to? It occurred to him he could get his bearings by the stars visible through the skylight. The patch of stars he saw was in Sagittarius and south-eastward; the door was north—or was it north by west? He tried to think. If he could get the door open he might retreat. It might be the thing was wounded. The suspense was beastly. "Look here!" he said, "if you don't come on, I shall come at you."

Then the thing began clambering up the side of the observatory, and he saw its black outline gradually blot out the skylight. Was it in retreat? He forgot about the door and watched as the dome shifted and creaked. Somehow he did not feel very frightened or excited now. He felt a curious sinking sensation inside him. The sharply-defined patch of light, with the black form moving across it, seemed to be growing smaller and smaller. That was curious. He began to feel very thirsty, and yet he did not feel inclined to get anything to drink. He seemed to be sliding down a long funnel.

He felt a burning sensation in his throat, and then he perceived it was broad daylight and that one of the Dyak servants was looking at him with a curious expression. Then there was the top of Thaddy's face upside down. Funny fellow, Thaddy, to go about like that! Then he grasped the situation better, and perceived that his head was on Thaddy's knee, and Thaddy was giving him brandy. And then he saw the eyepiece of the telescope with a lot of red smears on it. He began to remember.

"You've made this observatory in a pretty mess," said Thaddy.

The Dyak boy was beating up an egg in brandy. Woodhouse took this and sat up. He felt a sharp twinge of pain. His ankle was tied up, so were his arm and the side of his face. The smashed glass, redstained, lay about the floor, the telescope seat was overturned, and by the opposite wall was a dark pool. The door was open, and he saw the grey summit of the mountain against a brilliant background of blue sky.

"Pah!" said Woodhouse. "Who's been killing calves here? Take me out of it."

Then he remembered the Thing, and the fight he had had with it.

'What *was* it?" he said to Thaddy—"the Thing I fought with?"

"*You* know that best," said Thaddy. "But, anyhow, don't worry yourself now about it. Have some more to drink."

Thaddy, however, was curious enough, and it was a hard struggle between duty and inclination to keep Woodhouse quiet until he was decently put away in bed, and had slept upon the copious dose of meat extract Thaddy considered advisable. They then talked it over together.

"It was," said Woodhouse, "more like a big bat than anything else in the world. It had sharp, short ears, and soft fur, and its wings were leathery. Its teeth were little but devilish sharp, and its, jaws could not have been very strong or else it would have bitten through my ankle."

"It has pretty nearly," said Thaddy.

"It seemed to me to hit out with its claws pretty freely. That is about as much as I know about the beast. Our conversation was intimate, so to speak, and yet not confidential."

"The Dyak chaps talk about a Big Colugo, a Klangutang—whatever that may be. It does not often attack man, but I suppose you made it nervous. They say there is a Big Colugo, and something else that sounds like gobble. They all fly about at night. For my own part, I know there are flying foxes and flying lemurs about here, but they are none of them very big beasts."

"There are more things in heaven and earth," said Woodhouse—and Thaddy groaned at the quotation—"and more particularly in the forests of Borneo, than are dreamt of in our philosophies. On the whole, if the Borneo fauna is going to disgorge any more of its novelties upon me, I should prefer that it did so when I was not occupied in the observatory at night and alone."

H.G. WELLS

Leiningen Versus the Ants

"Unless they alter their course, and there's no reason why they should, they'll reach your plantation in two days at the latest."

Leiningen sucked placidly at a cigar about the size of a corn-cob and for a few seconds gazed without answering at the agitated District Commissioner. Then he took the cigar from his lips, and leaned slightly forward. With his bristling grey hairs, bulky nose and lucid eyes he had the look of an ageing and shabby eagle.

"Decent of you," he murmured, "paddling all this way just to give me the tip. But you're pulling my leg, of course, when you say I must do a bunk. Why, even a herd of saurians couldn't drive me from this plantation of mine."

The Brazilian official threw up lean and lanky arms and clawed the air with wildly distended fingers. "Leiningen!" he shouted. "You're insane! They're not creatures you can fight! Ten miles long, two miles wide—ants, nothing but ants! And every single one of them a fiend from hell; before you can spit three times they'll eat a full grown buffalo to the bones. I tell you if you don't clear out at once there'll be nothing left of you but a skeleton picked as clean as your own plantation."

Leiningen grinned. "Anyway, I'm not an old woman; I'm not going to run for it. And don't think I'm the kind of fathead who tries to fend off lightning with his fists either. I use my intelligence, old man. ... When I began this model farm and plantation three years ago I took into account all that could conceivably happen to it. And now I'm ready for anything and everything—including your ants."

The Brazilian rose heavily to his feet. "I've done my best," he gasped. "Your obstinacy endangers not only yourself but the lives of your four hundred workers. You don't know these ants!"

Leiningen accompanied him down to the river, where the Government launch was moored. The vessel cast off. ... Long after the launch had disappeared round the bend, Leiningen thought he could still hear that dimming, imploring voice: "You don't know them, I tell you! *You don't know them!*"

But the reported enemy was by no means unfamiliar to the planter. Before he started work on his settlement, he had lived long enough in the country to see for himself the fearful devastations sometimes wrought by these ravenous insects in their campaigns for food. But since then he had planned measures of defence accordingly, and these, he was convinced, were in every way adequate to withstand the approaching peril.

Yes, Leiningen had always known how to grapple with life. Even here, in this Brazilian wilderness, his brain had triumphed over every difficulty and danger it had so far encountered. First he had vanquished primal forces by cunning and organization, then he had enlisted the resources of modern science to increase miraculously the yield of his plantation. And now he was sure he would prove more than a match for the "irresistible" ants.

That same evening, however, Leiningen assembled his workers. He had no intention of waiting till the news reached their ears from other sources. Most of them had been born in the district; the cry "The ants are coming!" was to them an imperative signal for instant, panic-stricken flight, a spring for life itself. But so great was the Indians' trust in Leiningen, in Leiningen's word, and in Leiningen's wisdom, that they received his curt tidings, and his orders for the imminent struggle, with the calmness with which they were given. They waited, unafraid, alert, as if for the beginning of a new game or hunt which he had just described to them. The ants were indeed mighty, but not so mighty as the boss. Let them come!

They came at noon the second day. Their approach was announced by the wild unrest of the horses, scarcely controllable now either in stall or under rider, scenting from afar a vapour instinct with horror.

It was announced by a stampede of animals, timid and savage, hurtling past each other; jaguars and pumas flashing by nimble stags of the pampas; bulky tapirs, no longer hunters, themselves hunted, outpacing fleet kinkajous; maddened herds of cattle, heads lowered, nostrils snorting, rushing through tribes of loping monkeys, chattering in a dementia of terror; then followed the creeping and springing denizens of bush and steppe, big and little rodents, snakes and lizards.

Pell-mell the rabble swarmed down the hill to the plantation, scattered right and left before the barrier of the water-filled ditch, then sped onwards to the river, where, again hindered, they fled along its bank out of sight.

This water-filled ditch was one of the defence measures which Leiningen had long since prepared against the advent of the ants. It encompassed three sides of the plantation like a huge horseshoe. Twelve feet across, but not very deep, when dry it could hardly be described as an obstacle to either man or beast. But the ends of the "horseshoe" ran into the river which formed the northern boundary, and fourth side, of the plantation. And at the end nearer the house and outbuildings, in the middle of the plantation, Leiningen had constructed a dam by means of which water from the river could be diverted into the ditch.

So now, by opening the dam, he was able to fling an imposing girdle of water, a huge quadrilateral with the river as its base, completely around the plantation, like the moat encircling a medieval city. Unless the ants were clever enough to build rafts, they had no hope of reaching the plantation, Leiningen concluded.

The twelve-foot water ditch seemed to afford in itself all the security needed. But while awaiting the arrival of the ants, Leiningen made a further improvement. The western section of the ditch ran along the edge of a tamarind wood, and the branches of some great trees reached over the water. Leiningen now had them lopped so that ants could not descend from them within the "moat."

The women and children, then the herds of cattle, were escorted by peons on rafts over the river, to remain on the other side in absolute safety until the plunderers had departed. Leiningen gave this instruction, not because he believed the non-combatants were in any danger, but in order to avoid hampering the efficiency of the defenders.

Finally, he made a careful inspection of the "inner" moat— a smaller ditch lined with concrete, which extended around the hill on which stood the ranch house, barns, stables and other buildings. Into this concrete ditch emptied the inflow pipes from three great petrol tanks. If by some miracle the ants managed to cross the water and reach the plantation, this "rampart of petrol" would be an absolutely impassable protection for the besieged and their dwellings and stock. Such, at least, was Leiningen's opinion.

He stationed his men at irregular distances along the water ditch, the first line of defence. Then he lay down in his hammock and puffed drowsily away at his pipe until a peon came with the report that the ants had been observed far away in the south.

Leiningen mounted his horse, which at the feel of its master seemed to forget its uneasiness, and rode leisurely in the direction of the threatening offensive. The southern stretch of ditch—the upper side of the quadrilateral—was nearly three miles long; from its centre one could survey the entire countryside. This was destined to be the scene of the outbreak of war between Leiningen's brain and twenty square miles of life-destroying ants.

It was a sight one could never forget. Over the range of hills, as far as eye could see, crept a darkening hem, ever longer and broader, until the shadow spread across the slope from the east to west, then downwards, downwards, uncannily swift, and all the green herbage of that wide vista was being mown as by a giant sickle, leaving only the vast moving shadow, extending, deepening, and moving rapidly nearer.

When Leiningen's men, behind their barrier of water, perceived the approach of the long-expected foe, they gave vent to their suspense in screams and imprecations. But as the distance began to lessen between the "sons of hell" and the water ditch, they relapsed into silence. Before the advance of that awe-inspiring throng, their belief in the powers of the boss began to steadily dwindle.

Even Leiningen himself, who had ridden up just in time to restore their loss of heart by a display of unshakable calm, even he could not free himself from a qualm of malaise. Yonder were thousands of millions of voracious jaws bearing down upon him and only a suddenly insignificant, narrow ditch lay between him and his men and being gnawed to the bones "before you can spit three times."

Hadn't his brain for once taken on more than it could manage? If the blighters decided to rush the ditch, fill it to the brim with their corpses, there'd still be more than enough to destroy every trace of that cranium of his. The planter's chin jutted; they hadn't got him yet, and he'd see to it they never would. While he could think at all, he'd flout both death and the devil.

The hostile army was approaching in perfect formation; no human battalions, however well-drilled, could ever hope to rival the precision of that advance. Along a front that moved forward as uniformly as a straight line, the ants drew nearer and nearer to the water ditch. Then, when they learned through their scouts the nature of the obstacle, the two outlying wings of the army detached themselves from the main body and marched down the western and eastern sides of the ditch.

This surrounding manoeuvre took rather more than an hour to accomplish; no doubt the ants expected that at some point they would find a crossing.

During this outflanking movement by the wings, the army on the centre and southern front remained still. The besieged were therefore able to contemplate at their leisure the thumb-long, reddish-black, long-legged insects; some of the Indians believed they could see, too, intent on them, the brilliant, cold eyes, and the razor-edged mandibles, of this host of infinity.

It is not easy for the average person to imagine that an animal, not to mention an insect, can *think*. But now both the European brain of Leiningen and the primitive brains of the Indians began to stir with the unpleasant foreboding that inside every single one of that deluge of insects dwelt a thought. And that thought was: ditch or no ditch, we'll get your flesh!

Not until four o'clock did the wings reach the "horseshoe" ends of the ditch, only to find these ran into the great river. Through some kind of secret telegraphy, the report must have then flashed very swiftly along the entire enemy line. And Leiningen, riding—no longer casually—along his side of the ditch, noticed by energetic and widespread movements of troops that for some unknown reason the news of the check had its greatest effect on the southern front, where the main army was massed. Perhaps the failure to find a way over the ditch was persuading the ants to withdraw from the plantation in search of spoils more easily attainable.

An immense flood of ants, about a hundred yards in width, was pouring in a glimmering-black cataract down the far slope of the ditch. Many thousands were already drowning in the sluggish, creeping flow, but they were followed by troop after troop, who clambered over their sinking comrades, and then themselves served as dying bridges to the reserves hurrying on in their rear.

Shoals of ants were being carried away by the current into the middle of the ditch, where gradually they broke asunder and then, exhausted by their struggles, vanished below the surface. Nevertheless, the wavering, floundering hundred-yard front was remorselessly if slowly advancing towards the besieged on the other bank. Leiningen had been wrong when he supposed the enemy would first have to fill the ditch with their bodies before they could cross; instead, they merely needed to act as stepping-stones, as they swam and sank, to the hordes ever pressing onwards from behind.

Near Leiningen a few mounted herdsmen awaited his orders. He sent one to the weir—the river must be dammed more strongly to increase the speed and power of the water coursing through the ditch.

A second peon was dispatched to the outhouses to bring spades and petrol sprinklers. A third rode away to summon to the zone of the offensive all the men, except the observation posts, on the near-by sections of the ditch, which were not yet actively threatened.

The ants were getting across far more quickly than Leiningen would have deemed possible. Impelled by the mighty cascade behind them, they struggled nearer and nearer to the inner bank. The momentum of the attack was so great that neither the tardy flow of the stream nor its downward pull could exert its proper force; and into the gap left by every submerging insect hastened a dozen more.

When reinforcements reached Leiningen, the invaders were halfway over. The planter had to admit to himself that it was only by a stroke of luck for him that the ants were attempting the crossing on a relatively short front; had they assaulted simultaneously along the entire length of the ditch, the outlook for the defenders would have been black indeed.

Even as it was, it could hardly be described as rosy, though the planter seemed quite unaware that death in a gruesome form was drawing closer and closer. Such, indeed, was his aura of confidence that the Indians forgot their stupefied fear of the peril only a yard or two away; under the planter's supervision, they began fervidly digging up to the edge of the bank and throwing clods of earth and spadefuls of sand into the midst of the hostile fleet.

The petrol sprinklers, hitherto used to destroy pests and blights on the plantation, were also brought into action. Streams

petrol, idiot! Douse your paws in the petrol!" The
eased his pirouette as if transfixed, then tore off his shirt
nged his arm and the ants hanging to it up to the shoulder
of the large open tins of petrol. But even then the fierce
oles did not slacken; another peon had to help him squash
etach each separate insect.

Distracted by the episode, some defenders had turned away
n the ditch. And now cries of fury, a thudding of spades, and
ild trampling to and fro, showed that the ants had made full
e of the interval, though luckily only a few had managed to get
cross. The men set to work again desperately with the barrage
of earth and sand. Meanwhile an old Indian, who acted as medicine-
man to the plantation workers, gave the bitten peon a drink he
had prepared some hours before, which, he claimed, possessed
the virtue of dissolving and weakening ants' venom.

Leiningen surveyed his position. A dispassionate observer
would have estimated the odds against him at a thousand to one.
But then such an onlooker would have reckoned only by what
he saw—the advance of myriad battalions of ants against the
futile efforts of a few defenders—and not by the unseen activity
that can go on in a man's brain.

For the water in the ditch was beginning to rise; the stronger
damming of the river was making itself apparent.

Visibly the swiftness and power of the masses of water
increased, swirling into quicker and quicker movement its living
black surface, dispersing its pattern, carrying away more and
more of it on the hastening current.

Victory had been snatched from the very jaws of defeat. With
a hysterical shout of joy, the peons feverishly intensified their
bombardment of earth clods and sand.

of evil-reeking oil now soared and
disorder through the bombardment

The ants responded to these vigoro
of defence by further developments o.
clumps of huddling insects began to roll o
into the water. At the same time, Leiningen
were now attacking along an ever-widening fr
both of his men and his petrol sprinklers were
this rapid extension of the line of battle wa
overwhelming danger.

To add to his difficulties, the very clods of ear
into that black floating carpet often whirled fragmen
the defenders' side, and here and there dark ribbons wei
mounting the inner bank. True, wherever a man saw the
could still be driven back into the water by spadefuls of
or jets of petrol. But the file of defenders was too sparse
scattered to hold off at all points these landing parties, a.
though the peons toiled like madmen their plight became momently
more perilous.

One man struck with his spade at an enemy clump, did not
draw it back quickly enough from the water; in a trice the
wooden haft swarmed with upward-scurrying insects. With a
curse he dropped the spade into the ditch; too late, they were
already on his body. They lost no time; wherever they encountered
bare flesh they bit deeply; a few, bigger than the rest, carried in
their hindquarters a sting which injected a burning and paralysing
venom. Screaming, frantic with pain, the peon danced and twirled
like a dervish.

Realizing that another such casualty, yes, perhaps this alone,
might plunge his men into confusion and destroy their morale,
Leiningen roared in a bellow louder than the yells of the victim:

And now the wide cataract down the opposite bank was thinning and ceasing, as if the ants were becoming aware that they could not attain their aim. They were scurrying back up the slope to safety.

All the troops so far hurled into the ditch had been sacrificed in vain. Drowned and floundering insects eddied in thousands along the flow, while Indians running on the bank destroyed every swimmer that reached the farther side.

The news ran swiftly along the entire chain of outposts, and soon a long scattered line of laughing men could be seen hastening along the ditch towards the scene of victory.

For once they seemed to have lost all their native reserve, for it was in wild abandon now they celebrated the triumph—as if there were no longer thousands of millions of merciless, cold and hungry eyes watching them from the opposite bank, watching and waiting.

The sun sank behind the rim of the tamarind wood and twilight deepened into night. It was not only hoped but expected that the ants would remain quiet until dawn. But to defeat any forlorn attempt at a crossing, the flow of water through the ditch was powerfully increased by opening the dam still further.

In spite of this impregnable barrier, Leiningen was not yet altogether convinced that the ants would not venture another surprise attack. He ordered his men to camp along the bank overnight. He also detailed parties of them to patrol the ditch in two of his motor-cars and ceaselessly to illuminate the surface of the water with headlights and electric torches.

After having taken all precautions he deemed necessary, the farmer ate his supper with considerable appetite and went to bed. His slumbers were in no wise disturbed by the memory of the waiting, live, twenty square miles.

Dawn found a thoroughly refreshed and active Leiningen riding along the edge of the ditch. The planter saw before him a motionless and unaltered throng of besiegers. He studied the wide belt of water between them and the plantation, and for a moment almost regretted that the fight had ended so soon and so simply. In the comforting, matter-of-fact light of morning, it seemed to him now that the ants hadn't the ghost of a chance to cross the ditch. Even if they plunged headlong into it on all three fronts at once, the force of the now powerful current would inevitably sweep them away. He had got quite a thrill out of the fight—a pity it was already over.

He rode along the eastern and southern sections of the ditch and found everything in order. He reached the western section, opposite the tamarind wood, and there, contrary to the other battlefronts, he found the enemy very busy indeed. The trunks and branches of the trees and the creepers of the lianas, on the far bank of the ditch, fairly swarmed with industrious insects. But instead of eating the leaves there and then, they were merely gnawing through the stalks, so that a thick green shower fell steadily to the ground.

No doubt they were victualling columns sent to obtain provender for the rest of the army. The discovery did not surprise Leiningen. He did not need to be told that ants are intelligent, that certain species even use others as milch cows, watchdogs and slaves. He was well aware of their power of adaptation, their sense of discipline, their marvellous talent for organization.

His belief that a foray to supply the army was in progress was strengthened when he saw the leaves that fell to the ground being dragged to the troops waiting outside the wood. Then all at once he realized the aim that rain of green was intended to serve.

Each single leaf, pulled or pushed by dozens of toiling insects, was borne straight to the edge of the ditch. Even as Macbeth watched the approach of Birnam Wood in the hands of his enemies, Leiningen saw the tamarind wood move nearer and nearer in the mandibles of the ants. Unlike the fey Scot, however, he did not lose his nerve; no witches had prophesied his doom, and if they had he would have slept just as soundly. All the same, he was forced to admit to himself that the situation was now far more ominous than that of the day before.

He had thought it impossible for the ants to build rafts for themselves—well, here they were, coming in thousands, more than enough to bridge the ditch. Leaves after leaves rustled down the slope into the water, where the current drew them away from the bank and carried them into mid-stream. And every single leaf carried several ants. This time the farmer did not trust to the alacrity of his messengers. He galloped away, leaning from his saddle and yelling orders as he rushed past outpost after outpost: "Bring petrol pumps to the south-west front! Issue spades to every man along the line facing the wood!" And arrived at the eastern and southern sections, he dispatched every man except the observation posts to the menaced west.

Then, as he rode past the stretch where the ants had failed to cross the day before, he witnessed a brief but impressive scene. Down the slope of the distant hill there came towards him a singular being, writhing rather than running, an animal-like blackened statue with a shapeless head and four quivering feet that knuckled under almost ceaselessly. When the creature reached the far bank of the ditch and collapsed opposite Leiningen, he recognized it as a pampas stag, covered over and over with ants.

It had strayed near the zone of the army. As usual, they had attacked its eyes first. Blinded, it had reeled ... straight into the ranks of its persecutors, and now the beast swayed to and fro in its death agony.

With a shot from his rifle Leiningen put it out of its misery. Then he pulled out his watch. He hadn't a second to lose, but for life itself he would not have denied his curiosity the satisfaction of knowing how long the ants would take—for personal reasons, so to speak. After six minutes the white polished bones alone remained. That's how he himself would look before you can— Leiningen spat once, and put spurs to his horse. The zest with which the excitement of the novel contest had inspired him the day before had now vanished; in its place was a cold and violent purpose. He had underestimated the might of the enemy; he really would have to bestir himself if he hoped to outwit them.

The biggest danger now, he decided, was the point where the western section of the ditch curved southwards. And arrived there, he found his worst expectations justified. The very power of the current had huddled the leaves and their crews of ants so close together at the bend that the bridge was almost ready.

True, streams of petrol and clumps of earth still prevented a landing. But the number of floating leaves was increasing ever more swiftly. It could not be long now before a stretch of water a mile in length was decked by a green pontoon over which the ants could rush in millions.

Leiningen galloped to the weir. The damming of the river was controlled by a wheel on its bank. The planter ordered the man at the wheel first to lower the water in the ditch almost to vanishing point, next to wait a moment, then suddenly to let the river in again. This manoeuvre of lowering and raising the surface, of decreasing, then increasing, the flow of water through the ditch, was to be repeated over and over again until further notice.

This tactic was at first successful. The water in the ditch sank, and with it the film of leaves. The green fleet nearly reached the bed and the troops on the far bank swarmed down the slope to it. Then a violent flow of water at the original depth raced through the ditch, overwhelming leaves and ants and sweeping them along.

This intermittent rapid flushing prevented just in time the almost completed fording of the ditch. But it also flung here and there squads of the enemy vanguard simultaneously up the inner bank. These seemed to know their duty only too well, and lost no time accomplishing it. The air rang with the curses of bitten Indians. They had removed their shirts and pants to detect the quicker the upwards-hastening insects; when they saw one, they crushed it; and fortunately the onslaught as yet was only by skirmishers.

Again and again the water sank and rose, carrying leaves and drowned ants away with it. It lowered once more nearly to its bed; but this time the exhausted defenders waited in vain for the flush of destruction. Leiningen sensed disaster; something must have gone wrong with the machinery of the dam. Then a sweating peon tore up to him with the news— "They're over!"

While the besieged were concentrating upon the defence of the stretch opposite the wood, the seemingly unaffected line beyond the wood had become the theatre of decisive action. Here the defenders' front was sparse and scattered; everyone who could be spared had hurried away to the south.

Just as the man at the weir had lowered the water almost to the bed of the ditch, the ants on a wide front began another attempt at a direct crossing like that of the preceding day. Into the emptied bed poured an irresistible throng. Rushing across the ditch, they attained the inner bank before the slow-witted Indians fully grasped the situation. Their frantic screams dumbfounded the man at the weir. Before he could direct the river anew into the safeguarding bed he saw himself surrounded by raging ants. He ran like the others, ran for his life.

When Leiningen heard this, he knew the plantation was doomed. He wasted no time bemoaning the inevitable. For as long as there was the slightest chance of success he had stood his ground, and now any further resistance was both useless and dangerous. He fired three revolver shots into the air—the prearranged signal for his men to retreat instantly within the "inner moat." Then he rode towards the ranchhouse.

This was two miles from the point of invasion. There was therefore time enough to prepare the second line of defence against the advent of the ants. Of the three great petrol cisterns near the house, one had already been half emptied by the constant withdrawals needed for the pumps during the fight at the water ditch. The remaining petrol in it was now drawn off through underground pipes into the concrete trench which encircled the ranch-house and its outbuildings.

And there, drifting in twos and threes, Leiningen's men reached him. Most of them were obviously trying to preserve an air of calm and indifference, belied, however, by their restless glances and knitted brows. One could see their belief in a favourable outcome of the struggle was already considerably shaken.

The planter called his peons around him.

"Well, lads," he began, "we've lost the first round. But we'll smash the beggars yet, don't you worry. Anyone who thinks otherwise can draw his pay here and now and push off. There are rafts enough and to spare on the river and plenty of time still to reach 'em."

Not a man stirred.

Leiningen acknowledged this silent vote of confidence with a laugh that was half a grunt. "That's the stuff, lads. Too bad if you'd missed the rest of the show, eh? Well, the fun won't start till morning. Once these blighters turn tail, there'll be plenty of work for everyone and higher wages all round. And now run along and get something to eat; you've earned it all right."

The bridges over the concrete ditch were removed. Here and there solitary ants had reached the ditch; they gazed at the petrol meditatively, then scurried back again. Apparently they had little interest, at the moment, for what lay beyond the evil-reeking barrier; the abundant spoils of the plantation were the main attraction. Soon the trees, shrubs and beds for miles around were hulled with ants zealously gobbling the yield of long weary months of strenuous toil.

As twilight began to fall, a cordon of ants marched around the petrol trench, but as yet made no move towards its brink. Leiningen posted sentries with headlights and electric torches, then withdrew to his office and began to reckon up his losses. He estimated these as large, but, in comparison with his bank balance, by no means unbearable. He worked out in some detail a scheme of intensive cultivation which would enable him, before very long, to more than compensate himself for the damage now being wrought to his crops. It was with a contented mind that he finally betook himself to bed, where he slept deeply until dawn, undisturbed by any thought that next day little more might be left of him than a glistening skeleton.

He rose with the sun and went out on the flat roof of his house. And a scene like one from Dante lay around him; for miles in every direction there was nothing but a black, glittering multitude, a multitude of rested, sated, but none the less voracious ants; yes, look as far as one might, one could see nothing but that rustling black throng, except in the north, where the great river drew a boundary they could not hope to pass. But even the high stone breakwater, along the bank of the river, which Leiningen had built as a defence against inundations, was like the paths, the shorn trees and shrubs, the ground itself, black with ants.

So their greed was not glutted in razing that vast plantation? Not by a long chalk; they were all the more eager now on a rich and certain booty—four hundred men, numerous horses, and bursting granaries.

At first it seemed that the petrol trench would serve its purpose. The besiegers sensed the peril of swimming it, and made no move to plunge blindly over its brink. Instead they devised a better manoeuvre; they began to collect shreds of bark, twigs and dried leaves and dropped these into the petrol. Everything green, which could have been similarly used, had long since been eaten. After a time, though, a long procession could be seen bringing from the west the tamarind leaves used as rafts the day before.

Since the petrol, unlike the water in the outer ditch, was perfectly still, the refuse stayed where it was thrown. It was several hours before the ants succeeded in covering an appreciable part of the surface. At length, however, the invading forces were ready to proceed to a direct attack.

Their storm-troops swarmed down the concrete side, scrambled over the supporting surface of twigs and leaves, and impelled these over the few remaining streaks of open petrol until they reached the other side. Then they began to climb up this to make straight for the helpless garrison.

During the entire offensive the planter sat peacefully, watching them with interest, but not stirring a muscle. Moreover, he had ordered his men not to disturb in any way whatever the advancing horde. So they squatted listlessly along the bank of the ditch and waited for a sign from the boss.

The petrol was now covered with ants. A few had climbed the inner concrete wall and were scurrying towards the defenders. "Everyone back from the ditch!" roared Leiningen. The men rushed away, without the slightest idea of his plan. He stooped forward and cautiously dropped into the ditch a stone which split the floating carpet and its living freight, to reveal a gleaming patch of petrol. A match spurted, sank down to the oily surface—Leiningen sprang back; in a flash a towering rampart of fire encompassed the garrison.

This spectacular and instant repulse threw the Indians into ecstasy. They applauded, yelled and stamped, like children at a pantomime. Had it not been for the awe in which they held the boss, they would infallibly have carried him shoulder-high.

It was some time before the petrol burned down to the bed of the ditch and the wall of smoke and flame began to lower. The ants had retreated in a wide circle from the devastation, and innumerable charred fragments along the outer bank showed that the flames had spread from the holocaust in the ditch well into the ranks beyond, where they had wrought havoc far and wide.

Yet the perseverance of the ants was by no means broken; indeed, each set-back seemed only to whet it. The concrete cooled, the flicker of the dying flames wavered and vanished, petrol from the second tank poured into the trench—and the ants marched forward anew to the attack.

The foregoing scene repeated itself in every detail, except that on this occasion less time was needed to bridge the ditch, for the petrol was now already filmed by a layer of ash. Once again they withdrew; once again petrol flowed into the ditch. Would the creatures never learn that their self-sacrifice was utterly senseless? It really was senseless, wasn't it? Yes, of course it was senseless—provided the defenders had an *unlimited* supply of petrol.

When Leiningen reached this stage of reasoning he felt, for the first time since the arrival of the ants, that his confidence was deserting him. His skin began to creep; he loosened his collar. Once the devils were over the trench there wasn't a chance in hell for him and his men. God! What a prospect, to be eaten alive like that!

For the third time the flames immolated the attacking troops and burned down to extinction. Yet the ants were coming on again as if nothing had happened. And meanwhile Leiningen had made a discovery that chilled him to the bone—petrol was no longer flowing into the ditch. Something must be blocking the outflow pipe of the third and last cistern—a snake or a dead rat? Whatever it was, the ants could be held off no longer, unless petrol could by some method be led from the cistern into the ditch.

Then Leiningen remembered that in an outhouse near-by were two old disused fire-engines. Spry as never before in their lives, the peons dragged them out of the shed, connected their pumps to the cistern, uncoiled and laid the hose. They were just in time to aim a stream of petrol at a column of ants that had already crossed and drive them back down the incline into the ditch. Once more an oily girdle surrounded the garrison, once more it was possible to hold the position—for the moment.

It was obvious, however, that this last resource meant only the postponement of defeat and death. A few of the peons fell on their knees and began to pray; others, shrieking insanely, fired their revolvers at the black, advancing masses, as if they felt their despair was pitiful enough to sway fate itself to mercy.

At length two of the men's nerves broke; Leiningen saw a naked Indian leap over the north side of the petrol trench, quickly followed by a second. They sprinted with incredible speed towards the river. But their fleetness did not save them; long before they could attain the rafts, the enemy covered their bodies from head to foot....

In spite of this bloody warning, more and more men showed they were making up their minds to run the blockade. Anything, even a fight midstream against alligators, seemed better than powerlessly waiting for death to come and slowly consume their living bodies.

Leiningen flogged his brain till it reeled.

Then out of the inferno of his bewilderment rose a terrifying inspiration. Yes, one hope remained, and one alone. It might be possible to dam the great river completely, so that its waters would fill not only the water ditch but overflow into the entire gigantic 'saucer' of land in which lay the plantation.

The far bank of the river was too high for the waters to escape that way. The stone breakwater ran between the river and the plantation; its only gaps occurred where the 'horseshoe' ends of the water ditch passed into the river. So its waters would not only be forced to inundate into the plantation, they would also be held there by the breakwater until they rose to its own high level. In half an hour, perhaps even earlier, the plantation and its hostile army of occupation would be flooded.

The ranch-house and outbuildings stood upon rising ground. Their foundations were higher than the breakwater, so the flood would not reach them. And any remaining ants trying to ascend the slope could be repulsed by petrol.

It was possible—yes, if one could only get to the dam! A distance of nearly two miles lay between the ranch-house and the weir—two miles of ants. Those two peons had managed only a fifth of that distance at the cost of their lives. Was there an Indian daring enough, after that, to run the gauntlet five times as far? Hardly likely; and if there were, his prospect of getting back was almost nil.

No, there was only one thing for it, he'd have to make the attempt himself; he might just as well be running as sitting still, anyway, when the ants finally got him. Besides, there *was* a bit of a chance.

"Listen, lads!" he shouted. "You're frightened of those beggars, but you're a damn sight more frightened of me, and I'm proud of you. There's still a chance to save our lives—by flooding the plantation from the river. Now one of you might manage to get as far as the weir—but he'd never come back. Well, I'm not going to let you try it; if I did I'd be worse than one of those ants. No, I called the tune, and now I'm going to pay the piper.

"The moment I'm over the ditch, set fire to the petrol. That'll allow time for the flood to do the trick. Then all you have to do is to wait here all snug and quiet till I'm back. Yes, I'm coming back, trust me"—he grinned—"when I've finished my slimming cure."

He pulled on high leather boots, drew heavy gauntlets over his hands, and stuffed the spaces between breeches and boots, gauntlets and arms, shirt and neck, with rags soaked in petrol. With close-fitting mosquito goggles he shielded his eyes, knowing too well the ants' dodge of first robbing their victim of sight. Finally, he plugged his nostrils and ears with cottonwool, and let the peons drench his clothes with petrol.

Leiningen then remembered the paralysing effect of ants' venom, and the old Indian medicine-man gave him a gourd full of the medicine he had administered to the bitten peon at the water ditch. The planter drank it down without noticing its bitter taste; his mind was already at the weir.

He started off towards the north-west corner of the trench. With a bound he was over—and among the ants.

The beleaguered garrison had no opportunity to watch Leiningen's race against death. The ants were climbing the inner bank again—the lurid ring of petrol blazed aloft. For the fourth time that day the reflection from the fire shone on the sweating faces of the imprisoned men, and on the reddish-black cuirasses of their oppressors. The red-and-blue, dark-edged flames leaped vividly now, celebrating what? The funeral pyre of the four hundred, or of the hosts of destruction?

Leiningen ran. He ran in long equal strides, with only one thought, one sensation, in his being—he *must* get through. He dodged all trees and shrubs; except for the split seconds his soles touched the ground the ants should have no opportunity to alight on him. That they would get to him soon, despite the salve on his boots, the petrol in his clothes, he realized only too well, but he knew even more surely that he must, and that he would, get to the weir.

Apparently the salve was some use after all; not until he had reached half-way did he feel ants under his clothes, and a few on his face. Mechanically, in his stride, he struck at them, scarcely conscious of their bites. He 'saw he was drawing appreciably nearer the weir—the distance grew less and less—sank to five hundred—three—two—one hundred yards.

Then he was at the weir and gripping the ant-hulled wheel. Hardly had he seized it when a horde of infuriated ants flowed over his hands, arms and shoulders. He started the wheel—before it turned once on its axis the leaders were on his face. Leiningen strained like a madman, his lips pressed tight; if he opened them to draw breath...

He turned and turned; slowly the dam lowered until it reached the bed of the river. Already the water was overflowing the ditch. Another minute and the river was pouring through the near-by gap in the breakwater. The flooding of the plantation had begun.

Leiningen let go the wheel. Now, for the first time, he realized he was coated from head to foot with a layer of ants. In spite of the petrol, his clothes were full of them, several had got underneath all his clothes to his body. Now that he had completed his task he felt the smart raging over his flesh from the bites of sawing and piercing insects.

Frantic with pain, he almost plunged into the river. To be ripped and slashed to shreds by piranhas? Already he was running the return journey, knocking ants from his gloves and jacket, brushing them from his bloodied face, squashing them to death under his clothes.

One of the creatures bit him just below the rim of his goggles; he managed to tear it away, but the agony of the bite and its etching acid drilled into the eye-nerves; he saw now through circles of fire into a milky mist, then he ran for a time almost blinded, knowing that if he once tripped and fell...

The old Indian's brew didn't seem much good after all; it weakened the poison a bit, but didn't get rid of it. His heart pounded as if it would burst; blood roared in his ears; a giant's fist battered his lungs.

Then he could see again, but the burning girdle of petrol appeared infinitely far away; he could not last half that distance. Swift-changing pictures flashed through his head, episodes in his life, while in another part of his brain a cool and impartial onlooker informed that ant-blurred, gasping, exhausted bundle named Leiningen that such a rushing panorama of scenes from one's past is seen only in the moment before death.

A stone in the path ... too weak to avoid it ... the planter stumbled and collapsed. He tried to rise ... he must be pinned under a rock ... it was impossible ... the slightest movement was impossible...

Then all at once he saw, starkly clear and huge, and, right before his eyes, furred with ants, towering and swaying in its death agony, the pampas stag. In six minutes—gnawed to the bones. God! He *couldn't* die like that! And something outside him seemed to drag him to his feet. He tottered. He began to stagger forward again.

Through the blazing ring hurtled an apparition which, as soon as it reached the ground on the inner side, fell full length and did not move. Leiningen, at the moment he made that leap through the flames, lost consciousness for the first time in his life.

As he lay there, prostrate, with glazing eyes and lacerated face, he appeared as a man returned from the grave. The peons rushed to him, stripped off his clothes and tore away the ants. ... They carried him into the ranch-house.

As the curtain of flames lowered, one could see, in place of the illimitable host of ants, an extensive vista of water. The thwarted river had swept over the plantation, carrying with it the entire army. The water had collected and mounted in the great 'saucer' while the ants had in vain attempted to reach the hill on which stood the ranch-house. The girdle of flames held them back.

And so, imprisoned between water and fire, they had been delivered into the annihilation that was their god. And near the farther mouth of the water ditch, where the stone mole had its second gap, the ocean swept the lost battalions into the river, to vanish for ever.

The ring of fire dwindled as the water mounted to the petrol trench and quenched the dimming flames....

It swelled over ant-stippled shrubs and bushes, until it washed against the foot of the knoll whereon the besieged had taken refuge. For a while an alluvial of ants tried again and again to attain this dry land, only to be repulsed by streams of petrol back into the merciless flood.

Leiningen lay on his bed, his body swathed from head to foot in bandages. With fomentations and salves they had managed to stop the bleeding, and had dressed his many wounds.

Now the men thronged around him, one question in every face. Would he recover?

"He won't die," said the old man who had bandaged him, "if he doesn't want to."

The planter opened his eyes, "Everything in order?" he asked.

"They've gone," said his nurse. "To hell." He held out to his master a gourd full of a powerful sleeping draught. Leiningen gulped it down.

"I told you I'd come back," he murmured, "even if I am a bit streamlined."

He grinned and shut his eyes. He slept.

CARL STEPHENSON

The Law

The Afridi's face was pale by Eastern standards. To the ordinary observer it was devoid of any emotion, and the mouth was still. The man stood alone, with a certain dignity, and never moved when the senior Indian officer, a Sikh, stripped him of his belt. With an air of apparent indifference he heard the short sentence in Pushtu: 'You have worked in secret against the authority of the Sircar. You have designed to betray the regiment which has nurtured you, and are a thing of shame in the eyes of your brotherhood. Now it is ordered that from henceforth you have no place with us, and you have brought this sentence on your own head. You will go.'

The man drew himself up to his full height, turned abruptly about, and left the Durbar. The Colonel rose from the table; every face, British and Indian, betrayed emotion—relief, scorn, satisfaction—something. Only the offender had seemed unaffected.

It was nearly time for mess. Colonel Omney had changed and was sitting on his veranda, catching the fitful breeze from the river. He had neglected the club that night, from a disinclination to discuss the event of the morning. His regiment had always been his religion; he had believed in the ultimate power of the British example to affect character, even in the case of the wild tribesman of the frontier. Hitherto his creed had seemed justified. Other regiments had had cases of desertion, it is true; there were whispers of disloyalty among the tribes, particularly the large and turbulent tribe of Afridis; but his regiment had a clean sheet. He had good officers, carefully selected, and they had the confidence of their men; this had been proved a dozen times. And yet—here was this baffling case of Yakub Khan. For five years the man had been his own orderly; then he had been promoted for good intelligence work, and had fulfilled his early promise. He had been a certain candidate for further promotion to the rank of Indian Officer. And now he had been clearly proved to have been tampering with the loyalty of the younger Afridi's. There had been only one possible course—degradation—in public Durbar. The Colonel felt it deeply, personally. He had believed that he knew his man. His whole creed was upset. Yakub Khan was a decided score for the cynics.

The Colonel was thinking in this strain, when the man's Squadron Commander, Major Sefton, dropped in on his way to mess, and took one of the long chairs. The Major suggested an extra guard on the bungalow, adding:

'I know it sounds fidgety, Colonel, but I know my Afridi. He's mugra;[1] he took it badly—never saluted—and he's disappeared. Akbar Khan was keeping an eye on him, but he gave him the slip.

---

1.   Mugra = Surly.

I can't help thinking we should have sent him up the road under escort. I never trust an Afridi.'

'Won't do, Sefton. I don't like the effect on the men. These fellows always hide their feelings, as you know. He never flinched, but he was ashamed. He'll disappear—get back to his own people—hide his head. We've done with him.'

The Major lit a cigarette before he answered.

'Maybe, Colonel. But I had a good view of him when you read out that sentence. I always look at a man's eyes. That man's face never moved. You might have thought he never heard. But I saw the whites of his eyes—once; just a flicker, when you told him to go. That flicker meant that he is an Afridi as much as when he left his village to join us. We have never touched him; we never do touch them—really, fundamentally. Look at their lives—family feuds from generation to generation—*lex talionis*—nicks on the rifle-butt—it's in the blood. Sure as I sit here, Colonel, that flicker meant the old thing; it registered a new enemy. That man has only one idea now.'

The Colonel got up, saying:

'I fear you are one of the cynics, Sefton. Come and have a short drink. We have just time.' And they strolled over to the mess.

Yakub Khan had put off his khaki for ever. It had been hastened—that was all; he had never meant to die in it. It had suited his purpose to leave his village for a time, as he had shot the son of Sher Khan, and the old man had a large following and a good memory for faces. On his return, he must send old Sher Khan to join his son—then he could rest safe. Sher Khan would never expect him—unless that young Gul Haidar, who had started off on leave two days back, had spread the news. He would have to risk that. In any case Sher Khan was an old man, and might delay. He would start to-night, and be well over the pass at early dawn. He had but to finish his present business. That would be easy.

He had put on his ordinary national dress—a shirt of dark material, flowing free; loose pajamas of dingy white cloth; an untidy dark blue puggaree; a cartridge-belt round his waist. In his hand he carried a stolen service rifle, and a bundle. He crept from rock to rock in the dry river-bed, which commanded a view of the mess, making no sound. His aquiline, clean-cut face, with the curved nose and hard mouth, was impassive as he lay down behind a rock and watched the khitmatgars[2] laying the table inside.

It was very still; he could hear the horses a quarter of a mile away in the regimental stables, and some syces[3] singing. He wished he could take a horse—but that would only make him a prominent object on the road.

Now he could hear the sahebs going across to the mess. He could see the glow of their cigarettes. Yes, there was the Colonel saheb, with his Squadron saheb. They were coming outside, into the veranda. The light was good. In a few minutes it would be better. Ah, there was a khitmatgar attending on them; now he had gone; the chairs were in shadow—but when they stood up the moon would catch them. His eyes flickered—once.

There was the trumpet; no more trumpets for him; they would be going in now.... The Colonel and his friend were standing up, clear in the moonlight. They were looking towards the river-bed; the Major saheb was urging something.... Now!

2.   Khitmatgar = Waiter.
3.   Syce = Groom.

There was one rifle-shot from the direction of the river-bed, silence for a moment, almost till the echo had died away; the sound of a heavy fall—then a rushing—shouts—lights.

But the man in the river-bed had slipped away very quietly.

The pass looked desolate in that half-hour before sunrise. A long pale road wound down into the valley; not a hint of a tree; no sound at all; and, on either side, hills dimly red, and rocks everywhere. At the top of the pass the hills were steep on either side. Thirty yards east of the road, and near the top, was a big rock, reaching like a shelf from the hillside, and commanding the road below. There was loose débris on this shelf—shingle and stones; and it would have been hard, in that light, to pick out the man's head.

He lay still, his body quite hidden. His dirty tumbling brown puggaree was of a colour with the rocks. He had a rough red beard, and wild red hair. Little of his face showed, except the eyes—and they lay deep—grey-blue and cold. One would have said that he was an old man, for there were flecks of grey in the henna'd beard. His cheek lay against the breach of a martini rifle, evidently locally built, with clumsy sighting. Yet the butt, had it been visible would have shown a number of little nicks—proofs that the old man knew his weapon. The barrel was masked with some thin cloth. There was nothing for the sun to betray when it should rise.

The sun must have risen behind the hills. The light was improving. The old man watched the road. There were few early wayfarers. A party of men and women with donkeys, carrying

4.   Malik = Petty chief.

bundles of grass, wandered up from their last camp in the rough plain by the river. A malik[4] on his pony, with a small following of retainers, passed down on his way to a tribal jirgha.[5] A descending flock of sheep, driven by two lusty lads with black ringlets and carrying little bows, made a great dust in the road. They none of them saw the watcher. He watched the dust into the valley. There was a cloud of it where the sheep ran down the steep incline to the ford over the slender stream. It hung there for some time—and then, a black dot against the cloud, a man emerged. Nearer he came, hurrying, darting his head to observe the hills above; then his face was clear, pale against his dark blue puggaree; the cock of his rifle behind him; a point of light in his cartridge-belt. He was below the rock now; he looked up, noting the dark stones; he might have seen one stone stir ever so slightly; then the shot rang out, and he pitched forward on the road.

This time the echoes of the shot lingered long. In the silence that followed, there might have been heard a sound of scrambling, and the fall of a displaced pebble. Sher Khan, wild and unkempt, was shambling up the hill, threading the rocks. At the crest he stopped, clear against the arisen sun, and danced from foot to foot with rifle held above his head. Then he disappeared.

JOHN EYTON

---

5.   Jirgha = Session.

From the Primaeval Past

$\mathcal{I}$ discovered the pool near Rajpur on a hot summer's day some fifteen years ago. It was shaded by close-growing Sal trees, and looked cool and inviting. I took off my clothes and dived in.

The water was colder than I had expected. It was an icy, glacial cold. The sun never touched it for long, I supposed. Striking out vigorously, I swam to the other end of the pool and pulled myself up on the rocks, shivering.

But I wanted to swim. So I dived in again and did a gentle breast-stroke towards the middle of the pool. Something slid between my legs. Something slimy, pulpy. I could see no one, hear nothing. I swam away, but the floating, slippery thing followed me. I did not like it. Something curled around my leg. Not an underwater plant. Something that sucked at my foot. A long tongue licking at my calf. I struck out wildly, thrust myself away from whatever it was that sought my company. Something lonely, lurking in the shadows. Kicking up spray, I swam like a frightened porpoise fleeing from some terror of the deep.

Safely out of the water, I looked for a warm, sunny rock, and stood there looking down at the water.

Nothing stirred. The surface of the pool was now calm and undisturbed. Just a few fallen leaves floating around. Not a frog, not a fish, not a water-bird in sight. And that in itself seemed strange. For you would have expected some sort of pond life to have been in evidence.

But something lived in the pool, of that I was sure. Something very cold-blooded; colder and wetter than the water. Could it have been a corpse trapped in the weeds? I did not want to know; so I dressed and hurried away.

A few days later I left for Delhi, where I went to work in an ad agency, telling people how to beat the summer heat by drinking fizzy drinks that made you thirstier. The pool in the forest was forgotten. And it was ten years before I visited Rajpur again.

Leaving the small hotel where I was staying, I found myself walking through the same old Sal forest, drawn almost irresistibly towards the pool where I had not been able to finish my swim. I was not over-eager to swim there again, but I was curious to know if the pool still existed.

Well, it was there all right, although the surroundings had changed and a number of new houses and buildings had come up where formerly there had only been wilderness. And there was a fair amount of activity in the vicinity of the pool.

A number of labourers were busy with buckets and rubber pipes, doing their best to empty the pool. They had also dammed off and diverted the little stream that fed it.

Overseeing this operation was a well-dressed man in a white safari suit. I thought at first that he was an honorary forest warden, but it turned out that he was the owner of a new school that had come up nearby.

"Do you live in Rajpur?" he asked.

"I used to ... once upon a time ... Why are you draining the pool?"

"It's become a hazard," he said. "Two of my boys were drowned here recently. Both senior students. Of course they weren't supposed to be swimming here without permission, the pool is off limits. But you know what boys are like. Make a rule and they feel duty-bound to break it."

He told me his name, Kapoor, and led me back to his house, a newly-built bungalow with a wide cool verandah. His servant brought us glasses of cool *sherbet*. We sat in cane chairs overlooking the pool and the forest. Across a clearing, a gravelled road led to the school buildings, newly white-washed and glistening in the sun.

"Were the boys there at the same time?" I asked.

"Yes, they were friends. And they must have been attacked by fiends. Limbs twisted and broken, faces disfigured. But death was due to drowning—that was the verdict of the medical examiner."

We gazed down at the shallows of the pool, where a couple of men were still at work, the others having gone for their mid-day meal.

"Perhaps it would be better to leave the place alone," I said. "Put a barbed-wire fence around it. Keep your boys away. Thousands of years ago this valley was an inland sea. A few small pools and streams are all that is left of it."

"I want to fill it in and build something there. An open-air theatre, maybe. We can always create an artificial pond somewhere else."

Presently only one man remained at the pool, knee-deep in muddy, churned-up water. And Mr Kapoor and I both saw what happened next.

Something rose out of the bottom of the pool. It looked like a giant snail, but its head was part human, its body and limbs part squid or octopus. An enormous succubus. It stood taller than the man in the pool. A creature soft and slimy, a survivor from our primaeval past.

With a great sucking motion it enveloped the man completely, so that only his arms and legs could be seen thrashing about wildly and futilely. The succubus dragged him down under the water.

Kapoor and I left the verandah and ran to the edge of the pool. Bubbles rose from the green scum near the surface. All was still and silent. And then, like bubble-gum issuing from the mouth of a child, the mangled body of the man shot out of the water and came spinning towards us.

Dead and drowned and sucked dry of its fluids.

Naturally no more work was done at the pool. A labourer had slipped and fallen to his death on the rocks, that was the story that was put out. Kapoor swore me to secrecy. His school would have to close down if there were too many strange drownings and accidents in its vicinity. But he walled the place off from his property and made it practically inaccessible. The jungle's undergrowth now hides the approach.

The monsoon rains came and the pool filled up again. I can tell you how to get there, if you'd like to see it. But I wouldn't advise you to go for a swim.

RUSKIN BOND

The Road to the Shore

I

𝓘t was a favourite walk of mine, when the days were fine enough and the wind not too cutting, along the stone groyne that projected like some old abandoned undertaking from out of the soft sand and coarse grass of the foreshore. I suppose that at one time, before the great granite piers were built, it had marked the real end to the river; but its usefulness seemed to have long since been given over to the small boys who fished with high optimism from the stones, or performed acrobatics over the massive rusted railings.

There were a few wooden seats, too—you know the kind, devoid of paint and all hacked with the sprawling initials of successive generations of youth—clustered round the base of a stumpy tower that had once been white. I used to like to sit there and watch the traffic moving up and down the smoky river; a river which would have been depressing but for the bright colourings of the steamers' flags and funnels splashed across the background of innumerable dwellings that huddled and clung with the tenacity of mussels to the rising banks.

That particular afternoon I sat down on a seat occupied by two men—the other seats were taken up by either urchins or the smelly remnants of marine creatures that small boys delight to impale on fish-hooks—and began to fill the pipe I always enjoyed there in the salt-tanged air. I took no particular notice of these men, who seemed, judging from the lack of conversation, to be strangers to each other. Anyway I was rather interested in a steamer with sides well streaked with rust, which at that moment was passing a line over her stern to a dirty but efficient tugboat that poked its nose right under the counter. I can remember the young officer hanging over the rails right aft, signing with one hand to the sailors handling the heavy rope; the pilot running to the side of the bridge blowing a little shrill whistle, and the sudden white flurry of steam like a big piece of cotton-wool that had somehow attached itself to the buff-coloured funnel of the tug. Then came the sound, a single short blast, full of vigour and eagerness, and the cotton-wool was gone. Dense black smoke rose up, vertically and sudden, from the tug's stack, and in such volume that one wondered how so small a craft could manufacture the stuff so prodigiously; then ship and escort passed on, lost among the dim shapes of other hulls showing through the murk.

The children left the benches, noisily, and ran bare-footed over the flat stones towards the shore and the sand, their voices growing fainter as their darting figures diminished. I noticed, then, that one of the men—the one farthest from me—had stood up. He was short in stature, past middle age, but very respectably dressed; I saw that his clothes were good but far from new, the black overcoat a little shining at the shoulders; the bowler hat had lost the intensity of its black; the lower parts of his trousers were just a little frayed. A man, I thought, who had to be careful.

He did not immediately walk away, but with his back to me and the ferrule of his stick scratching on the stones, seemed to pause in deep and serious thought; then turning slowly he looked right over my head towards the east and the sea. It was then that I beheld his face for the first—and last—time. There was nothing conspicuous about it; no single feature that commanded attention; nothing out of place; just a pleasant, well-balanced countenance, ruddy, with the flush of health.

He turned away a little. His eyes, blue and frank, seemed to fasten on distant objects, as though searching sadly for some sign he alone expected. And then he spoke, as if to himself, in a voice that had the slight huskiness of a strong voice that is subdued.

'No. I will go now,' he said; 'I don't think I could bear to see her again. Let me know how you get on.' The stick swept up in a gesture of farewell and he started off over the bleached and sea-worn stones towards the shore, erect and unhurried, looking to neither right nor left.

'Good-bye, sir,' the sharer of my seat answered, with an elevation of the hand that seemed like a compromise between a salute and a mere wave, 'I will let you know.'

Now, I must confess to a normal amount of interest in my fellows, apart from the insatiable and morbid curiosity that seems to infect a quarter of the human race. Speculating on a man's occupation by a glance at his hands and face, or on the country that claims him by the dialect he utters, is a pastime that has its own charms—and often surprising results.

An idle pastime you may say; but as conversation often follows, I have indeed learned much from my idleness. I was surprised when the men spoke, thinking they had no knowledge of each other. The odd sentence or two sounded uncommonly like an allusion to some sordid family upheaval. I would have lost all further interest had not the young man bid me good afternoon as he rolled, with able fingers, a cigarette from coarse tobacco intended, I am sure, for a pipe. He might have been thirty, with a brown face and a strong jaw line; a straight nose and eyes that were dark and wonderfully alert, with little crows' feet at the corners. Like his older companion now half-way to the shore he wore clothes of a dark material. The interest, however, lay not in his clothes, but in his face, his strong voice, and brown hands that seemed to belong to an older man.

There was something these men had in common which I could not place; they bore a common stamp. The respect of the younger man for the elder (so often forgotten these days) discounted any relationship. Their voices, free of any trace of dialect, were of no assistance.

I returned the young man's greeting. 'Favourite walk of mine, this,' I added; 'interesting here. I like to watch the traffic on the river, to read the names of the steamers and wonder where they come from—and where they are bound. That one now, that's just come in ...'

'One of Baines's tramps,' he replied; 'saw her coming into Aden one morning with her plates red-hot and the foremast hanging over her bows like a broken bowsprit; couldn't see much for steam. She glowed like a brazier at night—until they scuttled her. Cotton, you know.'

He crossed his legs and blew a lot of strong smoke down his nostrils.

'Cotton, you say?" I was woefully ignorant. But the light dawned on his occupation.

'Yes. Queer stuff to stow. New paint in the hold is taboo, and oil! Especially oil. Got to check the oilcans up every now and then; those coolies oil the screws far too often if they are not watched. Spontaneous combustion, you know.'

'Really?' I answered, I hope, with a reasonable degree of intelligence.

'I suppose,' he went on, 'that the "old man" would be on the carpet for that. I can imagine the explanatory report to the owners, and the nice cutting letter in reply—you know the sort of thing—beginning, "Dear Captain. We fail to understand;" or, "We shudder to think," and so on. They always fail to understand.'

He stretched out a hand in a gesture of hopelessness.

'Yes,' he went on, without waiting for any comment from me, 'they always fail to understand. I would be mad to assume they were capable of any understanding in these things. How can they? They get up at eight, arrive at the office between nine and ten all rigged out in black and white complete with umbrella; read *The Times* and the mail, have coffee at eleven, chat with the typist, and pack up for lunch at one; tot up a few figures in the afternoon, dictate a few letters about four, then go home, exhausted, to a loving wife and family. I ask you, sir,' he said, looking at me with an eye of appealing and good-natured frankness, 'how can they understand?'

I said I really did not know, watching him inhale deeply of a smoke that would upset many a stomach. It seemed to inspire him to further efforts of loquacity, to deeper and less tolerant thought. A sea-bird, with a raucous scream passed very low, heading towards the sea, a study in white curves against the sombre black-grey dwellings of men on the far side of the river.

'No,' my companion began again, 'they will never understand. We don't expect them to; it is too much. I suppose when that Captain explained everything at the office, they would offer a lot of impracticable and idiotic suggestions on how to prevent cotton cargoes from taking fire in the Indian Ocean, with, "now Captain, if only you had done such and such, just consider, all this would never have happened; our steamer would not have lost twelve months freighting, apart from repairs, &c., and you could still have continued in our employ." Then they would send him home, for ever and ever, Amen.'

I murmured some sounds which I thought suitable. Politely I asked, 'Do you really mean to say…?'

He cut me off. 'I am saying it. These things happen. I follow a calling, sir, where all accidents are apparently someone's mistakes and retribution follows with unemotional alacrity.'

'Do you not then become—a little embittered?' I ventured. To my surprise he smiled, and his teeth looked strong and white against the ruddy weathered face.

'You can't become embittered against the sea or the ship, or the misfortunes that fall into the definition of "Acts of God." And as for the owners—why, have I not said what they always themselves admit—that they fail to understand?'

There was a silence after that, broken only by the ripple of water surging round the stones below and the impatient blasts of a siren somewhere up the smoky reaches of the river. I observed the keen eyes of my companion sweeping in a slow arc along the great stretch of the northern breakwater; but I think he was looking beyond even that. He seemed, like the other man, to gaze on far-off things. Quite suddenly, without shortening his vision, he remarked—

'I suppose that I, too, will come to it some day. *His* came late, and a man's chances at sixty are slender.' His head indicated by a slight sideways inclination the way to the shore.

'Your friend who sat here?'

'My friend? A former Captain of mine. I never quite looked upon him as a friend when I was with him out there. Don't misunderstand me, the word "friend" is not normally used in the relationship between the Master and second mate of a merchant steamer—and I was the second mate. There were two other officers, of course, and the engineers; an Indian crew from the Ratnagari district, Christian boys from the Goa coast and a Chinese carpenter. Quite a mixture of races and creeds like a League of Nations in embryo. But unlike that collection of vociferous citizens, dealers in high-level discord, we were a contented lot; free of even the petty upsets that can make life a trial in the cramped space available in a medium-sized steamer.

'There, you come to know a man as in no other calling; his virtues and his faults stand out clear and naked like the peaks and valleys of a mountain range that show black and sharp against a setting sun. Because there are no outside distractions you seek the company of your fellows with a spirit unknown between companions ashore, and with an understanding not of the surface, but which goes deep down into the heart of things. Because a man appears each day in a white shirt, trousers, and topee it is natural to associate him only with such rig. You never know his wordly possessions because, like the reverse face of the moon, they are invisible; but unlike the moon they excite no interest and are not even thought of. No, you come to know only him. You peep down into his soul.

'In his case it was different—he was the Master, above all three of us officers in rank, in experience, and in technical skill.

I know that he held the rare and esteemed certificate of Extra Master, Square Rigged. The very fact that he had suffered the head-winds and the cold fury of the Horn, had fought the frozen canvas on a royal yard swinging dizzily through the black night of the Southern Ocean, and lain waiting for wind in the burning calms of the Gulf of Siam, made us regard him with a deep professional reverence. When on the odd occasions at the cabin table he made reference to some episode in big square riggers before he took to steam, we felt humbled. Not uncomfortably so. Perhaps that is a point that only a seaman can appreciate. One thought, here is a man who is allowed, by a very critical Board of Trade, to command not only the largest steamship afloat, but also the largest sailing vessel; further, there is no higher acknowledgment of his art and skill but what he possesses. Our pride in technical matters was humbled. All the things we knew he also knew; beyond that there was a great field of experience, of knowledge and of achievement which was his alone. Had he not brought his ship, dismasted and battered, safely in under jury-rig after the whirling hell of a Bengal cyclone?

'And yet he never tried to make you humble. He did not delight, as some I have known, in alluding to you as "you steamboat-man" in that derisive manner that only makes you grind your teeth. No. He was quiet and alert, a little shy even, one might have said. And methodical to a fault; decisive too. Beside him, one derived that feeling of confidence that radiates only from the chosen few. Standing together on the blacked-out bridge searching for some unlighted island that was always something of a nightmare to pass in the dark, he would replace the night-glasses and say, "There we are now, keep her off half a point," or something like that, and your tension eased. You relaxed because your faith in him was strong. There was never any "You don't think you've passed it yet, Mister?" No, he was comfortably decisive.

'And yet, somehow, there was a great barrier behind which he sheltered. It seemed impossible to get close to the man, to know him, to understand him with the same vision as you understand the other officers, for instance. I realised after a while that he told you absolutely nothing of himself, that his conversations were limited to purely technical matters.

'He and I would take observations together by unusual methods. He knew all the methods I proposed—and others I had never heard of. We discussed the value of these things, and just when I thought, when I felt, that he was about to say something of himself, he would leave the bridge abruptly and take to walking his own deck quite quickly for perhaps a couple of hours without pause.

'We admired him, for his skill, for the confidence he dispersed. We liked his quiet manner, his fair judgment, his unobtrusive way of life. I think he was perhaps the nearest approach to a perfect shipmaster I shall ever meet. But he was not spoken of with any great depth of affection. In the club out there, when his name came up (as they always do), officers who knew him all gave the same answer, "Smart, isn't he? But deep, don't you think?"

'No. I don't think he was deep—not in that way. I think he was shy and therefore lonely. And I never heard him swear. That alone is unusual; more, it is remarkable in a profession where the use of descriptive words and colourful phrases is accepted, not as bad language, but as part of a necessary vocabulary. The heat alone is, at times out there, enough to warrant a special dictionary of its own.

'We traded to and fro, among the ports and harbours of the East. East of Suez—west of Guam. But our home port, as we liked to call it rather fondly, was up a great muddy river that lay sprawled like an immense brown and leafless tree that had fallen across a desert of yellow sand, with the roots growing out of the sea. On either bank the narrow, continuous belt of palms, dark green and close-packed, was the only relief in a flat and dreary immensity of sand, and always reminded me of green moss clinging for life to the body of the tree. Which was what the trees were doing. Nearest the water they were tall and splendid, but tapered to poor stunted things towards the desert. The river meant life: to the trees; to the dark-skinned people walking erect along the endless mud walls; to the jackals that howled in wailing packs at night; to the millions of croaking bull-frogs that put up a continuous vibrating screen of noise on which all the other sounds of the night were projected.

'But in daylight the river belonged to man—as much as this one before us. Ships came and went. Anchors splashed through the muddy waters with the cables rumbling noisily through the hawsepipes, flinging the mud of far-off places in parabolic showers over the bows. Tugboats churned the turbid and sickly smelling stream; native sailing craft, silent and with an air of deep and ancient mystery, glided without noise over the unchanging river. Yes, by day it was industrious, prosperous, civilised. But when the sun set, the night rushed over from the east like a hurrying shadow, filling the world with stars and the screaming voices of nature, of innumerable wild and unseen things that vied with each other for acoustic supremacy across the dark water between the darker forests.

'And with a majestic disregard the great river flowed on. It must have been doing that for a million years; flowing on—and carrying the mud to the sea. The sea won—it always does in the end—and the mud is dropping now ever as I talk, building up the banks and shoals that stretch, unseen and treacherous, in long irregular patches that are as unstable and varying as the sea itself is unalterable.

'Navigation and pilotage were difficult tasks among the tortuous channels and strong streams that were, at times, so unreliable. So we had many pilots and they were stationed in a large pilot-boat that lay at anchor just to seaward of the shoals. It was a good pilot-boat—once: as big as that tug over there.'

My young companion, by a nod of his head, brought me back to a grey English river where a large and dirty tug was making fast to a buoy. He paused only to relight the cigarette which for want of smoking had died out between his fingers. I was glad when he began again.

'Much cleaner, of course. Everything scrubbed, polished, and painted; just as it should be, and is out there in ships with big native crews. The brasswork shone like the proverbial dollar in the nigger's hand. Her pole masts were scraped and varnished; her awnings flat and without a wrinkle; her cable, as she swung at anchor, was whitewashed man-o'-war fashion. And her boats! Immaculate is the only word. She always looked like that, as if the paint had not quite dried.

'You may wonder why I, a seaman, should enlarge upon the virtues of a craft that I had not even set foot aboard. It is unnatural, not in keeping with the spirit of loyalty that grows upon a man sailing in even the crankiest tub that ever floated. Yet I must tell the facts as they were—she was a joy to behold as she lay like a faultless model upon a smiling sea. Every single ship that arrived and departed knew her. Every man admired her in silence: we do not often give tongue to such admiration in other ships, for we are a highly critical breed. But she was different. She had a profound influence, especially on the mate of every ship, injecting into him a restive discontent with his own past efforts. I don't think that the crew of a homeward-bounder realised what lay behind the suddenly acquired meticulousness that animated its chief officer. No ordinary clean-up and paint would do; the greatest efforts would not satisfy; the striving after such perfection would be a gallant but impossible task. And the mate of that pilot-boat, sipping his gin under the double awnings, was supremely unaware of the amount of human endeavour he stirred up.

'We saw quite a lot of her. Every few weeks we would return to find her resplendent and motionless at her anchorage, performing in silence her indispensable service. Sometimes, in the shimmering heat, when the surface of the sea was like unpolished pewter, when the horizon was lost completely and one had the impression of steaming through the sky itself, she would loom up, far away, resembling a string of barges piled high with celestial cargoes drifting deserted through space. It took two or three hours' steaming to weld the distorted images into the familiar shape we knew so well, into the thing we grew to look upon as a permanent mark among the treacherous shoals.

'And yet, with all her goodness, I came to hate her.

'It was a morning in early summer when we left the jetty up that river and dropped down the muddy steam with the great palms like a thick living fence on either bank. I remember the tug, disappearing round the bends ahead of us like a gaudy and immense water-beetle that refused to allow us to come nearer. Her bow waves, breaking on the low banks, washed the very roots of the trees and violently agitated the odd native boats moored here and there to the shore, causing the burnous-clad boatmen to shake their fists and call Allah to witness their righteousness.

'The heat, as usual, was dry and intense, though the hour was yet early. The air over the trees rose up like the air above a brazier; the desert beyond was a yellow blur, like a picture out of focus. But we get used to these things, and discomfort is a comparative term. We looked forward to the wet cold monsoon, but having encountered it preferred again the dry heat. But early summer is not too bad out there and that morning was as pleasant as most. We were glad to be off again; change and motion are good things. We would soon be at our old routine, our regular duties; our gin and quiet yarning in the hot evenings. And he— he would be back to his solitary meditation as he walked alone up and down his deck, thinking of God knows what. You see, he stood outside even when duty was over.

'The Goanese boy called me with the inevitable tea and toast at seven-thirty; I had turned in for a couple of hours while coming down the river, having been up all night. I could see, from my bunk, the shades of brown and blue of the shoals. The palms had disappeared: we had left the river behind. A floating buoy with red topmark went past the open ports of my room, the eddies rotating the thing like a spinning top. I knew then that we were in the dredged channel cut through the mud-banks to the sea. Another half-hour and we would be dropping the pilot.

'I drank my tepid tea at a single gulp—amazing what a paltry thing a cupful of tea is in that dehydrating heat—smoked, and dressed leisurely. Everything in that ship seemed to flow smoothly. No upsets. No shouting or bad temper; nothing to ruffle the placidity of our existence. I heard the native pilot coming from the bridge to get his bag. His duties up there were finished and the Master was taking her over towards the pilot-vessel to drop him. I could hear the mate, who had just come below, humming in the jerking fashion that accompanies the flourishing of a shaving-brush. He used to hum that same tune every morning at the same time, and I connect it now with the smell of a famous brand of shaving-soap. But I was just as much a creature of habit.

I picked up my topee, and, walking up the alleyway to his room, stood leaning in at his door for a few minutes' chat before going to the bridge for that most important of tasks—the pre-breakfast winding of the chronometers.

A sudden, shattering rattle of the telegraph chains in the casing above my head, brought us both in an infinitesimal period of time to the alert. I remember the bell in the engine-room sounding clear and urgent above the hum of the turbines; the look of questioning alarm and tenseness in the eyes of the mate as he swung away from the mirror, razor in hand; the sudden rush of feet on the bridge above us; confused warning shouts; but above all I remember the picture that I saw as I jerked my head up to look out of the forward port of the mate's room. On either side of the sunlit expanse of awning over our forecastle-head the flashing varnished masts of the pilot-vessel rose up, and in between them the big new-looking funnel protruded as if growing out of our stempost. I never realised, till then, how large that pilot-vessel was.

'And I never quite remember negotiating the intricacies of the narrow alleys or leaping over the eighteen-inch weather-boards in that sudden burst of energy that precipitated us both on to our own forecastle-head. The last of our Indian seamen was struggling with his sleeping-mat as if it were the most treasured relic that ever came out of Mecca. Perhaps for him it was. I felt the characteristic trembling of the deck that develops in a deep-laden ship when the engines are going full astern. Why the mate and I had raced forward I do not know. There was nothing we could do, now that our fore-end was cleared of men. Perhaps it was mere instinct to face up to a danger in the open.

'Then came the crunch. That, I think, is the only word. We struck her a little forward of amidships on her starboard side, and she, poor thing, was tied down by her own anchor and cable like a tethered goat feeling the impact of a jungle tiger; only our speed was slow—not above three or four knots. But fourteen thousand tons need some stopping even at that. With her cable under us keeping her jammed hard up against our port side, she slid and crunched and tore as she slipped aft. The mate and I stood still, appalled and helpless in the brilliant hot sunshine, listening to the sickening sounds and watching the slow disintegration of that craft before our eyes.

'Two or three of our awning spars, ripping the canvas, beat down on her light bridge like white flaying and chastising arms: there was a rending of wood and iron, the stanchions of her light super-structure were torn away, and the upper deck partially collapsed. I could see, as she came aft, that the heavy square timber running round her hull was shorn through and that the shell-plating showed a vertical gash. Her big grey motor-launch still immaculate, still hanging at the davits ready for service, seemed to float along our rail—until it came up against our midship house; it went to pieces in three seconds, the planking sprung up and showered everywhere, settling in a confused mass on our foredeck over the smashed engine. The big massive davits themselves seemed suddenly changed to warm wax; they bent and twisted so easily. And so it went on, down the full length of our port side, until finally she slid clear and the awful tearing, shearing, and groaning ceased as suddenly as it had begun.

'I looked at the mate. His face, half-covered still with drying soap-lather, looked blank; not surprised, not afraid, just blank. Perhaps I looked the same. I felt a little numbed. Something had happened that was quite new to me; something unpleasant; our way of life was upset. I wanted that boat to be whole again; back on her station intact and perfect.

' "Stand by to let go. Port anchor, Mister." I looked up to the bridge. It was the Master speaking and his voice was unchanged. The mate, safety razor still in hand, called out "Chippy, Chippy" to the Chinese carpenter, who, looking like an emaciated convalescent ignoring medical advice, was leaping up the iron ladder with his hammer for the windlass.

'I went quickly to the bridge and stood near the Master, admiring the cool precise manner he delivered his orders and got the ship brought up, thinking also that I seemed to be the only one affected by the recent accident. Nothing at that moment seemed very much altered; just a few broken awning spars and a heap of rubbish on our foredeck. The sea was unchanged; the sun penetrated the awning above our heads with its usual intensity. The matter of chronometer-winding seemed all-important. As for the vessel we had struck, she was now presenting her best side, and beyond having a slight list did not appear very much different.

'I was just finishing an entry in the chronometer journal when he entered the chartroom, sitting down on the settee with a little sigh like that of a man fatigued after a great exertion. It was a difficult moment; what could I say? To say nothing at all could be interpreted as a silent and unmanly accusation of guilt. To say, "Bad show, sir," would of course have been worse, and the words, "I'm sorry, sir," would have been a milk-and-water sort of remark when the issue was so deep.

'I felt that I wanted to sympathise, but didn't know how to start. I felt, too, at that moment, that it was the human and not the material issue which monopolised my thoughts. I was glad when he spoke.

' "That's the end for me, second mate," he said. And his voice was tragically soft and sad, like a man who speaks of the passing of an affectionate friend.

'I turned then. He looked old and weary, but not ashamed. When his eyes met mine they were disturbingly searching for some answer that eluded him. Perhaps for my judgment. As if that mattered! As if that could possibly alter the future for him. Perhaps for a sign of loss of faith in him, I don't know. But I knew that, for the time being, the barrier was down.

' "Not for you, sir!" I replied. "I wouldn't look at it quite like that, especially at your age." A great sympathy and a great loyalty was suddenly born within me. "Why the devil didn't she heave short? We might have missed her!"

'He put aside my suggestion of blame, wagging his head from side to side in the slow way of a man who does not understand and who is not satisfied. I observed the puzzled expression of his eyes.

' "She wouldn't sheer when I went astern," he said in a flat voice. "And she held on even with the helm hard over and a kick ahead." He looked old, defeated and puzzled. Some spark seemed to have died out. "No," he said after a little pause, "she tricked me. It is the end. There is no excuse."

'He got up slowly, without the customary vigour that had always been his, and went below to attend to the formalities with the master of the pilot-vessel who had just arrived aboard.

'For the next two weeks during our short trip away from that place this disciple of Lecky never deviated from his old routine, from his skilful navigational methods. He skirted coasts as he always had done—coasts that other ships avoided like the plague—in order to make the fullest use of favourable currents and tidal sets. His courage and self-confidence seemed in no way altered. During his years of shiphandling he must have saved his owners many thousands of pounds. We told ourselves that surely these things would be taken into account; that this man who by his skill and the winds of heaven could take a square rigger across the world, through storm and sun and the intricacies of the treacherous seas; who had handled without accident many steamers through all the vicissitudes of a ship's life; surely, we argued, the owners would be respectable, lenient, and do the right thing.

'Out of earshot, I say, we thrashed out the incident. The mate, the chief engineer, and myself checked over the steering system with meticulous regard. Not a single fault could we discover. The ship had always behaved well, and she continued to steer through the intense calms and the turbulent monsoon seas with her customary fidelity.

'And so we returned again to our loading port to find a small strange vessel doing pilotage duty on the station and the once perfect victim of our shearing steam lying torn and unkempt on a mud-bank up the river where she had been beached to prevent her sinking. And there was a new master too, ready to take over from him. It was a sad moment when he left us, but I think that in the firmness of our hand-clasps and the message in our eyes, he grasped and accepted with gratitude what we could not bring ourselves to say—the magnitude of our unbroken faith.

'I can see him now, his uniform suit dazzlingly white in the merciless glare of the sun, his face, a dark-red shadow beneath the pith helmet; his hand steady on the manrope of the shore gangway. He paused for perhaps two seconds, as if taking a last lingering survey of a ship that had defeated him; then his eyes hardened suddenly, he turned about and walked off with something approaching his old virile step, and he never once looked back.

'Something seemed to have gone with him too, from the ship. Things were never quite the same; the old ways were changed; the spirit of comradeship that had been the essence of our life seemed to have lost its fortifying property like a sparkling glass of wine that stands overlong and becomes flat and uninteresting. The tranquil course of our service became disturbed, as a placid sunny sea is altered by cat's-paws of wind. The mate and the chief engineer began counting the weeks when their service on the coast would be finished. The incident and our late master were not spoken of—the subject became taboo. And yet each of us gave it a considerable amount of thought. In the dark watches up there on her bridge I wrestled with the thing continually. What had happened? Why had we rammed the cursed beautiful thing? Was it an error of judgment, over-confidence, an example of the blind spot of a man's intelligence—or a mere mechanical defect of the ship? Perhaps some cursed and diabolical tidal stream acting down there on our deep-draughted hull? I couldn't answer my own questions. But I could picture the panelled London officer with the rows of ledgers on the shelves, the letter files, and the ten-foot builders' model of a similar ship in a glass case; nautical-looking calendars on the wall sent by firms selling rope and paint and canvas; the big table with the chart of the river approaches; match-boxes for models and a pencil for the wind; the glib talk of men whose brains are shrewd but whose knowledge of the sea begins at Brighton and ends in victualling allowances. I could hear the inevitable, damning questions.

"Now, just suppose, Captain, that you had given her a wider berth—say another couple of hundred yards! In the beautiful prevailing weather conditions that wouldn't have made a hazardous journey for the pilot's boat—would it now? And all this depressing and unfortunate business would never have occurred at all— would it? No. That's right. You see, what we really fail to understand…"

'You see, as he said, there was no excuse.'

II

'*W*ell,' my companion went on, 'we loaded for the Cape—
an uncomfortable run in July. We boiled and roasted in the river;
we staggered encrusted with salt through the dripping wind and
high head-seas of a fierce monsoon; we were blasted by the
howling westerly gales of a Cape winter, struggling up and over
and through the great swells that only the Southern Ocean can
produce. But I would like to pass on to the day we sailed from
Capetown.

'It was a grey, Cape day with a fresh westerly wind, a moderate
sea, and a threat of rain. We were glad to be away, eager to renew
our acquaintance with the heat and moil we so often cursed. In
ballast, we rolled our way round Cape Point and turned to the
east. Our new master, anxious to emulate some of his predecessor's
runs, laid the course close to the coast in order to make use of
the strong easterly counter current and thus avoid the well-
known Agulhas farther out. By noon we were doing, with strong
quartering wind and favourable set, about fifteen knots over the
ground—quite an achievement for us in a steamer that averaged
about ten.

'In the reeling chartroom I held on to the long table and studied
for a few minutes the large-scale chart laid out there. The great
swell bore us aloft and dragged us down into immense valleys, and
all the time without pause we rolled heavily forward along a
frowning coast. It was now my watch until four, so I went out
through the wheel-house to the port wing of the bridge where the
third mate passed me the usual information, then went below.
Normally he would return at half-past twelve to relieve me for the
mid-day meal. The master, following me out, stood by my side.

' "I have told Mr.——," he said, "to take his lunch first today. By the time he is finished we should be past that rock. I would like you to be up here then. We should pass a mile outside. Keep the bearings going and don't let her set in."

' "Yes; very good, sir," I replied. "I'll watch her." And with that he, too, went below. It was then fifteen minutes after noon. I should, I suppose, have felt flattered at his remark, but I thought the change in routine a discouraging thrust at the young third mate. Why could the Master not have stayed up himself? That was more usual. It hurt no one's pride. Perhaps, I thought, he was afraid that his soup would get cold.

'The rock he had mentioned was an isolated spot on the chart; for the coast is everywhere precipitous and steep-to, and comfortably free from out-lying dangers. A mile was a reasonable distance to pass the thing, which was awash at low water, under the existing conditions of daylight and good visibility.

'Well, I did keep the bearings going. Every few minutes I obtained a good fix, staying in the chartroom for as short a time as possible; for I was anxious to see the effect of the big swell on that rock. Between the bearings I swept the undulating offing for the tell-tale signs, but between the ship and the black forbidding coast, with the bases of its precipitous cliffs lost in a mist of wind-driven spume, there was nothing but an endless succession of crests, rearing lines of water racing on towards the shore.

'A position at twelve-thirty provided the first shock—it was well inside the soft-pencilled line laid down on the chart. She was setting in quickly. I wondered if I had made a mistake, but no, the cocked hat of the three bearings was small; I called, in Hindustani, to the quartermaster standing swaying and bare-footed on the grating.

' "Starboard—ten degrees!"

' "Ah, Sahib. Ten degress starboard."

'Dividers in hand, I measured the distance to run, and found it was two miles. That seems a long way, but at fifteen knots it is only eight minutes of time. I dropped the instruments as if they were hot, and stepped out again to search for that cursed outlying obstruction.

'A sudden startled cry from the wheel-house stepped up my normal heart-beats to hammer-blows inside my chest, jerking me to a state of instant alertness.

' "*Dekko*, sahib! *Dekko*, sahib!" He had seen the thing before me. There it was, fine on the port bow, just a cloud of mist that seemed to race backwards over the moving crests. A glance at the sky beyond showed the truth and dispelled the illusion of movement which the yawing of the ship's head, too, was creating.

'I relaxed inwardly; for the unseen danger is the father and mother of suspense, and suspense is a dangerous emotion. I gave the order for the helm to be put hard over, determined to get the danger well out on the port bow—on the beam if necessary—so long as I kept the ship well outside to seaward.

' "Hard over, sahib!"

'Five minutes, perhaps, to go. The mist was denser, bigger, higher. I jammed myself between a stanchion and the open door of the wheel-house, waiting for the swing of the ship's head. Nothing happened! Suspense returned with a tightening of the chest and abdomen that I had not before experienced. I stepped quickly into the wheel-house and looked at the polished brass helm indicator on the pedestal—it showed extreme starboard helm. Still she didn't swing.

'A sudden urge to do something practical—give some task to my hands—seized me. I pushed the man from the grating and took the wheel myself, saying, "Captain sahib *bolow. Juldi, juldi*," and the fellow disappeared like a frightened shadow.

'The forward windows of the wheel-house were open, for the wind was following. There it was, still fine on the port bow. A little black showed every now and then between the great crests of the swell; the spray was flung up and over in a great cloud of wind-driven drops. I could hear the singing of the turbines and the loud ticking of the wheelhouse clock above my head. The engine telegraph standing polished and gleaming held a sudden and silent fascination. No! I would not touch it. That would be fatal. I knew the time it takes to get the engines from full ahead to full astern even with the engineers waiting for it. I knew how far the ship would run before stopping. Time and distance had a new significance. I knew the immediate loss of steering that "full astern" incurs.

'I suppose that in those two minutes I was seized by some form of demoralising mental panic. I thought of lifeboats, their uses and their weaknesses; the awful hideous shock that would occur when she struck; I gripped those spokes with a fierce and crushing clasp. Where the devil was that *seccunni* and the Master? Why didn't he come? The perspiration began to form under the band of my peaked cap; a drop ran down my face, leaving a cold wet line. Through the mist that was forming over my eyeballs the black mass grew suddenly large and diabolically cruel, with the great swell creaming over it and the spray hurled skywards. I was left alone, with a ship that refused to steer, hurtling on to destruction. There it was, the bearing remaining constant. Fragments of stuff I knew off by heart flew to my tongue. I could hear myself repeating the words and the booming of the reef getting louder.

'"Nothing in these rules shall exonerate ... from the neglect to keep a proper look-out ... or of any precaution ... by the special circumstances of the case."

'The clock behind me stopped. A voice in my ear—and it was *his* voice—said very calmly, "She wouldn't steer for me either. She tricked me. It is the end and there is no excuse. Only you and I will understand."

'The ticking of the clock recommenced. There was a sudden rush of feet up the starboard ladder and the Master stood in front of me, his table napkin in his hand, his mouth not yet emptied of food.

' "Helm hard over?" His voice was curt.

' "Hard over, sir," I replied. "She won't come up."

'His broad back shut out the view of the rock, but I could still see the spray flying up in a great cloud like a hail-storm in reverse.

' "She's coming up now," he replied, and the words seemed like a cooling pack laid upon my burning forehead. I looked at the iron davit over the stem tracing a great yawing ellipse, sometimes on the sky, sometimes on the sea, but slowly, slowly creeping towards the south. And there was I, with the helm jammed hard against the stop and the native quartermaster standing with pendulous lips and protruding dark eyes beside me. I never knew his thoughts; but I wished at that moment for a little of the faith that the relic round his neck was imparting to his simple soul.

'The clock ticked on. Then a great noise grew out from ahead, drowning out all other noises of the ship. We were borne aloft on the crest of a Southern Ocean greybeard; the land was obscured by an immense cloud of upward flying spray that seemed to rise vertically from somewhere below our port bilges. Would the awful grinding crash and shudder never come?

'I glanced quickly through the port window and looked down through the moving screen of drops on to a black and glistening smooth stretch of rock that was the bottom of the sea. A second, and it was gone, covered with creaming water that roared across it in seething boiling anger. The whole fabric of the ship shuddered with the deafening thunder of the noise, with the roaring turbulence of ten thousand tons of water gone mad. But it was the vibration of sound alone, of the awful eternal contest of the greatest forces of the world.

'I saw the Master turn, shouting, but his voice was lost in that thunderous sound. Only by the gesture of his arm did I know his meaning. I let go the wheel to ease the helm. Instead of recoiling back to the midship position it stayed where it was, slack, without life. And the little black finger behind the glass of the pressure gauge showed no pressure in the hydraulic system, as if the fluid had frozen in the pipes with sheer fright. The murderous roar passed away astern, like dying thunder rolling behind high hills. The sounds of the ship crept back.

' "Cutting things a bit fine, aren't you?" The Master's voice sounded weak, puny as the cry of a child when the shouting of a multitude ceases. His face was strained; his eyes blinked once or twice quickly. He wiped his forehead and the back of his neck with the crumpled napkin. I read the blame in his eyes.

' "*She* is," I answered. "Some day she is going to commit suicide; but, by God, before that I will go through this steering system with a fine-tooth comb. I will discover why she chooses such moments as this to display her rottenness."

'He stepped aft beside me to observe the pressure gauges on the pedestal. "Nothing wrong with the steering. Usual pressure there," he said. "Keep her out a point for the set. I'll be up after I have my coffee."

'I looked at the gauges. The pressures were normal. He was right. And with a sense of defeat, of having been tricked, I stepped from the grating and gave the course to the Indian quartermaster.

'"*Atcha*, sahib," he said, smiling. "*Abi teke-ai*. Yes, now it is all right."'

My companion on the wooden bench ceased speaking, and by a quick sideways glance I saw that, for him at the moment, I did not exist: neither did the river nor the great granite breakwater spread out like a protecting arm from the northern shore. He seemed to be looking beyond, seeing the things, the big things of life which had been denied to me—until now. There was a trace of glistening moisture on the brown unfurrowed brow beneath the brim of his hat; his broad and freckled hands were still clasped together between his knees.

A sudden, powerful blast from the whistle of a big steamer emerging out of the murk brought him back from the undulating vastness of a Southern Ocean; from the burning delta of a great river.

A weak ray of winter afternoon sunshine piercing the grey pall overhead fell upon the bright new dry-dock paint of the steamer's boot-topping and topsides. She glided nearer on her way out to the sea with the low hum of turbines and the thumb of a half-immersed screw beating the water. Her ensign and house flag hung limp and lifeless in the still air.

Getting to his feet the young man read aloud the white-lettered legend on her bow, and his face was still hard.

'That,' he said, 'is the ship *he* could not bear to see again. Come, let us take the road to the shore.'

A.A. BELDON

The Three Sisters

Thirty years ago on a wet autumn evening the household of Mallett's Lodge was gathered round the death-bed of Ursula Mallow, the eldest of the three sisters who inhabited it. The dingy moth-eaten curtains of the old wooden bedstead were drawn apart, the light of a smoking oil-lamp falling upon the hopeless countenance of the dying woman as she turned her dull eyes upon her sisters. The room was in silence except for an occasional sob from the youngest sister, Eunice. Outside the rain fell steadily over the streaming marshes.

"Nothing is to be changed, Tabitha," gasped Ursula to the other sister, who bore a striking likeness to her, although her expression was harder and colder; "this room is to be locked up and never opened."

"Very well," said Tabitha brusquely; "though I don't see how it can matter to you then."

"It does matter," said her sister with startling energy. "How do you know, how do I know that I may not sometimes visit it?

I have lived in this house so long I am certain that I shall see it again. I *will* come back. Come back to watch over you both and see that no harm befalls you."

"You are talking wildly," said Tabitha, by no means moved at her sister's solicitude for her welfare. "Your mind is wandering; you know that I have no faith in such things."

Ursula sighed, and beckoning to Eunice, who was weeping silently at the bedside, placed her feeble arms around her neck and kissed her.

"Do not weep, dear," she said feebly. "Perhaps it is best so. A lonely woman's life is scarce worth living. We have no hopes, no aspirations; other women have had happy husbands and children, but we in this forgotten place have grown old together. I go first, but you must soon follow."

Tabitha, comfortably conscious of only forty years and an iron frame, shrugged her shoulders and smiled grimly.

"I go first," repeated Ursula in a new and strange voice as her heavy eyes slowly closed, "but I will come for each of you in turn, when your lease of life runs out. At that moment I will be with you to lead your steps whither I now go."

As she spoke the flickering lamp went out suddenly as though extinguished by a rapid hand, and the room was left in utter darkness. A strange suffocating noise issued from the bed, and when the trembling women had relighted the lamp, all that was left of Ursula Mallow was ready for the grave.

That night the survivors passed together. The dead woman had been a firm believer in the existence of that shadowy borderland which is said to form an unhallowed link between the living and the dead, and even stolid Tabitha, slightly unnerved by the events of the night, was not free from certain apprehensions that she might have been right.

With the bright morning their fears disappeared. The sun stole in at the window, and seeing the poor earthworn face on the pillow so touched it and glorified it that only its goodness and weakness were seen, and the beholders came to wonder how they could ever have felt any dread of aught so calm and peaceful. A day or two passed, and the body was transferred to a massive coffin long regarded as the finest piece of work of its kind ever turned out of the village carpenter's workshop. Then a slow and melancholy cortège headed by four bearers wound its solemn way across the marches to the family vault in the grey old church, and all that was left of Ursula was placed by the father and mother who had taken that self-same journey some thirty years before.

To Eunice as they toiled slowly home the day seemed strange and Sabbath-like, the flat prospect of marsh wilder and more forlorn than usual, the roar of the sea more depressing. Tabitha had no such fancies. The bulk of the dead woman's property had been left to Eunice, and her avaricious soul was sorely troubled and her proper sisterly feelings of regret for the deceased sadly interfered with in consequence.

"What are you going to do with all that money, Eunice?" she asked as they sat at their quiet tea.

"I shall leave it as it stands," said Eunice slowly. "We have both got sufficient to live upon, and I shall devote the income from it to supporting some beds in a children's hospital."

"If Ursula had wished it to go to a hospital," said Tabitha in her deep tones, "she would have left the money to it herself. I wonder you do not respect her wishes more."

"What else can I do with it then?" inquired Eunice.

"Save it," said the other with gleaming eyes, "save it."

Eunice shook her head.

"No," said she, "it shall go to the sick children, but the principal I will not touch, and if I die before you it shall become yours and you can do what you like with it."

"Very well," said Tabitha, smothering her anger by a strong effort; "I don't believe that was what Ursula meant you to do with it, and I don't believe she will rest quietly in the grave while you squander the money she stored so carefully."

"What do you mean?" asked Eunice with pale lips. "You are trying to frighten me; I thought that you did not believe in such things."

Tabitha made no answer, and to avoid the anxious inquiring gaze of her sister, drew her chair to the fire, and folding her gaunt arms, composed herself for a nap.

For some time life went on quietly in the old house. The room of the dead woman, in accordance with her last desire, was kept firmly locked, its dirty windows forming a strange contrast to the prim cleanliness of the others. Tabitha, never very talkative, became more taciturn than ever, and stalked about the house and the neglected garden like an unquiet spirit, her brow roughened into the deep wrinkles suggestive of much thought. As the winter came on, bringing with it the long dark evenings, the old house became more lonely than ever, and an air of mystery and dread seemed to hang over it and brood in its empty rooms and dark corridors. The deep silence of night was broken by strange noises for which neither the wind nor the rats could be held accountable. Old Martha, seated in her distant kitchen, heard strange sounds upon the stairs, and once, upon hurrying to them, fancied that she saw a dark figure squatting upon the landing, though a subsequent search with candle and spectacles failed to discover anything. Eunice was disturbed by several vague incidents, and, as she suffered from a complaint of the heart, rendered very ill by them. Even Tabitha admitted a strangeness about the house, but, confident in her piety and virtue, took no heed of it, her mind being fully employed in another direction.

Since the death of her sister all restraint upon her was removed, and she yielded herself up entirely to the stern and hard rules enforced by avarice upon its devotees. Her house-keeping expenses were kept rigidly separate from those of Eunice and her food limited to the coarsest dishes, while in the matter of clothes the old servant was by far the better dressed. Seated alone in her bedroom this uncouth, hard-featured creature revelled in her possessions, grudging even the expense of the candle-end which enabled her to behold them. So completely did this passion change her that both Eunice and Martha became afraid of her, and lay awake in their beds night after night trembling at the chinking of the coins at her unholy vigils.

One day Eunice ventured to remonstrate. "Why don't you bank your money, Tabitha?" she said; "it is surely not safe to keep such large sums in such a lonely house."

"Large sums!" repeated the exasperated Tabitha, "large sums; what nonsense is this? You know well that I have barely sufficient to keep me."

"It's a great temptation to housebreakers," said her sister, not pressing the point. "I made sure last night that I heard somebody in the house."

"Did you?" said Tabitha, grasping her arm, a horrible look on her face. "So did I. I thought they went to Ursula's room, and I got out of bed and went on the stairs to listen."

"Well?" said Eunice faintly, fascinated by the look on her sister's face.

"There was *something* there," said Tabitha slowly. "I'll swear it, for I stood on the landing by her door and listened; something scuffling on the floor round and round the room. At first I thought it was the cat, but when I went up there this morning the door was still locked, and the cat was in the kitchen."

"Oh, let us leave this dreadful house," moaned Eunice.

"What!" said her sister grimly; "afraid of poor Ursula? Why should you be? Your own sister who nursed you when you were a babe, and who perhaps even now comes and watches over your slumbers."

"Oh!" said Eunice, pressing her hand to her side, "if I saw her I should die. I should think that she had come for me as she said she would. O God! have mercy on me, I am dying."

She reeled as she spoke, and before Tabitha could save her, sank senseless to the floor.

"Get some water," cried Tabitha, as old Martha came hurrying up the stairs, "Eunice has fainted."

The old woman, with a timid glance at her, retired, reappearing shortly afterwards with the water, with which she proceeded to restore her much-loved mistress to her senses. Tabitha, as soon as this was accomplished, stalked off to her room, leaving her sister and Martha sitting drearily enough in the small parlour, watching the fire and conversing in whispers.

It was clear to the old servant that this state of things could not last much longer, and she repeatedly urged her mistress to leave a house so lonely and so mysterious. To her great delight Eunice at length consented, despite the fierce opposition of her sister, and at the mere idea of leaving gained greatly in health and spirits. A small but comfortable house was hired in Morville, and arrangements made for a speedy change.

It was the last night in the old house, and all the wild spirits of the marshes, the wind and the sea seemed to have joined forces for one supreme effort. When the wind dropped, as it did at brief intervals, the sea was heard moaning on the distant beach, strangely mingled with the desolate warning of the bell-buoy as it rocked to the waves. Then the wind rose again, and the noise of the sea was lost in the fierce gusts which, finding no obstacle on the open marshes, swept with their full fury upon the house by the creek. The strange voices of the air shrieked in its chimneys, windows rattled, doors slammed, and even the very curtains seemed to live and move.

Eunice was in bed, awake. A small night-light in a saucer of oil shed a sickly glare upon the worm-eaten old furniture, distorting the most innocent articles into ghastly shapes. A wilder gust than usual almost deprived her of the protection afforded by that poor light, and she lay listening fearfully to the creakings and other noises on the stairs, bitterly regretting that she had not asked Martha to sleep with her. But it was not too late even now. She slipped hastily to the floor, crossed to the huge wardrobe, and was in the very act of taking her dressing-gown from its peg when an unmistakable footfall was heard on the stairs. The robe dropped from her shaking fingers, and with a quickly beating heart she regained her bed.

The sounds ceased and a deep silence followed, which she herself was unable to break although she strove hard to do so. A wild gust of wind shook the windows and nearly extinguished the light, and when its flame had regained its accustomed steadiness she saw that the door was slowly opening, while the huge shadow of a hand blotted the papered wall. Still her tongue refused its office. The door flew open with a crash, a cloaked figure entered and, throwing aside its coverings, she saw with a horror past all expression the napkin-bound face of the dead Ursula smiling terribly at her. In her last extremity she raised her faded eyes above for succour, and then as the figure noiselessly advanced and laid its cold hand upon her brow, the soul of Eunice Mallow left its body with a wild shriek and made its way to the Eternal.

Martha, roused by the cry, and shivering with dread, rushed to the door and gazed in terror at the figure which stood leaning over the bedside. As she watched, it slowly removed the cowl and the napkin and exposed the fell face of Tabitha, so strangely contorted between fear and triumph that she hardly recognised it.

"Who's there?" cried Tabitha in a terrible voice as she saw the old woman's shadow on the wall.

"I thought I heard a cry," said Martha, entering. "Did anybody call?"

"Yes, Eunice," said the other, regarding her closely. "I, too, heard the cry, and hurried to her. What makes her so strange? Is she in a trance?"

"Aye," said the old woman, falling on her knees by the bed and sobbing bitterly, "the trance of death. Ah, my dear, my poor lonely girl, that this should be the end of it! She has died of fright," said the old woman, pointing to the eyes, which even yet retained their horror. "She has seen something *devilish*."

Tabitha's gaze fell. "She has always suffered with her heart," she muttered; "the night has frightened her; it frightened me."

She stood upright by the foot of the bed as Martha drew the sheet over the face of the dead woman.

"First Ursula, then Eunice," said Tabitha, drawing a deep breath. "I can't stay here. I'll dress and wait for the morning."

She left the room as she spoke, and with bent head proceeded to her own. Martha remained by the bedside, and gently closing the staring eyes, fell on her knees and prayed long and earnestly for the departed soul. Overcome with grief and fear, she remained with bowed head until a sudden sharp cry from Tabitha brought her to her feet.

"Well," said the old woman, going to the door.

"Where are you?" cried Tabitha, somewhat reassured by her voice.

"In Miss Eunice's bedroom. Do you want anything?"

"Come down at once. Quick! I am unwell."

Her voice rose suddenly to a scream. "Quick! For God's sake! Quick, or I shall go mad. *There is some strange woman in the house.*"

The old woman stumbled hastily down the dark stairs. "What is the matter?" she cried, entering the room. "Who is it? What do you mean?"

"I saw it," said Tabitha, grasping her convulsively by the shoulder. "I was coming to you when I saw the figure of a woman in front of me going up the stairs. Is it—can it be Ursula come for the soul of Eunice, as she said she would?"

"Or for yours?" said Martha, the words coming from her in some odd fashion, despite herself.

Tabitha, with a ghastly look, fell cowering by her side, clutching tremulously at her clothes. "Light the lamps," she cried hysterically. "Light a fire, make a noise; oh, this dreadful darkness! Will it never be day!"

"Soon, soon," said Martha, overcoming her repugnance and trying to pacify her. "When the day comes you will laugh at these fears."

"I murdered her," screamed the miserable woman, "I killed her with fright. Why did she not give me the money? 'Twas no use to her. Ah! *Look there!*"

Martha, with a horrible fear, followed her glance to the door, but saw nothing.

"It's Ursula," said Tabitha, from between her teeth. "Keep her off! Keep her off!"

The old woman, who by some unknown sense seemed to feel the presence of a third person in the room, moved a step forward and stood before her. As she did so Tabitha waved her arms as though to free herself from the touch of a detaining hand, half-rose to her feet, and without a word fell dead before her.

At this the old woman's courage forsook her, and with a great cry she rushed from the room, eager to escape from this house of death and mystery. The bolts of the great door were stiff with age, and strange voices seemed to ring in her ears as she strove wildly to unfasten them. Her brain whirled. She thought that the dead in their distant rooms called to her, and that a devil stood on the step outside laughing and holding the door against her. Then with a supreme effort she flung it open, and heedless of her night-clothes passed into the bitter night. The path across the marshes was lost in the darkness, but she found it; the planks over the ditches slippery and narrow, but she crossed them in safety, until at last, her feet bleeding and her breath coming in great gasps, she entered the village and sank down more dead than alive on a cottage doorstep.

W.W. Jacobs

The Ivory God

At six o'clock Thurston put down his pen, pushed his chair back from the table at which he had been writing, and rose to his feet with a series of gestures indicative of mental and physical fatigue. He glanced at the few sheets of manuscript which represented the result of a long day's labour, and he frowned, as if in anger or distaste.

He had written, or tried to write, from ten o'clock until one, and again from two until six; and his entire product after seven hours' work was comparatively infinitesimal. He had felt no enthusiasm; he had been unable to concentrate his thoughts; the whole thing had been distasteful to him. As he glanced around him he asked himself for the thousandth time whether the game was worth the candle.

More from force of habit than from genuine desire to do it, Thurston proceeded to make some sort of toilet for the evening. He shaved and washed carefully; he put on a clean linen shirt and a dark lounge suit; he was unduly particular about the fold of his tie; in several small ways he showed that he had a gentleman like love of cleanliness and orderly habits.

He did everything very slowly. It would have been evident to anyone who might have had an opportunity of watching him that he had no engagement to keep. In point of fact, he had few friends with whom he could have kept any engagement. He was, as he now never cared to remind himself, one of the very loneliest men living. For a while he had reminded himself of this pertinent truth somewhat often; then he wearied of the thought, and put it from him. The fact of the loneliness, however, remained.

Thurston lived in two rooms at the top of a house which stood in a quiet street near the British Museum—a street of an aspect so grey and pathetic that you wondered at first sight of it whether laughter or children's voices were ever heard there. The two rooms opened one into the other by means of a tolding door. Thurston had furnished them himself when he first came to town.

One room contained a camp bedstead, a chest of drawers, a dressing-table, a wash-stand, a bath, and a hard-bottomed chair. The floor was stained and polished, and destitute of carpet; but there was a thick bearskin rug at the bedside. It was absolutely destitute of luxuries or of pictures, but it possessed a first-rate reading-lamp, attached to the wall at the head of the bed.

The other room knew the luxury of books; its walls were covered with them to half their height. The books related chiefly to philosophy, theology, history, metaphysics. There was little that was light, but a table was strewn with the reviews of several countries, all purchased second-hand and when a month old.

A desk, littered with papers, stood in the window; an armchair was placed near the hearth; two other chairs of an easyish sort occurred, sometimes here, sometimes there; a small table, big enough for one person to eat at, was in the middle of the room, which, unlike the sleeping-chamber, was softly carpeted and luxuriant in thick rugs.

It also possessed some luxuries in the way of pictures; but these, to the English eye of ordinary knowledge, were of a strange taste, being Japanese. One skilled in such matters might have told you that they were all by the most celebrated Japanese artists. Even then you would have felt some uneasiness at the prospect of being continually shut up in a room whose decorations were so purely Eastern.

In these two rooms Thurston had spent five years, every day corresponding to another day. He prepared his own breakfast when he wished for it; he read or wrote when he desired to do so; he lunched and dined out; he spent his evenings reading or thinking or dreaming. It was a strange life altogether; but it was his. But, then, the few people who knew Thurston said he was a strange man, a man who spoke little, laughed never, smiled seldom, and who was quite young, in spite of everything. In point of fact, he was twenty-seven years old.

At twenty-two he had left Oxford with some reputation as a scholar and a mystic, and had come to town with the set purpose of following a literary career. Whether he had any ambitions at that time is a debatable question. It is quite certain that at twenty-seven none of them had been carried out. He had a little money of his own—sufficient to pay his rent, his housekeeping expenses, his tailor's bills and so on; and there was, therefore, no need to keep his nose to the grindstone.

But he had made no name. He sometimes exhibited a rather heavy, rather pedantic, rather wearisome sort of article to one or other of the leading reviews—the sort of article which is spoken of with great respect by the critics, and read by only a few experts— but to the general public he was as unknown as an unborn babe.

The people who had any dealings with him said that he was unsociable; he had no conversation. If by any chance he was induced to lunch or dine with you, his sole notion seemed to be to get away as quickly as possible. It was evident that he was one of those men who like to be alone.

There were times, however, when Thurston felt his loneliness; and one of them was hanging heavily about him on this particular evening. He had found it difficult to write during the day; and more than once he had caught himself wishing that a friend would come in to break the solitude. But he would have been hard put to it to say where such a friend was to be found.

He never encouraged anyone to visit him at his rooms. One or two men—old college acquaintances—had tracked him down and called upon him, but quickly discovered that they were not wanted. It was not that Thurston wished to be rude; it was simply that a certain shyness and loneliness ran in his blood and his temperament, and made him incapable of entertaining his fellow-creatures. He was essentially an anchorite; and yet there were times when his flesh called for something which it would have found it hard to define in words.

As Thurston drew on his overcoat a light tap came at his door, and he went across and opened it, not without some feeling of surprise that anyone should be there. In the faint light at the top of the landing he saw a man whom he did not recognise—a tall, sloping-shouldered man, whose back was somewhat bowed, whose knees bent in—a man who made a succession of angles in his clothes. Thurston could see that he was shabbily attired, that his hair was long, greasy, and unclean; he had a vague notion that an unwashed atmosphere hung heavily all round and about his visitor. He held the door half open, staring at the man; the man blinked at him.

"Mr. Thurston?" he said inquiringly.

"Well?" replied Thurston.

The man sighed heavily.

"I was sent to you, sir, by Mr. Evanson. I have something to show you which he thought you would like to see. He thought you might not be indisposed to buy it from me. May I come in and show it to you, Mr. Thurston?" said the man, indicating a small parcel which he carried in the crook of one arm.

"I am not disposed to buy anything," answered Thurston, keeping his place.

"But this, sir, is something very uncommon. It is seldom that any collector has such a chance of securing such a valuable curiosity," urged the visitor. "At any rate it will do you no harm to look at it, Mr. Thurston."

"Well," said Thurston, impassively and hesitatingly, "you may bring it in, then, but I really don't want to see it, and I shan't buy it, whatever it may be."

He turned away, and made preparations for lighting a lamp. The man with the parcel lingered at the threshold until the lamp had been placed on the centre table, and the apartment was bathed in a clear, powerful light.

"Now, then," said Thurston, still impassive as ever, "come forward, and let me see what it is! Mr. Evanson has no business to send you to me. I'm merely an acquaintance of his, and I'm certainly not a collector. What is it you have to show me?"

The untidy and unwashed person took small notice of this impatient outburst. He advanced to the table, placed his parcel near the lamp, and proceeded to divest it of its wrappings. He kept himself between Thurston and the parcel while this was going on, and he did not speak until he suddenly turned round, and said, with a note of pride and triumph in his voice:

"There, Mr. Thurston, look at that!"

Thurston, during the unfolding of the parcel, had fallen into a sort of day-dream. He came out of it with a start, and looked at the object which his visitor had placed on the table in the full light of the lamp. A sudden gleam came into his rather dull eyes; a sudden exclamation burst from his lips.

"Ah!" he said.

The man smiled, and rubbed his hands. He chuckled.

"I thought that would move you, Mr. Thurston!" he said. "It's a beauty, isn't it?"

Thurston made no answer to this. He advanced to the table and stood at its edge, contemplating the thing which his visitor had been so anxious to exhibit. He found himself staring at an ivory statue of the god Ganesha, and wondering at the exquisite beauty of the workmanship, the subtle tints of the ivory, the atmosphere of the mystic East, which its mere dumb presence suggested and conveyed.

It was not a thing of any great size—its height was some ten inches, its breadth six; a cigar-box would have held it. And to Thurston, steeped to the lips in the odour and colour of the Orient, it represented a world of art and of dreams. He stared at the god; the god stared at him out of a pair of amethyst eyes, cunningly set into the creamy white of the ivory. A strange intoxication stole into Thurston's soul. He heard himself presently talking in set fashion, calmly, methodically, as though he were in a shop, buying something. He heard his visitor's replies.

"You want to sell this?"

"Yes, sir, I want to sell it. I'll tell you how I came by it, too, Mr. Thurston. All's above-board; and Mr. Evanson, he knows me well, and knew me before I fell on hard times. It was this way, sir: My father was in the army at the time of the Mutiny, and he saw a good deal of fighting out in India—Delhi and Lucknow and elsewhere—and he brought home a good many curiosities, and that image amongst them. It's the image of some Hindu god, so I'm told, and, of course, anybody can see that the workmanship is excellent. My father gave it to me on his deathbed, and charged me never to part with it, because there's some legend about its bringing luck with it. But it's brought no luck to me," continued Thurston's visitor, with a dismal laugh. "I've been down on my luck for some time. However, it will bring luck if you're agreeable to buy it, sir. Perhaps that's where the luck comes in."

"What price do you set upon it?" asked Thurston mechanically.

"Well, sir, I, of course, don't know anything about these matters. I was recommended to take the carving to Mr. Evanson," said the man, "and he advised me to see you. I should be quite satisfied to take what he said he thought it was worth."

"What was that?" said Thurston.

"Twenty pounds, sir."

The man uttered these words with some anxiety, and his eyes fastened themselves on Thurston's face, as if to watch the effect. Thurston, however, was still fascinated by the ivory god, and neither eyes nor lips betrayed anything. He remained silent for some moments. At last he started, as from a reverie.

"I am quite prepared to accept Mr. Evanson's estimate of the carving's value," he said. "I will give you twenty pounds for it."

The man bowed his untidy head, and sighed deeply. It was evident that the prospect of immediate possession of twenty pounds was very grateful to him.

"Thank you, sir," he said.

Thurston went over to his desk, unlocked a drawer, and produced a cash box, which, on examination, proved to contain twenty-two pound notes and gold. He counted out twenty to his visitor, put two pounds in his own pocket, restored the depleted cashbox to its drawer and locked it up again, and then, asking the vendor his name and address, wrote out a formal receipt. Five minutes later the unkempt person was descending the stairs, happy in the possession of a small fortune, and Thurston was left alone with the ivory god.

The clanging of the street door, far below, plunged the house into a weird silence. In its midst Thurston sighed deeply. There was a strange feeling within him that he had suddenly come into possession of something which he had been wanting all his life. It was akin to the feeling of the lover to whom the much-desired object of affection is at last given.

When the stranger first unwrapped the ivory god and revealed its strange charms to his eyes, Thurston became aware of a sense of satisfaction. This sense was now increasing to a point of something like delight. He drew in his nether lip, and began to utter a soft, sibilant sound, not unlike the purring of a cat. Not for many years had he experienced such a keen feeling of pleasure as that which now filled him.

He began looking about him for a suitable place wherein to enshrine his new acquisition. He glanced at the chimney-piece, already ornamented profusely with carvings from China, Japan, and India, with stones and vases from Peru, and turned away dissatisfied. The ivory god, he said to himself, must have a better setting than the chimney-piece offered. He wanted to have it near him while he wrote. There was something in the lines, in the dull white of the ivory, in the subtle purple tints of the amethyst eyes, which bade fair to soothe and to fascinate. He wished to have the ivory god upon his desk.

Looking about the room, he caught sight of a little triptych which he had bought years ago in Venice, admiring it more for the fineness of the wood and the carving than for the elementary art of the figure of Christ which was placed in the centre niche. Its dark wood, he thought, would make an admirable setting to the pallid tint of the ivory; and without hesitation he took it down from the wall, wrenched away the crucifix from the middle compartment, and installed the figure of the Hindu god in its place. Then he placed the triptych on the ledge above his desk, and stood back from it, admiring the bizarre effect. The amethyst eyes of the ivory god seemed to smile into his own.

Thurston tore himself away from his treasure at last, and went out to dine. He walked through the gloom of the badly-lighted London streets, until he came to the quiet restaurant wherein a certain corner had come to be almost sacred to him. He ate and drank mechanically and sparingly. A small quantity of plainly cooked food satisfied him at all times; he drank no wine or spirits or ale; after dinner he smoked a cigarette to the accompaniment of a cup of coffee, and glanced over his evening newspaper, handed to him by a waiter who knew him for an old and regular customer. Altogether he spent an hour at this restaurant; and on this particular evening there was an itching desire within him all the time to get back to his rooms. He wanted to examine the ivory god again, to look at it, to wonder about it. It was with a feeling of relief and of anticipation of coming pleasure that he finally paid his bill and went quickly away.

Thurston shut himself into his room with a great sense of satisfaction. He was alone in the midst of five millions of people—alone with the only things for which he cared, his books and his curiosities. Other men might dine and wine, go to theatres, balls, social functions. He cared for none of these things. He knew joys which were far deeper, far better worth having, and he could command their presence whenever he pleased to do so. So he fastened his outer door, drew a warm curtain over the inner one, turned up his lamp, and stirred his fire, and looked round about him with a sense of comfort. He saw the ivory god shining in the triptych above his desk, and caught the gleam of its amethyst eyes; and he was once more aware of the feeling that it in some strange way rounded off his life. He was glad to have it and to see it there, sitting above his altar like a presiding deity.

Thurston's next proceedings were significant and explanatory. He divested himself of his overcoat, and of the smartish morning-coat beneath it, and slipped into an old velvet jacket of undoubted antiquity; and, that done, he exchanged his boots for a comfortable and well-worn pair of slippers. And then, having made sure of his preliminaries, he unlocked a cupboard and produced a small decanter of curious shape, half filled with a golden-brown liquid, which seemed to sparkle and coruscate in the lamplight.

He set it on the table in the centre of the room, placed a glass of singular beauty—a deep crystal bowl set in twisted columns— at its side, and proceeded to heat water in a kettle. When the water was heated he made a careful mixture of it and the golden-brown liquid in the glass; and after that he curled himself up in an easy-chair facing the ivory god, with the glass and the decanter at his side.

Thurston had become a slave to the opium habit. Beginning the use of that attractive and insidious drug as a cure for some slight complaint, he had increased his doses, until at twenty-seven he made no excuses to himself for consuming it in large quantities.

During the day he took it in the form of pills, each containing a few grains; at night, following the example of De Quincey, he indulged in laudanum negus, sometimes sitting up until the grey of the morning broke in upon his dreams and fantasies.

He had long since relinquished all thought of giving up the habit. It had destroyed his moral courage once and for all, and had taken complete possession of him, mentally and physically. Under the influence of opium he was indifferent to everything in the world; and it was rarely that its influence was not upon him.

As the subtle charm of the drug stole through his brain, Thurston yielded himself up to the dreams which it induced.

His eyes were fixed on the ivory god. He began to speculate on its history, on the strange things which those amethyst eyes must have seen, on the deeds of blood, the mystic panorama of Eastern life, with its gorgeous colouring, its strange suggestion, which they must have watched unmoved. The phantasmagoria of a hundred worlds began to float, and finally to crystallise, before him.

In his estimation the carving was hundreds upon hundreds of years old. It must certainly have had its original abiding place in a temple or palace, and of itself formed some part of the gorgeous picture which was rapidly shaping itself in Thurston's imagination.

Thurston's evenings were usually spent in a dream of bliss which was itself a source of deep mental content. He was surprised, on this occasion, to find that contemplation of the ivory god was leading him into a state of unusual unrest.

A strange desire to sit down at his desk—literally at the feet of the god—and write, filled him with strenuous force. It was years since he had ever written anything at night, and the mere thought of doing so now made him almost afraid. But the fear vanished quickly; and he was presently conscious of nothing but that he was shortly going to sit down at his desk. It was as if the ivory god had laid some command upon him. He turned up the flame of his spirit-lamp, heated more water, and mixed himself more of the drug. A little later he found himself laying out paper on his blotting-pad, and examining the nib of a pen. And after a time, as if it had been the most natural thing in the world, he settled himself in his elbow-chair, and after one long, searching look at the ivory god, he dipped his pen in the ink and began to write:

"This is the Story of the Loves and Hates of Men and Women that have long been Dust; the Story of a Day when the Red Earth was Young, and the Gods sat steadfast in their Places; the Story of a Time and Times; and behold it has never been told to Human Ear till Now!"

After that came a long night of work—of work such as Thurston had never before done in his life. It was ten o'clock when he wrote the first words on the top sheet of the pile of manuscript paper which he had laid ready to hand. As each successive hour struck on the silver-voiced clock on the chimney-piece it did but interrupt the gentle scribbling of a rapidly-moving pen.

On Thurston's left hand stood the spirit-lamp, the kettle, the decanter, the glass! Now and then he turned to these things and mixed the drug. On his right hand there gradually accumulated a pile of closely-written manuscript. Above him, the amethyst eyes grew purple in the lamplight, the ivory god stared into the gloom beyond the writer's head.

The grey light stole through the cracks and crannies of the shutters, and found Thurston still writing. Much later, the old woman who acted as bedmaker and charwoman knocked loudly at the outer door. Thurston shouted to her to go away and leave him alone; and his pen travelled on and on as if it would never stop.

It was about three days after this that a famous publisher, with whom Thurston was acquainted in slight fashion, was somewhat astonished to find the latter waiting for him in his private room.

He stared at Thurston curiously, noting with the keen eye of a practical man of the world that his visitor wore a strange expression, and seemed to be wrapped in an atmosphere of mystery.

He was shaved and washed, and wore his best garments; but there was a strange pallor on his face, a strange light in his eyes, and his voice was as unnaturally steady as the cold, almost lifeless hand which he placed within the publisher's palm.

The publisher, who had never been able to understand Thurston's strangeness of manner, reverted to an earlier suspicion, and wondered if his visitor had been drinking; but he failed to perceive either twitch or tremor in face or hand, and his visitor's voice was even and firm to the verge of monotony.

"Some time ago," said Thurston, "you were good enough to suggest to me that I should write a romance of Eastern life. It seemed to you that I possessed the necessary knowledge of the East to attempt such a book."

"Quite so," said the other. "I don't know any man better fitted. You've been working in that direction all your life, haven't you? In fact, it's been a wonder to me that you never thought of the thing yourself."

Thurston produced a parcel of manuscript.

"I have here," he said, "a considerable portion of such a work. There is much that I might say to you about it, but at present I prefer not to say anything. Yes, it is not ordinary work, and I should like some assurance from you that it shall be read for you by someone competent to judge of its merits."

"I'll give it to Flintford to read," said the publisher. "How does his name strike you? He's about the best man I can think of."

"I am quite prepared to accept Mr. Flintford's judgment," replied Thurston. "Indeed, I intended suggesting his name to you. Then I will leave this portion of the manuscript with you?"

"Do," answered the publisher. "I'll send it on to Flintford by special messenger at once, and ask him to read it. About the rest of the book, now——"

"The remaining portion," said Thurston, "will be delivered to you when it is written." And with that and a frigid shaking of the publisher's outstretched hand he went away, walking through the outer office, as one of the clerks said, like a ghost.

The next morning Flintford walked into the publisher's office, looking very much excited.

"I say!" he exclaimed. "Where did you get that manuscript which you sent me yesterday? And have you got the rest?"

"Well, what of it?" asked the publisher, ignoring the second part of the question. "Is it good stuff? Will it do? Would it sell?"

"Good! My dear sir, it is the most wonderful piece of imaginative work I ever read in my life. It is amazing, stupendous— quite confusing in its brilliance. I began it last night. I went on reading it until breakfast-time this morning," answered Flintford. "I never read anything quite like it. Indeed, I wouldn't have believed that we had a brain amongst us that could have imagined such a work. Look here! You know I am by no means an enthusiastic person. Well, this book, if it keeps up that level all through, is the biggest find of the last half-century. For sheer imagination the man beats Poe hollow!"

"You think it will make a hit?" inquired the publisher.

"It is the greatest thing I ever had put before me," answered the critic. "I cannot understand the power in it. Who is the man? How does he come to be able to re-create Hindu life as it must have been thousands of years ago? Where did he get such an overwhelming imagination? There's something that's almost unholy, unearthly, about the whole thing. It is a great book—a rare book. I should like to see the author."

"I will try to get him here at three this afternoon," said the publisher. "Come in after lunch. I may tell you that he is a strange person—never done anything but an occasional article in the heavy reviews, but, I fancy, cram full of the East."

"That," said the critic, "is evident. I'll come at three."

At three o'clock Thurston was shown into the publisher's private room, and introduced to the great critic. Thurston, if possible, was more ghostlike than ever; more emotionless; more insensible to any outward influence. He sat with fixed passionless eyes, listening, while the critic praised his work and asked questions. It was not until all this had been said that he spoke.

"I think I may take you both into my confidence," he said. "I conclude, Mr. Mayne, that you will publish this book, and therefore I see no reason why you and Mr. Flintford should be kept in ignorance as to its real history. I may tell you that the story is not mine at all; it is being dictated to me. The circumstances are peculiar; but I feel sure that Mr. Flintford, with his knowledge of the East, will quite understand. I recently came into possession of an image of the god Ganesha, wonderfully wrought in ivory and adorned with amethyst eyes. The story of which you have read some portion is being dictated to me by this image, or, more probably, by this god represented by it. I think you will understand," he said, turning to Flintford with an air which had something appealing in it.

"Yes," said Flintford quietly, "I quite understand."

"I felt the influence of the god," continued Thurston, "as soon as I saw the image. It is a strange, a very fascinating influence. It impelled me to write against my will; and then I found that I was but a mouthpiece. Everything has been put into my lips— I should say, pen. Clearly, what I have written is the story of the image."

"And when," asked Flintford kindly, "when do you suppose the end of this story will be reached, Mr. Thurston?"

Thurston produced another packet of manuscript. He laid it on the publisher's desk.

"I believe," he said, "I believe that end will come to-night. If"—here he glanced from one face to the other— "if you would like to see the ivory statue, and could call to-morrow morning about noon, I will show it to you. It is certain that it possesses a strange influence."

When Thurston had gone away the two men looked at each other.

"Mad as a hatter!" said the publisher.

The critic shook his head.

"It seems strange," he said; "but, really, I don't think so. Does he drink?"

"I used to think he did," replied the publisher. "He has done work for me now and then, and he sometimes came here with all the symptoms of intoxication upon him, and yet he was always clear-headed and capable, if incoherent of speech. What I don't understand just now is the frightful deliberation with which he speaks, the sort of unearthly coldness and composure of his manner. But—I say!—to tell us that the book is being dictated to him by an ivory statue: surely that is an evidence of insanity!"

"Oh, but then genius and insanity are closely allied," said Flintford. "Well, let us call upon him to-morrow. In the meantime I'll take the manuscript he left with you. I expect it will cost me another sleepless night. You can't get away from it when you once begin—it's a live thing, Mayne."

"Come round about noon to-morrow," said Mayne.

It was half-past twelve next day when they climbed the stairs to Thurston's rooms. They knocked for some time at the outer door and evoked no answer; then Flintford climbed another flight of stairs and discovered the bedmaker woman, who resided nearer the sky, and appeared from a feast wherein onions had played a principal part.

"Mr. Thurston, sir? And indeed I'aven't set eyes on 'im this morning, sir. Which 'is conduck 'ave of late been most extrornary— me not being able to make no beds, nor nothing," said she. "A lit'ry gent, sir, which from long ixperience is very trying to anybody to deal with. You might knock again, sir; and if so as he doesn't answer, why, I must open the door with my key, and see if the poor gentleman isn't well, for never a word did he give me at ten o'clock."

When the door was opened at last, they found Thurston quite dead. His arms were crossed over the final page of his manuscript; his head was bowed upon them, as if, tired out with his long spell of labour, he had laid it down there and gone to sleep. Above him, the ivory god looked out of its amethyst eyes into the shadowy corner of the silent room.

J.S. FLETCHER

The Duel

I

The doctors could do no more for the Dowager Lady Berrick. When the medical advisers of a lady who has reached seventy years of age recommend the mild climate of the South of France, they mean in plain language that they have arrived at the end of their resources. Her ladyship gave the mild climate a fair trial, and then decided (as she herself expressed it) to 'die at home.' Travelling slowly, she had reached Paris at the date when I last heard of her. It was then the beginning of November. A week later, I met with her nephew, Lewis Romayne, at the club.

'What brings you to London at this time of year?' I asked.

'The fatality that pursues me,' he answered grimly. 'I am one of the unluckiest men living.'

He was thirty years old; he was not married; he was the enviable possessor of the tine old country seat, called Vange

Abbey; he had no poor relations; and he was one of the handsomest men in England. When I add that I am, myself, a retired army officer, with a wretched income, a disagreeable wife, four ugly children, and a burden of fifty years on my back, no one will be surprised to hear that I answered Romayne, with bitter sincerity, in these words:

'I wish to Heaven I could change places with you!'

'I wish to Heaven you could!' he burst out, with equal sincerity on his side. 'Read that.'

He handed me a letter addressed to him by the travelling medical attendant of Lady Berrick. After resting in Paris, the patient had continued her homeward journey as far as Boulogne. In her suffering condition, she was liable to sudden fits of caprice. An insurmountable horror of the Channel passage had got possession of her: she positively refused to be taken on board the steamboat. In this difficulty, the lady who held the post of her 'companion' had ventured on a suggestion. Would Lady Berrick consent to make the Channel passage if her nephew came to Boulogne expressly to accompany her on the voyage? The reply had been so immediately favourable, that the doctor lost no time in communicating with Mr. Lewis Romayne. This was the substance of the letter.

It was needless to ask any more questions—Romayne was plainly on his way to Boulogne. I gave him some useful information. 'Try the oysters,' I said, 'at the restaurant on the pier.'

He never even thanked me. He was thinking entirely of himself.

'Just look at my position,' he said. 'I detest Boulogne; I cordially share my aunt's horror of the Channel passage; I had looked forward to some months of happy retirement in the country among my books—and what happens to me? I am brought to London in this season of fogs, to travel by the tidal train at seven to-morrow morning—and all for a woman with whom I have no sympathies in common. If I am not an unlucky man— who is?'

He spoke in a tone of vehement irritation which seemed to me, under the circumstances, to be simply absurd. But *my* nervous system is not the irritable system—sorely tried by night study and strong tea—of my friend Romayne. 'It's only a matter of two days,' I remarked, by way of reconciling him to his situation.

'How do I know that?' he retorted. 'In two days the weather may be stormy. In two days she may be too ill to be moved. Unfortunately, I am her heir; and I am told I must submit to any whim that seizes her. I'm rich enough already; I don't want her money. Besides, I dislike all travelling—and especially travelling alone. You are an idle man. If you were a good friend, you would offer to go with me." He added, with the delicacy which was one of the redeeming points in his wayward character, 'Of course as my guest.'

I had known him long enough not to take offence at his reminding me, in this considerate way, that I was a poor man. The proposed change of scene tempted me. What did I care for the Channel passage? Besides, there was the irresistible attraction of getting away from home.

The end of it was that I accepted Romayne's invitation.

II

Shortly after noon, on the next day, we were established at Boulogne—near Lady Berrick, but not at her hotel. 'If we live in the same house,' Romayne reminded me, 'we shall be bored by the companion and the doctor. Meetings on the stairs, you know, and exchanging bows and small talk.' He hated those trivial conventionalities of society, in which other people delight. When somebody once asked him in what company he felt most at ease? he made a shocking answer—he said, 'In the company of dogs.'

I waited for him on the pier while he went to see her ladyship. He joined me again with his bitterest smile. 'What did I tell you? She is not well enough to see me to-day. The doctor looks grave, and the companion puts her handkerchief to her eyes. We may be kept in this place for weeks to come.'

The afternoon proved to be rainy. Our early dinner was a bad one. This last circumstance tried his temper sorely. He was no gourmand; the question of cookery was (with him) purely a matter of digestion. Those late hours of study and that abuse of tea to which I have already alluded, had sadly injured his stomach. The doctors warned him of serious consequences to his nervous system, unless he altered his habits. He had little faith in medical science, and he greatly overrated the restorative capacity of his constitution. So far as I know, he had always neglected the doctors' advice.

The weather cleared towards evening, and we went out for a walk. We passed a church—a Roman Catholic church, of course—the doors of which were still open. Some poor women were kneeling at their prayers in the dim light. 'Wait a minute,' said Romayne. 'I am in a vile temper. Let me try to put myself into a better frame of mind.'

I followed him into the church. He knelt down in a dark corner by himself. I confess I was surprised. He had been baptised in the Church of England; but, so far as outward practice was concerned, he belonged to no religious community. I had often heard him speak with sincere reverence and admiration of the spirit of Christianity—but he never, to my knowledge, attended any place of public worship. When we met again outside the church, I asked if he had been converted to the Roman Catholic faith.

'No,' he said. 'I hate the inveterate striving of that priesthood after social influence and political power as cordially as the fiercest Protestant living. But let us not forget that the Church of Rome has great merits to set against great faults. Its system is administered with an admirable knowledge of the higher needs of human nature. Take as one example what you have just seen. The solemn tranquillity of that church, the poor people praying near me, the few words of prayer by which I silently united myself to my fellow-creatures have calmed me, and done me good. In *our* country I should have found the church closed, out of service hours.' He took my arm, and abruptly changed the subject. 'How will you occupy yourself,' he asked, 'if my aunt receives me to-morrow?'

I assured him that I should easily find ways and means of getting through the time. The next morning a message came from Lady Berrick, to say that she would see her nephew after breakfast. Left by myself, I walked towards the pier, and met with a man who asked me to hire his boat. He had lines and bait, at my service. Most unfortunately, as the event proved, I decided on occupying an hour or two by sea fishing.

The wind shifted while we were out, and before we could get back to the harbour, the tide had turned against us. It was six o'clock when I arrived at the hotel. A little open carriage was waiting at the door. I found Romayne impatiently expecting me, and no signs of dinner on the table. He informed me that he had accepted an invitation, in which I was included, and promised to explain everything in the carriage.

Our driver took the road that led towards the High Town. I subordinated my curiosity to my sense of politeness, and asked for news of his aunt's health.

'She is seriously ill, poor soul,' he said. 'I am sorry I spoke so petulantly and so unfairly when we met at the club. The near prospect of death has developed qualities in her nature which I ought to have seen before this. No matter how it may be delayed, I will patiently wait her time for the crossing to England.'

So long as he believed himself to be in the right, he was, as to his actions and opinions, one of the most obstinate men I ever met with. But once let him be convinced that he was wrong, and he rushed into the other extreme—became needlessly distrustful of himself, and needlessly eager in seizing his opportunity of making atonement. In this latter mood he was capable (with the best intentions) of committing acts of the most childish imprudence. With some misgivings, I asked how he had amused himself in my absence.

'I waited for you,' he said, ''till I lost all patience, and went out for a walk. First, I thought of going to the beach, but the smell of the harbour drove me back into the town; and there, oddly enough, I met with a man, a certain Captain Peterkin, who had been a friend of mine at college.'

'A visitor to Boulogne?' I inquired.

'Not exactly.'

'A resident?'

'Yes. The fact is, I lost sight of Peterkin when I left Oxford— and since that time he seems to have drifted into difficulties. We had a long talk. He is living here, he tells me, until his affairs are settled.'

I needed no further enlightenment—Captain Peterkin stood as plainly revealed to me as if I had known him for years. 'Isn't it a little imprudent,' I said, 'to renew your acquaintance with a man of that sort? Couldn't you have passed him, with a bow?'

Romayne smiled uneasily. 'I dare say you're right,' he answered. 'But, remember, I had left my aunt, feeling ashamed of the unjust way in which I had thought and spoken of her. How did I know that I mightn't be wronging an old friend next, if I kept Peterkin at a distance? His present position may be as much his misfortune, poor fellow, as his fault. I was half inclined to pass him, as you say—but I distrusted my own judgment. He held out his hand, and he was so glad to see me. It can't be helped now. I shall be anxious to hear your opinion of him.'

'Are we going to dine with Captain Peterkin?"

'Yes. I happened to mention that wretched dinner yesterday at our hotel. He said, "Come to my boarding-house. Out of Paris, there isn't such a table d'hôte in France." I tried to get off it— not caring, as you know, to go among strangers—I said I had a friend with me. He invited you most cordially to accompany me. More excuses on my part only led to a painful result. I hurt Peterkin's feelings. "I'm down in the world," he said, "and I'm not fit company for you and your friends. I beg your pardon for taking the liberty of inviting you!" he turned away with the tears in his eyes. What could I do?'

I thought to myself, 'You could have lent him five pounds, and got rid of his invitation without the slightest difficulty.' If I had returned in reasonable time to go out with Romayne, we might not have met the captain—or, if we had met him, my presence would have prevented the confidential talk and the invitation that followed. I felt I was to blame —and yet, how could I help it? It was useless to remonstrate: the mischief was done.

We left the Old Town on our right hand, and drove on, past a little colony of suburban villas, to a house standing by itself, surrounded by a stone wall. As we crossed the front garden on our way to the door, I noticed against the side of the house two kennels, inhabited by two large watch-dogs. Was the proprietor afraid of thieves?

III

The moment we were introduced to the drawing-room, my suspicions of the company we were likely to meet with were fully confirmed.

'Cards, billiards, and betting'—there was the inscription legibly written on the manner and appearance of Captain Peterkin. The bright-eyed yellow old lady who kept the boarding-house would have been worth five thousand pounds in jewellery alone, if the ornaments which profusely covered her had been genuine precious stones. The younger ladies present had their cheeks as highly rouged and their eyelids as elaborately pencilled in black as if they were going on the stage, instead of going to dinner. We found these fair creatures drinking Madeira as a whet to their appetites. Among the men, there were two who struck me as the most finished and complete blackguards whom I had ever met with in all my experience, at home and abroad. One, with a brown face and a broken nose, was presented to us by the title of 'Commander,' and was described as a person of great wealth and distinction in Peru, travelling for amusement. The other wore a military uniform and decorations, and was spoken of as 'the General.' A bold bullying manner, a fat sodden face, little leering eyes, and greasy-looking hands, made this man so repellent to me that I privately longed to kick him. Romayne had evidently been announced, before our arrival, as a landed gentleman with a large income. Men and women vied in servile attentions to him. When we went into the dining-room, the fascinating creature who sat next to him held her fan before her face, and so made a private interview of it between the rich Englishman and herself. With regard to the dinner, I shall only report that it justified Captain Peterkin's boast, in some degree at least. The wine was good, and the conversation became gay to the verge of indelicacy. Usually the most temperate of men, Romayne was tempted by his neighbours into drinking freely. I was unfortunately seated at the opposite extremity of the table, and I had no opportunity of warning him.

The dinner reached its conclusion, and we all returned together, on the foreign plan, to coffee and cigars in the drawing-room. The women smoked, and drank liqueurs as well as coffee, with the men. One of them went to the piano, and a little impromptu ball followed, the ladies dancing with their cigarettes in their mouths. Keeping my eyes and ears on the alert, I saw an innocent-looking table, with a surface of rosewood, suddenly develop a substance of green cloth. At the same time, a neat little roulette-table made its appearance from a hiding-place in a sofa. Passing near the venerable landlady, I heard her ask the servant, in a whisper, 'if the dogs were loose?' After what I had observed, I could only conclude that the dogs were used as a patrol, to give the alarm in case of a descent of the police. It was plainly high time to thank Captain Peterkin for his hospitality, and to take our leave.

'We have had enough of this,' I whispered to Romayne in English. 'Let us go.'

In these days it is a delusion to suppose that you can speak confidentially in the English language, when French people are within hearing. One of the ladies asked Romayne, tenderly, if he was tired of her already. Another reminded him that it was raining heavily (as we could all hear), and suggested waiting until it cleared up. The hideous General waved his greasy hand in the direction of the card table, and said, 'The game is waiting for us.'

Romayne was excited, but not stupefied, by the wine he had drunk. He answered, discreetly enough, 'I must beg you to excuse me; I am a poor card player.'

The General suddenly looked grave. 'You are speaking, sir, under a strange misapprehension,' he said. 'Our game is lansquenet—essentially a game of chance. With luck, the poorest player is a match for the whole table.'

Romayne persisted in his refusal. As a matter of course, I supported him, with all needful care to avoid giving offence. The General took offence, nevertheless. He crossed his arms on his breast, and looked at us fiercely.

'Does this mean, gentlemen, that you distrust the company?' he asked.

The broken-nosed Commander, hearing the question, immediately joined us, in the interests of peace—bearing with him the elements of persuasion, under the form of a lady on his arm.

The lady stepped briskly forward, and tapped the General on the shoulder with her fan. '*I* am one of the company,' she said, 'and I am sure Mr. Romayne doesn't distrust *me*.' She turned to Romayne with her most irresistible smile. 'A gentleman always plays cards,' she resumed, 'when he has a lady for a partner. Let us join our interests at the table—and, dear Mr. Romayne, don't risk too much!' She put her pretty little purse into his hand, and looked as if she had been in love with him for half her lifetime.

The fatal influence of the sex, assisted by wine, produced the inevitable result. Romayne allowed himself to be led to the card table. For a moment the General delayed the beginning of the game. After what had happened, it was necessary that he should assert the strict sense of justice that was in him. 'We are all honourable men,' he began.

'And brave men,' the Commander added, admiring the General.

'And brave men,' the General admitted, admiring the Commander. 'Gentlemen, if I have been led into expressing myself with unnecessary warmth of feeling, I apologise, and regret it.'

'Nobly spoken!' the Commander pronounced. The General put his hand on his heart and bowed. The game began.

As the poorest man of the two, I had escaped the attentions lavished by the ladies on Romayne. At the same time, I was obliged to pay for my dinner, by taking some part in the proceedings of the evening. Small stakes were allowed, I found, at roulette; and, besides, the heavy chances in favour of the table made it hardly worth while to run the risk of cheating in this case. I placed myself next to the least rascally-looking man in the company, and played roulette.

For a wonder, I was successful at the first attempt. My neighbour handed me my winnings. 'I have lost every farthing I possess,' he whispered to me, piteously, 'and I have a wife and children at home.' I lent the poor wretch five francs. He smiled faintly as he looked at the money. 'It reminds me,' he said, 'of my last transaction, when I borrowed of that gentleman there, who is betting on the General's luck at the card table. Beware of employing him as I did. What do you think I got for my note of hand of four thousand francs? A hundred bottles of champagne, fifty bottles of ink, fifty bottles of blacking, three dozen handkerchiefs, two pictures by unknown masters, two shawls, one hundred maps, *and*—five francs.'

'We went on playing. My luck deserted me; I lost, and lost, and lost again. From time to time I looked round at the card table. The 'deal' had fallen early to the General, and it seemed to be indefinitely prolonged. A heap of notes and gold (won mainly from Romayne, as I afterwards discovered) lay before him. As for my neighbour, the unhappy possessor of the bottles of blacking, the pictures by unknown masters, and the rest of it, he won, and then rashly presumed on his good fortune. Deprived of his last farthing, he retired into a corner of the room, and consoled himself with a cigar. I had just risen, to follow his example, when a furious uproar burst out at the card table.

I saw Romayne spring up, and snatch the cards out of the General's hand. 'You scoundrel!' he shouted, 'you are cheating!' The General started to his feet in a fury. 'You lie!' he cried. I attempted to interfere, but Romayne had already seen the necessity of controlling himself. 'A gentleman doesn't accept an insult from a swindler,' he said coolly. 'Accept this, then!' the General answered—and spat on him. In an instant Romayne knocked him down.

The blow was dealt straight between his eyes: he was a gross big-boned man, and he fell heavily. For the time he was stunned. The women ran, screaming, out of the room. The peaceable Commander trembled from head to foot. Two of the men present, who, to give them their due, were no cowards, locked the doors. 'You don't go,' they said, 'till we see whether he recovers or not.' Cold water, assisted by the landlady's smelling salts, brought the General to his senses after a while. He whispered something to one of his friends, who immediately turned to me. 'The General challenges Mr. Romayne,' he said. 'As one of his seconds, I demand an appointment for to-morrow morning.' I refused to make any appointment unless the doors were first unlocked, and we were left free to depart. 'Our carriage is waiting outside,' I added. 'If it returns to the hotel without us, there will be an inquiry.' This latter consideration had its effect. On their side, the doors were opened. On our side, the appointment was made. We left the house.

V

We were punctual to the appointed hour—eight o'clock.

The second who acted with me was a French gentleman, a relative of one of the officers who had brought the challenge. At his suggestion, we had chosen the pistol as our weapon. Romayne, like most Englishmen at the present time, knew nothing of the use of the sword. He was almost equally inexperienced with the pistol.

Our opponents were late. They kept us waiting for more than ten minutes. It was not pleasant weather to wait in. The day had dawned damp and drizzling. A thick white fog was slowly rolling in on us from the sea.

When they did appear, the General was not among them. A tall, well-dressed young man saluted Romayne with stern courtesy, and said to a stranger who accompanied him, 'Explain the circumstances.'

The stranger proved to be a surgeon. He entered at once on the necessary explanation. The General was too ill to appear. He had been attacked that morning by a fit—the consequence of the blow that he had received. Under these circumstances, his eldest son (Maurice) was now on the ground to fight the duel, on his father's behalf; attended by the General's seconds, and with the General's full approval.

We instantly refused to allow the duel to take place, Romayne loudly declaring that he had no quarrel with the General's son. Upon this, Maurice broke away from his seconds; drew off one of his gloves; and stepping close up to Romayne, struck him on the face with the glove. 'Have you no quarrel with me now?' the young Frenchman asked. 'Must I spit on you, as my father did?' His seconds dragged him away, and apologised to us for the outbreak. But the mischief was done. Romayne's fiery temper flashed in his eyes. 'Load the pistols,' he said. After the insult publicly offered to him, and the outrage publicly threatened, there was no other course to take.

It had been left to us to produce the pistols. We therefore requested the seconds of our opponent to examine, and to load them. While this was being done, the advancing sea-fog so completely enveloped us, that the duellists were unable to see each other. We were obliged to wait for the chance of a partial clearing in the atmosphere. Romayne's temper had become calm again. The generosity of his nature spoke in the words which he now addressed to his seconds.

'After all,' he said, 'the young man is a good son—he is bent on redressing what he believes to be his father's wrong. Does his flipping his glove in my face matter to me? I think I shall fire in the air.'

'I shall refuse to act as your second if you do,' answered the French gentleman who was assisting us. 'The General's son is famous for his skill with the pistol. If you didn't see it in his face just now, I did—he means to kill you. Defend your life, sir!' I spoke quite as strongly, to the same purpose, when my turn came. Romayne yielded—he placed himself unreservedly in our hands.

In a quarter of an hour the fog lifted a little. We measured the distance, having previously arranged (at my suggestion) that the two men should both fire at the same moment, at a given signal. Romayne's composure, as they faced each other, was, in a man of his irritable nervous temperament, really wonderful. I placed him sideways, in a position which in some degree lessened his danger, by lessening the surface exposed to the bullet. My French colleague put the pistol into his hand, and gave him the last word of advice. 'Let your arm hang loosely down, with the barrel of the pistol pointing straight to the ground. When you hear the signal, only lift your arm as far as the elbow; keep the elbow pressed against your side—and fire.' We could do no more for him. As we drew aside—I own it—my tongue was like a cinder in my mouth, and a horrid inner cold crept through me to the marrow of my bones.

The signal was given, and the two shots were fired at the same time.

My first look was at Romayne. He took off his hat, and handed it to me with a smile. His adversary's bullet had cut a piece out of the brim of his hat, on the right side. He had literally escaped by a hairbreadth.

While I was congratulating him, the fog gathered again more thickly than ever. Looking anxiously towards the ground occupied by our adversaries, we could only see vague, shadowy forms hurriedly crossing and re-crossing each other in the mist. Something had happened! My French colleague took my arm and pressed it significantly. 'Leave *me* to inquire,' he said. Romayne tried to follow; I held him back—we neither of us exchanged a word.

The fog thickened and thickened, until nothing was to be seen. Once we heard the surgeon's voice, calling impatiently for a light to help him. No light appeared that *we* could see. Dreary as the fog itself, the silence gathered round us again. On a sudden it was broken, horribly broken, by another voice, strange to both of us, shrieking hysterically through the impenetrable mist. 'Where is he?' the voice cried, in the French language. 'Assassin! Assassin! Where are you?' Was it a woman? or was it a boy? We heard nothing more. The effect upon Romayne was terrible to see. He who had calmly confronted the weapon lifted to kill him, shuddered dumbly like a terror-stricken animal. I put my arm round him, and hurried him away from the place.

We waited at the hotel until our French friend joined us. After a brief interval he appeared, announcing that the surgeon would follow him.

The duel had ended fatally. The chance course of the bullet, urged by Romayne's unpractised hand, had struck the General's son just above the right nostril—had penetrated to the back of his neck—and had communicated a fatal shock to the spinal marrow. He was a dead man before they could take him back to his father's house.

So far, our fears were confirmed. But there was something else to tell, for which our worst presentiments had not prepared us.

A younger brother of the fallen man (a boy of thirteen years old) had secretly followed the duelling party, on their way from his father's house—had hidden himself—and had seen the dreadful end. The seconds only knew of it when he burst out of his place of concealment, and fell on his knees by his dying brother's side. His were the frightful cries which we had heard from invisible lips. The slayer of his brother was the 'assassin' whom he had vainly tried to discover through the fathomless obscurity of the mist.

We both looked at Romayne. He silently looked back at us, like a man turned to stone. I tried to reason with him.

'Your life was at your opponent's mercy,' I said. 'It was *he* who was skilled in the use of the pistol; your risk was infinitely greater than his. Are you responsible for an accident? Rouse yourself, Romayne! Think of the time to come, when all this will be forgotten.'

'Never,' he said, 'to the end of my life.'

He made that reply in dull monotonous tones. His eyes looked wearily and vacantly straight before him. I spoke to him again. He remained impenetrably silent; he appeared not to hear, or not to understand me. The surgeon came in, while I was still at a loss what to say or do next. Without waiting to be asked for his opinion, he observed Romayne attentively, and then drew me away into the next room.

'Your friend is suffering from a severe nervous shock,' he said. 'Can you tell me anything of his habits of life?'

I mentioned the prolonged night studies, and the excessive use of tea. The surgeon shook his head.

'If you want my advice,' he proceeded, 'take him home at once. Don't subject him to further excitement, when the result of the duel is known in the town. If it ends in our appearing in a court of law, it will be a mere formality in this case, and you can surrender when the time comes. Leave me your address in London.'

I felt that the wisest thing I could do was to follow his advice. The boat crossed to Folkestone at an early hour that day—we had no time to lose. Romayne offered no objection to our return to England; he seemed perfectly careless of what became of him. 'Leave me quiet,' he said: 'and do as you like.' I wrote a few lines to Lady Berrick's medical attendant, informing him of the circumstances. A quarter of an hour afterwards we were on board the steamboat.

WILKIE COLLINS from *The Black Robe* (1883)

The Beast with Five Fingers

*T*he story, I suppose, begins with Adrian Borlsover, whom I met when I was a little boy and he an old man. My father had called to appeal for a subscription, and before he left, Mr. Borlsover laid his right hand in blessing on my head. I shall never forget the awe in which I gazed up at his face and realised for the first time that eyes might be dark and beautiful and shining, and yet not able to see.

For Adrian Borlsover was blind.

He was an extraordinary man, who came of an eccentric stock. Borlsover sons for some reason always seemed to marry very ordinary women which perhaps accounted for the fact that no Borlsover had been a genius, and only one Borlsover had been mad. But they were great champions of little causes, generous patrons of odd sciences, founders of querulous sects, trustworthy guides to the bypath meadows of erudition.

Adrian was an authority on the fertilisation of orchids. He had held at one time the family living at Borlsover Conyers, until a congenital weakness of the lungs obliged him to seek a less rigorous climate in the sunny south-coast watering-place where I had seen him. Occasionally he would relieve one or other of the local clergy. My father described him as a fine preacher, who gave long and inspiring sermons from what many men would have considered unprofitable texts. "An excellent proof," he would add, "of the truth of the doctrine of direct verbal inspiration."

Adrian Borlsover was exceedingly clever with his hands. His penmanship was exquisite. He illustrated all his scientific papers, made his own woodcuts, and carved the reredos that is at present the chief feature of interest in the church at Borlsover Conyers. He had an exceedingly clever knack in cutting silhouettes for young ladies and paper pigs and cows for little children, and made more than one complicated wind instrument of his own devising.

When he was fifty years old Adrian Borlsover lost his sight. In a wonderfully short time he adapted himself to the new conditions of life. He quickly learnt to read Braille. So marvellous indeed was his sense of touch, that he was still able to maintain his interest in botany. The mere passing of his long supple fingers over a flower was sufficient means for its identification, though occasionally he would use his lips. I have found several letters of his among my father's correspondence; in no case was there anything to show that he was afflicted with blindness, and this in spite of the fact that he exercised undue economy in the spacing of lines. Towards the close of his life Adrian Borlsover was credited with powers of touch that seemed almost uncanny. It has been said that he could tell at once the colour of a ribbon placed between his fingers. My father would neither confirm nor deny the story.

Adrian Borlsover was a bachelor. His elder brother, Charles, had married late in life, leaving one son, Eustace, who lived in the gloomy Georgian mansion at Borlsover Conyers, where he could work undisturbed in collecting material for his great book on heredity.

Like his uncle, he was a remarkable man. The Borlsovers had always been born naturalists, but Eustace possessed in a special degree the power of systematising his knowledge. He had received his university education in Germany; and then, after post-graduate work in Vienna and Naples, had travelled for four years in South America and the East, getting together a huge store of material for a new study into the processes of variation.

He lived alone at Borlsover Conyers with Saunders, his secretary, a man who bore a somewhat dubious reputation in the district, but whose powers as a mathematician, combined with his business abilities, were invaluable to Eustace.

Uncle and nephew saw little of each other. The visits of Eustace were confined to a week in the summer or autumn—tedious weeks, that dragged almost as slowly as the bath-chair in which the old man was drawn along the sunny sea-front. In their way the two men were fond of each other, though their intimacy would, doubtless, have been greater, had they shared the same religious views. Adrian held to the old-fashioned evangelical dogmas of his early manhood; his nephew for many years had been thinking of embracing Buddhism. Both men possessed, too, the reticence the Borlsovers had always shown, and which their enemies sometimes called hypocrisy. With Adrian it was a reticence as to the things he had left undone; but with Eustace it seemed that the curtain which he was so careful to leave undrawn hid something more than a half-empty chamber.

Two years before his death Adrian Borlsover developed, unknown to himself, the not uncommon power of automatic writing. Eustace made the discovery by accident. Adrian was sitting reading in bed, the forefinger of his left hand tracing the Braille characters, when his nephew noticed that a pencil the old man held in his right hand was moving slowly along the opposite page. He left his seat in the window and sat down beside the bed. The right hand continued to move, and now he could see plainly that they were letters and words which it was forming.

"Adrian Borlsover," wrote the hand, "Eustace Borlsover, Charles Borlsover, Francis Borlsover, Sigismund Borlsover, Adrian Borlsover, Eustace Borlsover, Saville Borlsover. B for Borlsover. Honesty is the Best Policy. Beautiful Belinda Borlsover."

"What curious nonsense!" said Eustace to himself.

"King George ascended the throne in 1760," wrote the hand. "Crowd, a noun of multitude; a collection of individuals. Adrian Borlsover, Eustace Borlsover,"

"It seems to me," said his uncle, closing the book, "that you had much better make the most of the afternoon sunshine and take your walk now."

"I think perhaps I will," Eustace answered as he picked up the volume. "I won't go far, and when I come back, I can read to you those articles in *Nature* about which we were speaking."

He went along the promenade, but stopped at the first shelter, and, seating himself in the corner best protected from the wind, he examined the book at leisure. Nearly every page was scored with a meaningless jumble of pencil-marks; rows of capital letters, short words, long words, complete sentences, copy-book tags. The whole thing, in fact had the appearance of a copy-book, and, on a more careful scrutiny, Eustace thought that there was ample evidence to show that the handwriting at the beginning of the book, good though it was, was not nearly so good as the handwriting at the end.

He left his uncle at the end of October with a promise to return early in December. It seemed to him quite clear that the old man's power of automatic writing was developing rapidly, and for the first time he looked forward to a visit that would combine duty with interest.

But on his return he was at first disappointed. His uncle, he thought, looked older. He was listless, too, preferring others to read to him and dictating nearly all his letters. Not until the day before he left had Eustace an opportunity of observing Adrian Borlsover's new-found faculty.

The old man, propped up in bed with pillows, had sunk into a light sleep. His two hands lay on the coverlet, his left hand tightly clasping his right. Eustace took an empty manuscript-book and placed a pencil within reach of the fingers of the right hand. They snatched at it eagerly, then dropped the pencil to loose the left hand from its restraining grasp.

"Perhaps to prevent interference I had better hold that hand," said Eustace to himself, as he watched the pencil. Almost immediately it began to write.

"Blundering Borlsovers, unnecessarily unnatural, extraordinarily eccentric, culpably curious."

"Who are you?" asked Eustace in a low voice.

"Never you mind," wrote the hand of Adrian.

"Is it my uncle who is writing?"

"O my prophetic soul, mine uncle!"

"Is it anyone I know?"

"Silly Eustace, you'll see me very soon."

"When shall I see you?"

"When poor old Adrian's dead."

"Where shall I see you?"

"Where shall you not?"

Instead of speaking his next question, Eustace wrote it. "What is the time?"

The fingers dropped the pencil and moved three or four times across the paper. Then, picking up the pencil, they wrote: "Ten minutes before four. Put your book away, Eustace. Adrian mustn't find us working at this sort of thing. He doesn't know what to make of it, and I won't have poor old Adrian disturbed. Au revoir!"

Adrian Borlsover awoke with a start.

"I've been dreaming again," he said; "such queer dreams of leaguered cities and forgotten towns. You were mixed up in this one, Eustace, though I can't remember how. Eustace, I want to warn you. Don't walk in doubtful paths. Choose your friends well. Your poor grandfather..."

A fit of coughing put an end to what he was saying, but Eustace saw that the hand was still writing. He managed unnoticed to draw the book away. "I'll light the gas," he said, "and ring for tea." On the other side of the bed-curtain he saw the last sentences that had been written.

"It's too late, Adrian," he read. "We're friends already, aren't we, Eustace Borlsover?"

On the following day Eustace left. He thought his uncle looked ill when he said good-bye, and the old man spoke despondently of the failure his life had been.

"Nonsense, uncle," said his nephew. "You have got over your difficulties in a way not one in a hundred thousand would have done. Everyone marvels at your splendid perseverance in teaching your hand to take the place of your lost sight. To me it's been a revelation of the possibilities of education."

"Education," said his uncle dreamily, as if the word had started a new train of thought. "Education is good so long as you know to whom and for what purpose you give it. But with the lower orders of men, the base and more sordid spirits, I have grave doubts as to its results. Well, good-bye, Eustace; I may not see you again. You are a true Borlsover, with all the Borlsover faults. Marry, Eustace. Marry some good, sensible girl. And if by any chance I don't see you again, my will is at my solicitor's. I've not left you any legacy, because I know you're well provided for; but I thought you might like to have my books. Oh, and there's just one other thing. You know, before the end people often lose control over themselves and make absurd requests. Don't pay any attention to them, Eustace. Good-bye!" and he held out his hand. Eustace took it. It remained in his a fraction of a second longer than he had expected and gripped him with a virility that was surprising. There was, too, in its touch a subtle sense of intimacy.

"Why, uncle," he said, "I shall see you alive and well for many long years to come."

* * * * *

Two months later Adrian Borlsover died.

Eustace Borlsover was in Naples at the time. He read the obituary notice in the *Morning Post* on the day announced for the funeral.

"Poor old fellow!" he said. "I wonder whether I shall find room for all his books."

The question occurred to him again with greater force when, three days later, he found himself standing in the library at Borlsover Conyers, a huge room built for use and not for beauty in the year of Waterloo by a Borlsover who was an ardent admirer of the great Napoleon. It was arranged on the plan of many college libraries, with tall projecting bookcases forming deep recesses of dusty silence, fit graves for the old hates of forgotten controversy, the dead passions of forgotten lives. At the end of the room, behind the bust of some unknown eighteenth-century divine, an ugly iron corkscrew stair led to a shelf-lined gallery. Nearly every shelf was full.

"I must talk to Saunders about it," said Eustace. "I suppose that we shall have to have the billiard-room fitted up with bookcases."

The two men met for the first time after many weeks in the dining-room that evening.

"Hallo!" said Eustace, standing before the fire with his hands in his pockets. "How goes the world, Saunders? Why these dress togs?" He himself was wearing an old shooting-jacket. He did not believe in mourning, as he had told his uncle on his last visit; and, though he usually went in for quiet-coloured ties, he wore this evening one of an ugly red, in order to shock Morton, the butler, and to make them thrash out the whole question of mourning for themselves in the servants' hall. Eustace was a true Borlsover. "The world," said Saunders, "goes the same as usual, confoundedly slow. The dress togs are accounted for by an invitation from Captain Lockwood to bridge."

"How are you getting there?"

"There's something the matter with the car, so I've told Jackson to drive me round in the dogcart. Any objection?"

"O dear me, no! We've had all things in common for far too many years for me to raise objections at this hour of the day."

"You'll find your correspondence in the library," went on Saunders. "Most of it I've seen to. There are a few private letters I haven't opened. There's also a box with a rat or something inside it that came by the evening post. Very likely it's the six-toed beast Terry was sending us to cross with the four-toed albino. I didn't look because I didn't want to mess up my things; but I should gather from the way it's jumping about that it's pretty hungry."

"Oh, I'll see to it," said Eustace, "while you and the captain earn an honest penny."

Dinner over and Saunders gone, Eustace went into the library. Though the fire had been lit, the room was by no means cheerful.

"We'll have all the lights on, at any rate," he said, as he turned the switches. "And, Morton," he added, when the butler brought the coffee, "get me a screwdriver or something to undo this box. Whatever the animal is, he's kicking up the deuce of a row. What is it? Why are you dawdling?"

"If you please, sir, when the postman brought it, he told me that they'd bored the holes in the lid at the post office. There were no breathing holes in the lid, sir, and they didn't want the animal to die. That is all, sir."

"It's culpably careless of the man, whoever he was," said Eustace, as he removed the screws, "packing an animal like this in a wooden box with no means of getting air. Confound it all! I meant to ask Morton to bring me a cage to put it in. Now I suppose I shall have to get one myself."

He placed a heavy book on the lid from which the screws had been removed, and went into the billiard-room. As he came back into the library with an empty cage in his hand, he heard the sound of something falling, and then of something scuttling along the floor.

"Bother it! The beast's got out. How in the world am I to find it again in this library?"

To search for it did indeed seem hopeless. He tried to follow the sound of the scuttling in one of the recesses, where the animal seemed to be running behind the books on the shelves; but it was impossible to locate it. Eustace resolved to go on quietly reading. Very likely the animal might gain confidence and show itself. Saunders seemed to have dealt in his usual methodical manner with most of the correspondence. There were still the private letters.

What was that? Two sharp clicks and the lights in the hideous candelabra that hung from the ceiling suddenly went out.

"I wonder if something has gone wrong with the fuse," said Eustace, as he went to the switches by the door. Then he stopped. There was a noise at the other end of the room, as if something was crawling up the iron corkscrew stair. "If it's gone into the gallery," he said, "well and good." He hastily turned on the lights, crossed the room, and climbed up the stair. But he could see nothing. His grandfather had placed a little gate at the top of the stair, so that children could run and romp in the gallery without fear of accident. This Eustace closed, and, having considerably narrowed the circle of his search, returned to his desk by the fire.

How gloomy the library was! There was no sense of intimacy about the room. The few busts that an eighteenth-century Borlsover had brought back from the grand tour might have been in keeping in the old library. Here they seemed out of place. They made the room feel cold in spite of the heavy red damask curtains and great gilt cornices.

With a crash two heavy books fell from the gallery to the floor; then, as Borlsover looked, another, and yet another.

"Very well. You'll starve for this, my beauty!" he said. "We'll do some little experiments on the metabolism of rats deprived of water. Go on! Chuck them down! I think I've got the upper hand." He turned once more to his correspondence. The letter was from the family solicitor. It spoke of his uncle's death, and of the valuable collection of books that had been left to him in the will.

"There was one request [he read] which certainly came as a surprise to me. As you know, Mr. Adrian Borlsover had left instructions that his body was to be buried in as simple a manner as possible at Eastbourne. He expressed a desire that there should be neither wreaths nor flowers of any kind, and hoped that his friends and relatives would not consider it necessary to wear mourning. The day before his death we received a letter cancelling these instructions. He wished the body to be embalmed (he gave us the address of the man we were to employ—Pennifer, Ludgate Hill), with orders that his right hand should be sent to you stating that it was at your special request. The other arrangements about the funeral remained unaltered."

"Good Lord," said Eustace, "what in the world was the old boy driving at? And what in the name of all that's holy is that?"

Someone was in the gallery. Someone had pulled the cord attached to one of the blinds, and it had rolled up with a snap. Someone must be in the gallery, for a second blind did the same. Someone must be walking round the gallery, for one after the other the blinds sprang up, letting in the moonlight.

"I haven't got to the bottom of this yet," said Eustace, "but I will do, before the night is very much older"; and he hurried up the corkscrew stair. He had just got to the top, when the lights went out a second time, and he heard again the scuttling along the floor. Quickly he stole on tiptoe in the dim moonshine in the direction of the noise, feeling, as he went, for one of the switches. His fingers touched the metal knob at last. He turned on the electric light.

About ten yards in front of him, crawling along the floor, was a man's hand. Eustace stared at it in utter amazement. It was moving quickly in the manner of a geometer caterpillar, the fingers humped up one moment, flattened out the next; the thumb appeared to give a crablike motion to the while. Whole he was looking, too surprised to stir, the hand disappeared round the corner. Eustace ran forward. He no longer saw it, but he could hear it, as it squeezed its way behind the books on one of the shelves. A heavy volume had been displaced. There was a gap in the row of books, where it had got in. In his fear lest it should escape him again, he seized the first book that came to his hand and plugged it into the hole. Then, emptying two shelves of their contents, he took the wooden boards and propped them up in front to make his barrier doubly sure.

"I wish Saunders was back," he said; "one can't tackle this sort of thing alone." It was after eleven, and there seemed little likelihood of Saunders returning before twelve. He did not dare to leave the shelf unwatched, even to run downstairs to ring the bell. Morton, the butler, often used to come round about eleven to see that the windows were fastened, but he might not come. Eustace was thoroughly unstrung. At last he heard steps down below.

"Morton!" he shouted. "Morton!"

"Sir?"

"Has Mr. Saunders got back yet?"

"Not yet, sir."

"Well, bring me some brandy, and hurry up about it. I'm up in the gallery, you duffer."

"Thanks," said Eustace, as he emptied the glass. "Don't go to bed yet, Morton. There are a lot of books that have fallen down by accident. Bring them up and put them back on their shelves."

Morton had never seen Borlsover in so talkative a mood as on that night. "Here," said Eustace, when the books had been put back and dusted, "you might hold up these boards for me,

Morton. That beast in the box got out, and I've been chasing it all over the place."

"I think I can hear it chawing at the books, sir. They're not valuable, I hope? I think that's the carriage, sir; I'll go and call Mr. Saunders."

It seemed to Eustace that he was away for five minutes, but it could hardly have been more than one, when he returned with Saunders. "All right, Morton, you can go now. I'm up here, Saunders."

"What's all the row?" asked Saunders, as he lounged forward with his hands in his pockets. The luck had been with him all the evening. He was completely satisfied, both with himself and with Captain Lockwood's taste in wines. "What's the matter? You look to me to be in an absolutely blue funk."

"That old devil of an uncle of mine," began Eustace—"Oh, I can't explain it all. It's his hand that's been playing Old Harry all the evening. But I've got it cornered behind these books. You've got to help me to catch it."

"What's up with you, Eustace? What's the game?"

"It's no game, you silly idiot! If you don't believe me, take out one of those books and put your hand in and feel."

"All right," said Saunders; "but wait till I've rolled up my sleeve. The accumulated dust of centuries, eh?" He took off his coat, knelt down, and thrust his arm along the shelf.

"There's something there right enough," he said. "It's got a funny, stumpy end to it, whatever it is, and nips like a crab. Ah! no, you don't!" He pulled his hand out in a flash. "Shove in a book quickly. Now it can't get out."

"What was it?" asked Eustace.

"Something that wanted very much to get hold of me. I felt what seemed like a thumb and forefinger. Give me some brandy."

"How are we to get it out of there?"

"What about a landing-net?"

"No good. It would be too smart for us. I tell you, Saunders, it can cover the ground far faster than I can walk. But I think I see how we can manage it. The two books at the end of the shelf are big ones, that go right back against the wall. The others are very thin. I'll take out one at a time, and you slide the rest along, until we have it squashed between the end two."

It certainly seemed to be the best plan. One by one as they took out the books, the space behind grew smaller and smaller. There was something in it that was certainly very much alive. Once they caught sight of fingers feeling for a way of escape. At last they had it pressed between the two big books.

"There's muscle there, if there isn't warm flesh and blood," said Saunders, as he held them together. "It seems to be a hand right enough, too. I suppose this is a sort of infectious hallucination. I've read about such cases before."

"Infectious fiddlesticks!" said Eustace, his face white with anger; "bring the thing downstairs. We'll get it back into the box."

It was not altogether easy, but they were successful at last. "Drive in the screws," said Eustace; "we won't run any risks. Put the box in this old desk of mine. There's nothing in it that I want. Here's the key. Thank goodness there's nothing wrong with the lock."

"Quite a lively evening," said Saunders. "Now let's hear more about your uncle."

They sat up together until early morning. Saunders had no desire for sleep. Eustace was trying to explain and to forget; to conceal from himself a fear that he had never felt before—the fear of walking alone down the long corridor to his bedroom.

* * * * *

"Whatever it was," said Eustace to Saunders on the following morning, "I propose that we drop the subject. There's nothing to keep us here for the next ten days. We'll motor up to the Lakes and get some climbing."

"And see nobody all day, and sit bored to death with each other every night. Not for me, thanks. Why not run up to town? Run's the exact word in this case, isn't it? We're both in such a blessed funk. Pull yourself together, Eustace, and let's have another look at the hand."

"As you like," said Eustace; "there's the key."

They went into the library and opened the desk. The box was as they had left it on the previous night.

"What are you waiting for?" asked Eustace.

"I am waiting for you to volunteer to open the lid. However, since you seem to funk it, allow me. There doesn't seem to be the likelihood of any rumpus this morning at all events." He opened the lid and picked out the hand.

"Cold?" asked Eustace.

"Tepid. A bit below blood heat by the feel. Soft and supple too. If it's the embalming, it's a sort of embalming I've never seen before. Is it your uncle's hand?"

"Oh yes, it's his all right," said Eustace. "I should know those long thin fingers anywhere. Put it back in the box, Saunders. Never mind about the screws. I'll lock the desk, so that there'll be no chance of its getting out. We'll compromise by motoring up to town for a week. If we can get off soon after lunch, we ought to be at Grantham or Stamford by night."

"Right," said Saunders, "and to-morrow—oh, well, by tomorrow we shall have forgotten all about this beastly thing."

If, when the morrow came, they had not forgotten, it was certainly true that at the end of the week they were able to tell a very vivid ghost-story at the little supper Eustace gave on Hallow E'en.

"You don't want us to believe that it's true, Mr. Borlsover? How perfectly awful!"

"I'll take my oath on it, and so would Saunders here; wouldn't you, old chap?"

"Any number of oaths," said Saunders. "It was a long thin hand, you know, and it gripped me just like that."

"Don't, Mr. Saunders! Don't! How perfectly horrid! Now tell us another one, do! Only a really creepy one, please."

"Here's a pretty mess!" said Eustace on the following day, as he threw a letter across the table to Saunders. "It's your affair, though. Mrs. Merrit, if I understand it, gives a month's notice."

"Oh, that's quite absurd on Mrs. Merrit's part," replied Saunders. "She doesn't know what she's talking about. Let's see what she says."

"Dear Sir [he read]. This is to let you know that I must give you a month's notice as from Tuesday, the 13th. For a long time I've felt the place too big for me; but when Jane Parfit and Emma Laidlaw go off with scarcely as much as an 'If you please,' after frightening the wits out of the other girls, so that they can't turn out a room by themselves or walk alone down the stairs for fear of treading on half-frozen toads or hearing it run along the passages at night, all I can say is that it's no place for me. So I must ask you, Mr. Borlsover, sir, to find a new housekeeper, that has no objection to large and lonely houses, which some people do say, not that I believe them for a minute, my poor mother always having been a Wesleyan, are haunted.

"Yours faithfully,
"Elizabeth Merrit.

"P.S.—I should be obliged if you would give my respects to Mr. Saunders. I hope that he won't run any risks with his cold."

"Saunders," said Eustace, "you've always had a wonderful way with you in dealing with servants. You mustn't let poor old Merrit go."

"Of course she shan't go," said Saunders. "She's probably only angling for a rise in salary. I'll write to her this morning."

"No. There's nothing like a personal interview. We've had enough of town. We'll go back to-morrow, and you must work your cold for all it's worth. Don't forget that it's got on to the chest, and will require weeks of feeding up and nursing."

"All right; I think I can manage Mrs. Merrit."

But Mrs. Merrit was more obstinate than he had thought. She was very sorry to hear of Mr. Saunders's cold, and how he lay awake all night in London coughing; very sorry indeed. She'd change his room for him gladly and get the south room aired, and wouldn't he have a hot basin of bread and milk last thing at night? But she was afraid that she would have to leave at the end of the month.

"Try her with an increase of salary," was the advice of Eustace.

It was no use. Mrs. Merrit was obdurate, though she knew of a Mrs. Goddard, who had been housekeeper to Lord Gargrave, who might be glad to come at the salary mentioned.

"What's the matter with the servants, Morton?" asked Eustace that evening, when he brought the coffee into the library. "What's all this about Mrs. Merrit wanting to leave?"

"If you please, sir, I was going to mention it myself. I have a confession to make, sir. When I found your note, asking me to open that desk and take out the box with the rat, I broke the lock, as you told me, and was glad to do it, because I could hear the animal in the box making a great noise, and I thought it wanted food. So I took out the box, sir, and got a cage, and was going to transfer it, when the animal got away."

"What in the world are you talking about? I never wrote any such note."

"Excuse me, sir; it was the note I picked up here on the floor on the day you and Mr. Saunders left. I have it in my pocket now."

It certainly seemed to be in Eustace's handwriting. It was written in pencil, and began somewhat abruptly.

"Get a hammer, Morton," he read, "or some other tool and break open the lock in the old desk in the library. Take out the box that is inside. You need not do anything else. The lid is already open. Eustace Borlsover."

"And you opened the desk?"

"Yes, sir; and, as I was getting the cage ready, the animal hopped out."

"What animal?"

"The animal inside the box, sir."

"What did it look like?"

"Well, sir, I couldn't tell you," said Morton nervously. "My back was turned, and it was half way down the room when I looked up."

"What was its colour?" asked Saunders. "Black?"

"Oh no, sir; a greyish white. It crept along in a very funny way, sir. I don't think it had a tail."

"What did you do then?"

"I tried to catch it; but it was no use. So I set the rat-traps and kept the library shut. Then that girl, Emma Laidlaw, left the door open when she was cleaning, and I think it must have escaped."

"And you think it is the animal that's been frightening the maids?"

"Well, no sir, not quite. They said it was—you'll excuse me, sir—a hand that they saw. Emma trod on it once at the bottom of the stairs. She thought then it was a half-frozen toad, only white. And then Parfit was washing up the dishes in the scullery. She wasn't thinking about anything in particular. It was close on dusk. She took her hands out of the water and was drying them absent-minded like on the roller towel, when she found she was drying someone else's hand as well, only colder than hers."

"What nonsense!" exclaimed Saunders.

"Exactly sir; that's what I told her; but we couldn't get her to stop."

"You don't believe all this?" said Eustace, turning suddenly towards the butler.

"Me, sir? Oh no, sir! I've not seen anything."

"Nor heard anything?"

"Well, sir, if you must know, the bells do ring at odd times, and there's nobody there when we go; and when we go round to draw the blinds of a night, as often as not somebody's been there before us. But, as I says to Mrs. Merrit, a young monkey might do wonderful things, and we all know that Mr. Borlsover has had some strange animals about the place."

"Very well, Morton, that will do."

"What do you make of it?" asked Saunders, when they were alone. "I mean of the letter he said you wrote."

"Oh, that's simple enough," said Eustace. "See the paper it's written on? I stopped using that paper years ago, but there were a few odd sheets and envelopes left in the old desk. We never fastened up the lid of the box before locking it in. The hand got out, found a pencil, wrote this note, and shoved it through the crack on to the floor, where Morton found it. That's plain as daylight."

"But the hand couldn't write!"

"Couldn't it? You've not seen it do the things I've seen."

And he told Saunders more of what had happened at East-bourne.

"Well," said Saunders, "in that case we have at least an explanation of the legacy. It was the hand which wrote, unknown to your uncle, that letter to your solicitor bequeathing itself to you. Your uncle had no more to do with that request than I. In fact, it would seem that he had some idea of this automatic writing and feared it."

"Then if it's not my uncle, what is it?"

"I suppose some people might say that a disembodied spirit had got your uncle to educate and prepare a little body for it. Now it's got into that little body and is off on its own."

"Well, what are we to do?"

"We'll keep our eyes open," said Saunders, "and try to catch it. If we can't do that, we shall have to wait till the bally clockwork runs down. After all, if it's flesh and blood, it can't live for ever."

For two days nothing happened. Then Saunders saw it sliding down the banister in the hall. He was taken unawares and lost a full second before he started in pursuit, only to find that the thing had escaped him. Three days later Eustace, writing alone in the library at night, saw it sitting on an open book at the other end of the room. The fingers crept over the page, as if it were reading; but before he had time to get up from his seat, it had taken the alarm, and was pulling itself up the curtains. Eustace watched it grimly, as it hung on to the cornice with three fingers and flicked thumb and forefinger at him in an expression of scornful derision.

"I know what I'll do," he said. "If I only get it into the open, I'll set the dogs on to it."

He spoke to Saunders of the suggestion.

"It's a jolly good idea," he said; "only we won't wait till we find it out of doors. We'll get the dogs. There are the two terriers and the under-keeper's Irish mongrel, that's on to rats like a flash. Your spaniel has not got spirit enough for this sort of game."

They brought the dogs into the house, and the keeper's Irish mongrel chewed up the slippers, and the terriers tripped up Morton, as he waited at table; but all three were welcome. Even false security is better than no security at all.

For a fortnight nothing happened. Then the hand was caught, not by the dogs, but by Mrs. Merrit's grey parrot. The bird was in the habit of periodically removing the pins that kept its seed-and water-tin in place, and of escaping through the holes in the side of the cage. When once at liberty, Peter would show no inclination to return, and would often be about the house for days. Now, after six consecutive weeks of captivity, Peter had again discovered a new way of unloosing his bolts and was at large, exploring the tapestried forests of the curtains and singing songs in praise of liberty from cornice and picture rail.

"It's no use your trying to catch him," said Eustace to Mrs. Merrit, as she came into the study one afternoon towards dusk with a step-ladder. "You'd much better leave Peter alone. Starve him into surrender, Mrs. Merrit; and don't leave bananas and seed about for him to peck at when he fancies he's hungry. You're far too soft-hearted."

"Well, sir, I see he's right out of reach now on that picture-rail; so, if you wouldn't mind closing the door, sir, when you leave the room, I'll bring his cage in to-night and put some meat inside it. He's that fond of meat, though it does make him pull out his feathers to suck the quills. They *do* say that if you cook——"

"Never mind, Mrs. Merrit," said Eustace, who was busy writing; "that will do; I'll keep an eye on the bird."

For a short time there was silence in the room.

"Scratch poor Peter," said the bird. "Scratch poor old Peter!"

"Be quiet, you beastly bird!"

"Poor old Peter! Scratch poor Peter; do!"

"I'm more likely to wring your neck, if I get hold of you." He looked up at the picture-rail, and there was the hand, holding on to a hook with three fingers, and slowly scratching the head of the parrot with the fourth. Eustace ran to the bell and pressed it hard; then across to the window, which he closed with a bang. Frightened by the noise, the parrot shook its wings preparatory to flight, and, as it did so, the fingers of the hand got hold of it by the throat. There was a shrill scream from Peter, as he fluttered across the room, wheeling round in circles that ever descended, borne down under the weight that clung to him. The bird dropped at last quite suddenly, and Eustace saw fingers and feathers rolled into an inextricable mass on the floor. The struggle abruptly ceased, as finger and thumb squeezed the neck; the bird's eyes rolled up to show the white, and there was a faint, half-choked gurgle. But, before the fingers had time to loose their hold, Eustace had them in his own.

"Send Mr. Saunders here at once," he said to the maid who came in answer to the bell. "Tell him I want him immediately."

Then he went with the hand to the fire. There was a ragged gash across the back, where the bird's beak had torn it, but no blood oozed from the wound. He noted with disgust that the nails had grown long and discoloured.

"I'll burn the beastly thing," he said. But he could not burn it. He tried to throw it into the flames, but his own hands, as if impelled by some old primitive feeling, would not let him. And so Saunders found him, pale and irresolute, with the hand still clasped tightly in his fingers.

"I've got it at last," he said, in a tone of triumph.

"Good, let's have a look at it."

"Not when it's loose. Get me some nails and a hammer and a board of some sort."

"Can you hold it all right?"

"Yes, the thing's quite limp; tired out with throttling poor old Peter, I should say."

"And now," said Saunders, when he returned with the things, "what are we going to do?"

"Drive a nail through it first, so that it can't get away. Then we can take our time over examining it."

"Do it yourself," said Saunders. "I don't mind helping you with guinea-pigs occasionally, when there's something to be learned, partly because I don't fear a guinea-pig's revenge. This thing's different."

"Oh, my aunt!" he giggled hysterically, "look at it now." For the hand was writhing in agonised contortions, squirming and wriggling upon the nail like a worm upon the hook.

"Well," said Saunders, "you've done it now. I'll leave you to examine it."

"Don't go, in heaven's name! Cover it up, man; cover it up! Shove a cloth over it! Here!" and he pulled off the antimacassar from the back of a chair and wrapped the board in it. "Now get the keys from my pocket and open the safe. Chuck the other things out. Oh, Lord, it's getting itself into frightful knots! Open it quick!" He threw the thing in and banged the door.

"We'll keep it there till it dies," he said. "May I burn in hell, if I ever open the door of that safe again."

* * * * *

Mrs. Merrit departed at the end of the month. Her successor, Mrs. Handyside, certainly was more successful in the management of the servants. Early in her rule she declared that she would stand no nonsense, and gossip soon withered and died.

"I shouldn't be surprised if Eustace married one of these days," said Saunders. "Well, I'm in no hurry for such an event. I know him far too well for the future Mrs. Borlsover to like me. It will be the same old story again; a long friendship slowly made—marriage—and a long friendship quickly forgotten."

But Eustace did not follow the advice of his uncle and marry. Old habits crept over and covered his new experience. He was, if anything, less morose, and showed a great inclination to take his natural part in country society.

Then came the burglary. The man, it was said, broke into the house by way of the conservatory. It was really little more than an attempt, for they only succeeded in carrying away a few pieces of plate from the pantry. The safe in the study was certainly found open and empty, but, as Mr. Borlsover informed the police inspector, he had kept nothing of value in it during the last six months.

"Then you're lucky in getting off so easily, sir," the man replied. "By the way they have gone about their business I should say they were experienced cracksmen. They must have caught the alarm when they were just beginning their evening's work."

"Yes," said Eustace, "I suppose I am lucky."

"I've no doubt," said the inspector, "that we shall be able to trace the men. I've said that they must have been old hands at the game. The way they got in and opened the safe shows that. But there's one little thing that puzzles me. One of them was careless enough not to wear gloves, and I'm bothered if I know what he was trying to do. I've traced his finger-marks on the new varnish on the window-sashes in every one of the downstairs rooms. They are very distinctive ones too."

"Right hand or left or both?" asked Eustace.

"Oh, right every time. That's the funny thing. He must have been a foolhardy fellow, and I rather think it was him that wrote that." He took out a slip of paper from his pocket. "That's what he wrote, sir: 'I've got out, Eustace Borlsover, but I'll be back before long.' Some jailbird just escaped, I suppose. It will make it all the easier for us to trace him. Do you know the writing, sir?"

"No," said Eustace. "It's not the writing of anyone I know."

"I'm not going to stay here any longer," said Eustace to Saunders at luncheon. "I've got on far better during the last six months than I expected, but I'm not going to run the risk of seeing that thing again. I shall go up to town this afternoon. Get Morton to put my things together, and join me with the car at Brighton on the day after to-morrow. And bring the proofs of those two papers with you. We'll run over them together."

"How long are you going to be away?"

"I can't say for certain, but be prepared to stay for some time. We've stuck to work pretty closely through the summer, and I for one need a holiday. I'll engage the rooms at Brighton. You'll find it best to break the journey at Hitchin. I'll wire to you there at the 'Crown' to tell you the Brighton address."

The house he chose at Brighton was in a terrace. He had been there before. It was kept by his old college gyp, a man of discreet silence, who was admirably partnered by an excellent cook. The rooms were on the first floor. The two bedrooms were at the back, and opened out of each other. "Mr. Saunders can have the smaller one, though it is the only one with a fire-place," he said. "I'll stick to the larger of the two, since it's got a bath-room adjoining. I wonder what time he'll arrive with the car."

Saunders came about seven, cold and cross and dirty. "We'll light the fire in the dining-room," said Eustace, "and get Prince to unpack some of the things while we are at dinner. What were the roads like?"

"Rotten. Swimming with mud, and a beastly cold wind against us all day. And this is July. Dear Old England!"

"Yes," said Eustace, "I think we might do worse than leave Old England for a few months."

They turned in soon after twelve.

"You oughtn't to feel cold, Saunders," said Eustace, "when you can afford to sport a great fur-lined coat like this. You do yourself very well, all things considered. Look at those gloves, for instance. Who could possibly feel cold when wearing them?"

"They are far too clumsy, though, for driving. Try them on and see"; and he tossed them through the door on to Eustace's bed and went on with his unpacking. A minute later he heard a shrill cry of terror. "Oh, Lord," he heard, "it's in the glove! Quick, Saunders, quick!" Then came a smacking thud. Eustace had thrown it from him. "I've chucked it into the bath-room," he gasped; "it's hit the wall and fallen into the bath. Come now, if you want to help." Saunders, with a lighted candle in his hand, looked over the edge of the bath. There it was, old and maimed, dumb and blind, with a ragged hole in the middle, crawling, staggering, trying to creep up the slippery sides, only to fall back helpless.

"Stay there," said Saunders. "I'll empty a collar-box or something, and we'll jam it in. It can't get out while I'm away."

"Yes, it can," shouted Eustace. "It's getting out now; it's climbing up the plug-chain.—No, you brute, you filthy brute, you don't!—Come back, Saunders; it's getting away from me. I can't hold it; it's all slippery. Curse its claws! Shut the window, you idiot! It's got out!" There was the sound of something dropping on to the hard flag-stones below, and Eustace fell back fainting.

* * * * *

For a fortnight he was ill.

"I don't know what to make of it," the doctor said to Saunders. "I can only suppose that Mr. Borlsover has suffered some great emotional shock. You had better let me send someone to help you nurse him. And by all means indulge that whim of his never to be left alone in the dark. I would keep a light burning all night, if I were you. But he *must* have more fresh air. It's perfectly absurd, this hatred of open windows."

Eustace would have no one with him but Saunders. "I don't want the other man," he said. "They'd smuggle it in somehow. I know they would."

"Don't worry about it, old chap. This sort of thing can't go on indefinitely. You know I saw it this time as well as you. It wasn't half so active. It won't go on living much longer, especially after that fall. I heard it hit the flags myself. As soon as you're a bit stronger, we'll leave this place, not bag and baggage, but with only the clothes on our backs, so that it won't be able to hide anywhere. We'll escape it that way. We won't give any address, and we won't have any parcels sent after us. Cheer up, Eustace! You'll be well enough to leave in a day or two. The doctor says I can take you out in a chair to-morrow."

"What have I done?" asked Eustace. "Why does it come after me? I'm no worse than other men. I'm no worse than you, Saunders; you know I'm not. It was you who was at the bottom of that dirty business in San Diego, and that was fifteen years ago."

"It's not that, of course," said Saunders. "We are in the

twentieth century, and even the parsons have dropped the idea of your old sins finding you out. Before you caught the hand in the library, it was filled with pure malevolence—to you and all mankind. After you spiked it through with that nail, it naturally forgot about other people and concentrated its attention on you. It was shut up in that safe, you know, for nearly six months. That gives plenty of time for thinking of revenge."

Eustace Borlsover would not leave his room, but he thought there might be something in Saunders's suggestion of a sudden departure from Brighton. He began rapidly to regain his strength.

"We'll go on the first of September," he said.

* * * * *

The evening of the thirty-first of August was oppressively warm. Though at midday the windows had been wide open, they had been shut an hour or so before dusk. Mrs. Prince had long since ceased to wonder at the strange habits of the gentlemen on the first floor. Soon after their arrival she had been told to take down the heavy window curtains in the two bedrooms, and day by day the rooms had seemed to grow more bare. Nothing was left lying about.

"Mr. Borlsover doesn't like to have any place where dirt can collect," Saunders had said as an excuse. "He likes to see into all the corners of the room."

"Couldn't I open the window just a little?" he said to Eustace that evening. "We're simply roasting in here, you know."

"No, leave well alone. We're not a couple of boarding-school misses fresh from a course of hygiene lectures. Get the chess-board out."

They sat down and played. At ten o'clock Mrs. Prince came to the door with a note. "I am sorry I didn't bring it before," she said, "but it was left in the letter-box."

"Open it, Saunders, and see if it wants answering."

It was very brief. There was neither address nor signature.

"Will eleven o'clock to-night be suitable for our last appointment?"

"Who is it from?" asked Borlsover.

"It was meant for me," said Saunders. "There's no answer, Mrs. Prince," and he put the paper into his pocket.

"A dunning letter from a tailor; I suppose he must have got wind of our leaving."

It was a clever lie, and Eustace asked no more questions. They went on with their game.

On the landing outside Saunders could hear the grandfather's clock whispering the seconds, blurting out the quarter-hours.

"Check," said Eustace. The clock struck eleven. At the same time there was a gentle knocking on the door; it seemed to come from the bottom panel.

"Who's there?" asked Eustace.

There was no answer.

"Mrs. Prince, is that you?"

"She is up above," said Saunders; "I can hear her walking about the room."

"Then lock the door; bolt it too. Your move, Saunders."

While Saunders sat with his eyes on the chess-board, Eustace walked over to the window and examined the fastenings. He did the same in Saunders's room, and the bathroom. There were no doors between the three rooms, or he would have shut and locked them too.

"Now, Saunders," he said, "don't stay all night over your move. I've had time to smoke one cigarette already. It's bad to keep an invalid waiting. There's only one possible thing for you to do. What was that?"

"The ivy blowing against the window. There, it's your move now, Eustace."

"It wasn't the ivy, you idiot! It was someone tapping at the window"; and he pulled up the blind. On the outer side of the window, clinging to the sash, was the hand.

"What is it that it's holding?"

"It's a pocket-knife. It's going to try to open the window by pushing back the fastener with the blade."

"Well, let it try," said Eustace. "Those fasteners screw down; they can't be opened that way. Anyhow, we'll close the shutters. It's your move, Saunders; I've played."

But Saunders found it impossible to fix his attention on the game. He could not understand Eustace, who seemed all at once to have lost his fear. "What do you say to some wine?" he asked. "You seem to be taking things coolly, but I don't mind confessing that I'm in a blessed funk."

"You've no need to be. There's nothing supernatural about that hand, Saunders. I mean it seems to be governed by the laws of time and space. It's not the sort of thing that vanishes into thin air or slides through oaken doors. And since that's so, I defy it to get in here. We'll leave the place in the morning. I for one have bottomed the depths of fear. Fill your glass, man! The windows are all shuttered; the door is locked and bolted. Pledge me my Uncle Adrian! Drink, man! What are you waiting for?"

Saunders was standing with his glass half raised. "It can get in," he said hoarsely; "it can get in. We've forgotten. There's the fire-place in my bed-room. It will come down the chimney."

"Quick!" said Eustace, as he rushed into the other room; "we haven't a minute to lose. What can we do? Light the fire, Saunders. Give me a match, quick!"

"They must be all in the other room. I'll get them."

"Hurry, man, for goodness' sake! Look in the bookcase! Look in the bath-room! Here, come and stand here; I'll look."

"Be quick!" shouted Saunders. "I can hear something!"

"Then plug a sheet from your bed up the chimney. No, here's a match!" He had found one at last that had slipped into a crack in the floor.

"Is the fire laid? Good, but it may not burn. I know—the oil from that old reading-lamp and this cotton-wool. Now the match, quick! Pull the sheet away, you fool! We don't want it now."

There was a great roar from the grate, as the flames shot up. Saunders had been a fraction of a second too late with the sheet. The oil had fallen on to it. It, too, was burning.

"The whole place will be on fire!" cried Eustace, as he tried to beat out the flames with a blanket. "It's no good! I can't manage it. You must open the door, Saunders, and get help."

Saunders ran to the door and fumbled with the bolts. The key was stiff in the lock. "Hurry," shouted Eustace, "or the heat will be too much for me." The key turned in the lock at last. For half a second Saunders stopped to look back. Afterwards he could never be quite sure as to what he had seen, but at the time he thought that something black and charred was creeping slowly, very slowly, from the mass of flames towards Eustace Borlsover. For a moment he thought of returning to his friend; but the noise and the smell of the burning sent him running down the passage, crying: "Fire! Fire!" He rushed to the telephone to summon help, and then back to the bath-room—he should have thought of that before—for water. As he burst into the bedroom there came a scream of terror which ended suddenly, and then the sound of a heavy fall.

* * * * *

This is the story which I heard on successive Saturday evenings from the senior mathematical master at a second-rate suburban school. For Saunders has had to earn a living in a way which other men might reckon less congenial than his old manner of life. I had mentioned by chance the name of Adrian Borlsover, and wondered at the time why he changed the conversation with such unusual abruptness. A week later Saunders began to tell me something of his own history; sordid enough, though shielded with a reserve I could well understand, for it had to cover not only his failings, but those of a dead friend. Of the final tragedy he was at first especially loath to speak; and it was only gradually that I was able to piece together the narrative of the preceding pages. Saunders was reluctant to draw any conclusions. At one time he thought that the fingered beast had been animated by the spirit of Sigismund Borlsover, a sinister eighteenth-century ancestor, who, according to legend, built and worshipped in the ugly pagan temple that overlooked the lake. At another time Saunders believed the spirit to belong to a man whom Eustace had once employed as a laboratory assistant, "a black-haired, spiteful little brute," he said, "who died cursing his doctor, because the fellow couldn't help him to live to settle some paltry score with Borlsover."

From the point of view of direct contemporary evidence, Saunders's story is practically uncorroborated. All the letters mentioned in the narrative were destroyed, with the exception of the last note which Eustace received, or rather which he would have received, had not Saunders intercepted it. That I have seen myself. The handwriting was thin and shaky, the handwriting of an old man. I remember the Greek "e" was used in "appointment." A little thing that amused me at the time was that Saunders seemed to keep the note pressed between the pages of his Bible.

I had seen Adrian Borlsover once. Saunders I learnt to know well. It was by chance, however, and not by design, that I met a third person of the story, Morton, the butler. Saunders and I were walking in the Zoological Gardens one Sunday afternoon, when he called my attention to an old man who was standing before the door of the Reptile House.

"Why, Morton," he said, clapping him on the back, "how is the world treating you?"

"Poorly, Mr. Saunders," said the old fellow, though his face lighted up at the greeting. "The winters drag terribly nowadays. There don't seem no summers or springs."

"You haven't found what you were looking for, I suppose?"

"No, sir, not yet; but I shall some day. I always told them that Mr. Borlsover kept some queer animals."

"And what is he looking for?" I asked, when we had parted from him.

"A beast with five fingers," said Saunders. "This afternoon, since he has been in the Reptile House, I suppose it will be a reptile with a hand. Next week it will be a monkey with practically no body. The poor old chap is a born materialist."

W.F. HARVEY

Miss Bracegirdle Does Her Duty

"*T*his is the room, madame."

"Ah, thank you—thank you."

"Does it appear satisfactory to madame?"

"Oh, yes. Thank you—quite."

"Does madame require anything further?"

"Er—if not too late, may I have a hot bath?"

"*Parfaitement*, madame. The bathroom is at the end of the passage on the left. I will go and prepare it for madame."

"There is one thing more. I have had a very long journey. I am very tired. Will you please see that I am not disturbed in the morning until I ring?"

"Certainly, madame."

Millicent Bracegirdle was speaking the truth—she *was* tired. But then, in the sleepy cathedral town of Easingstoke, from which she came, it was customary for everyone to speak the truth. It was customary, moreover, for everyone to lead simple, self-denying lives—to give up their time to good works and elevating thoughts. One had only to glance at little Miss Bracegirdle to see that in her were epitomised all the virtues and ideals of Easingstoke. Indeed, it was the pursuit of duty which had brought her to the Hôtel de l'Ouest at Bordeaux on this summer's night. She had travelled from Easingstoke to London, then without a break to Dover, crossed that horrid stretch of sea to Calais, entrained for Paris, where of necessity she had to spend four hours—a terrifying experience—and then had come on to Bordeaux, arriving at midnight. The reason of this journey being that someone had to come to Bordeaux to meet her young sister-in-law, who was arriving the next day from South America. The sister-in-law was married to a missionary in Paraguay, but the climate not agreeing with her, she was returning to England. Her dear brother, the dean, would have come himself, but the claims on his time were so extensive, the parishioners would miss him so—it was clearly Millicent's duty to go.

She had never been out of England before, and she had a horror of travel, and an ingrained distrust of foreigners. She spoke a little French, sufficient for the purpose of travel and for obtaining any modest necessities, but not sufficient for carrying on any kind of conversation. She did not deplore this latter fact, for she was of opinion that French people were not the kind of people that one would naturally want to have conversation with; broadly speaking, they were not quite "nice," in spite of their ingratiating manners.

She unpacked her valise, placed her things about the room, tried to thrust back the little stabs of home-sickness as she visualised her darling room at the deanery. How strange and hard

and unfriendly seemed these foreign hotel bedrooms! No chintz
and lavender and photographs of all the dear family, the dean,
the nephews and nieces, the interior of the Cathedral during
harvest festival; no samplers and needlework or coloured
reproductions of the paintings by Marcus Stone. Oh, dear, how
foolish she was! What *did* she expect?

She disrobed, and donned a dressing-gown; then, armed with
a sponge-bag and towel, she crept timidly down the passage to
the bathroom, after closing her bedroom door and turning out
the light. The gay bathroom cheered her. She wallowed luxuriously
in the hot water, regarding her slim legs with quiet satisfaction.
And for the first time since leaving home there came to her a
pleasant moment, a sense of enjoyment in her adventure. After
all, it *was* rather an adventure, and her life had been peculiarly
devoid of it. What queer lives some people must live, travelling
about, having experiences! How old was she? Not really old—
not by any means. Forty-two? Forty-three? She had shut herself
up so. She hardly ever regarded the potentialities of age. As the
world went, she was a well-preserved woman for her age. A life
of self-abnegation, simple living, healthy walking, and fresh air
had kept her younger than these hurrying, pampered, city people.

Love? Yes, once when she was a young girl—he was a
schoolmaster, a most estimable, kind gentleman. They were never
engaged—not actually, but it was a kind of understood thing. For
three years it went on, this pleasant understanding and friendship.
He was so gentle, so distinguished and considerate. She would
have been happy to have continued in this strain for ever. But
there was something lacking—Stephen had curious restless lapses.
From the physical aspect of marriage she shrank—yes, even with
Stephen, who was gentleness and kindness itself. And then, one
day—one day he went away, vanished, and never returned. They
told her he had married one of the country girls, a girl who used

to work in Mrs. Forbes's dairy—not a very nice girl, she feared, one of those fast, pretty, foolish women. Heigho! Well, she had lived that down, destructive as the blow appeared at the time. One lives everything down in time. There is always work, living for others, faith, duty. At the same time she could sympathise with people who found satisfaction in unusual experiences. There would be lots to tell the dear dean when she wrote to him on the morrow: nearly losing her spectacles on the restaurant-car, the amusing remarks of an American child on the train to Paris, the curious food everywhere, nothing simple and plain; the two English ladies at the hotel in Paris who told her about the death of their uncle—the poor man being taken ill on Friday and dying on Sunday afternoon, just before tea-time; the kindness of the hotel proprietor, who had sat up for her; the prettiness of the chambermaid. Oh, yes, everyone was really very kind. The French people, after all, were very nice. She had seen nothing—nothing but what was quite nice and decorous. There would be lots to tell the dean to-morrow.

Her body glowed with the friction of the towel. She again donned her night attire and her thick woollen dressing-gown. She tidied up the bathroom carefully in exactly the same way she was accustomed to do at home; then once more gripped her sponge-bag and towel, and turning out the light she crept down the passage to her room. Entering the room, she switched on the light and shut the door quickly. Then one of those ridiculous things happened, just the kind of thing you would expect to happen in a foreign hotel. The handle of the door came off in her hand. She ejaculated a quiet "Bother!" and sought to replace it with one hand, the other being occupied with the towel and sponge-bag. In doing this she behaved foolishly, for, thrusting the knob carelessly against the steel pin without properly securing it, she only succeeded in pushing the pin farther into the door, and the knob was not adjusted. She uttered another little "Bother!" and put her sponge-bag and towel down on the floor. She then tried to recover the pin with her left hand, but it had gone in too far.

"How very foolish!" she thought. "I shall have to ring for the chambermaid—and perhaps the poor girl has gone to bed."

She turned and faced the room, and suddenly the awful horror was upon her.

There was a man asleep in her bed!

The sight of that swarthy face on the pillow, with its black tousled hair and heavy moustache, produced in her the most terrible moment of her life. Her heart nearly stopped. For some seconds she could neither think nor scream, and her first thought was:

"I mustn't scream!"

She stood there like one paralysed, staring at the man's head and the great curved hunch of his body under the clothes. When she began to think she thought very quickly and all her thoughts worked together. The first vivid realisation was that it wasn't the man's fault; it was *her* fault. *She was in the wrong room.* It was the man's room. The rooms were identical, but there were all his things about, his clothes thrown carelessly over chairs, his collar and tie on the wardrobe, his great heavy boots and the strange yellow trunk. She must get out—somehow, anyhow. She clutched once more at the door, feverishly driving her fingernails into the hole where the elusive pin had vanished. She tried to force her fingers in the crack and open the door that way, but it was of no avail. She was to all intents and purposes locked in— locked in a bedroom in a strange hotel, alone with a man—a foreigner—a *Frenchman*!

She must think—she must think! She switched off the light. If the light was off he might not wake up. It might give her time to think how to act. It was surprising that he had not awakened. If he *did* wake up, what would he do? How could she explain herself? He wouldn't believe her. No one would believe her. In an English hotel it would be difficult enough, but here, where she wasn't known, where they were all foreigners and consequently antagonistic—merciful heavens!

She *must* get out. Should she wake the man? No, she couldn't do that. He might murder her. He might—oh, it was too awful to contemplate! Should she scream? Ring for the chambermaid? But no; it would be the same thing. People would come rushing. They would find her there in the strange man's bedroom after midnight—she, Millicent Bracegirdle, sister of the Dean of Easingstoke! Easingstoke! Visions of Easingstoke flashed through her alarmed mind. Visions of the news arriving, women whispering around tea-tables: "Have you heard, my dear? Really no one would have imagined! Her poor brother! He will, of course, have to resign you know, my dear. Have a little more cream, my love."

Would they put her in prison? She might be in the room for the purpose of stealing or she might be in the room for the purpose of breaking every one of the ten commandments. There was no explaining it away. She was a ruined woman, suddenly and irretrievably, unless she could open the door. The chimney? Should she climb up the chimney? But where would that lead to? And then she thought of the man pulling her down by the legs when she was already smothered in soot. Any moment he might wake up. She thought she heard the chambermaid going along the passage. If she had wanted to scream, she ought to have screamed before. The maid would know she had left the bathroom some minutes ago. Was she going to her room?

An abrupt and desperate plan formed in her mind. It was already getting on for one o'clock. The man was probably a quite harmless commercial traveller or businessman. He would probably get up about seven or eight o'clock, dress quickly, and go out. She would hide under his bed until he went. Only a matter of a few hours. Men don't look under their beds, although she made a religious practice of doing so herself. When he went he would be sure to open the door all right. The handle would be lying on the floor as though it had droped off in the night. He would probably ring for the chambermaid, or open it with a penknife. Men are so clever at those things. When he had gone she would creep out and steal back to her room, and then there would be no necessity to give any explanation to anyone. But heavens! What an experience! Once under the white frill of that bed, she would be safe until the morning. In daylight nothing seemed so terrifying. With feline precaution she went down on her hands and knees and crept towards the bed. What a lucky thing there was that broad white frill! She lifted it at the foot of the bed and crept under. There was just sufficient depth to take her slim body. The floor was fortunately carpeted all over, but it seemed very close and dusty. Suppose she coughed or sneezed! Anything might happen. Of course, it would be much more difficult to explain her presence under the bed than to explain her presence just inside the door. She held her breath in suspense. No sound came from above, but under the frill it was difficult to hear anything. It was almost more nerve-racking than hearing everything— listening for signs and portents. This temporary escape, in any case, would give her time to regard the predicament detachedly. Up to the present she had not been able to focus the full significance of her action. She had, in truth, lost her head. She had been like a wild animal, consumed with the sole idea of escape—a mouse or a cat would do this kind of thing—take cover and lie low. If only it hadn't all happened *abroad*!

She tried to frame sentences of explanation in French, but French escaped her. And then they talked so rapidly, these people. They didn't listen. The situation was intolerable. Would she be able to endure a night of it? At present she was not altogether uncomfortable, only stuffy and—very, very frightened. But she had to face six or seven or eight hours of it, and perhaps even then discovery in the end! The minutes flashed by as she turned the matter over and over in her head. There was no solution. She began to wish she had screamed or awakened the man. She saw now that that would have been the wisest and most politic thing to do; but she had allowed ten minutes or a quarter of an hour to elapse from the moment when the chambermaid would know that she had left the bathroom. They would want an explanation of what she had been doing in the man's bedroom all that time. Why hadn't she screamed before?

She lifted the frill an inch or two and listened. She thought she heard the man breathing, but she couldn't be sure. In any case, it gave her more air. She became a little bolder, and thrust her face partly through the frill so that she could breathe freely. She tried to steady her nerves by concentrating on the fact that— well, there it was. She had done it. She must make the best of it. Perhaps it would be all right, after all.

"Of course, I shan't sleep," she kept on thinking. "I shan't be able to. In any case, it will be safe not to sleep. I must be on the watch."

She set her teeth and waited grimly. Now that she had made up her mind to see the thing through in this manner she felt a little calmer. She almost smiled as she reflected that there would certainly be something to tell the dear dean when she wrote to him to-morrow. How would he take it? Of course he would believe it—he had never doubted a single word that she had uttered in her life—but the story would sound so preposterous. In Easingstoke it would be almost impossible to imagine such an experience. She, Millicent Bracegirdle, spending a night under a strange man's bed in a foreign hotel! What would those women think? Fanny Shields and that garrulous old Mrs. Rusbridger? Perhaps—yes, perhaps it would be advisable to tell the dear dean to let the story go no farther. One could hardly expect Mrs. Rusbridger to not make implications—exaggerate. Oh, dear! What were they all doing now? They would all be asleep, everyone in Easingstoke. Her dear brother always retired at 10.15. He would be sleeping calmly and placidly the sleep of the just—breathing the clear sweet air of Sussex, not this—oh, it *was* stuffy! She felt a great desire to cough. She mustn't do that.

Yes, at 9.30 all the servants were summoned to the library. There was a short service—never more than fifteen minutes; her brother didn't believe in a great deal of ritual—then at 10 o'clock cocoa for everyone. At 10.15 bed for everyone. The dear, sweet bedroom, with the narrow white bed, by the side of which she had knelt every night so long as she could remember—even in her dear mother's day—and said her prayers.

Prayers! Yes, that was a curious thing. This was the first night in her life experience when she had not said her prayers on retiring. The situation was certainly very peculiar—exceptional, one might call it. God would understand and forgive such a lapse. And yet, after all, why—what was to prevent her saying her prayers? Of course, she couldn't kneel in the proper devotional attitude, that would be a physical impossibility; nevertheless, perhaps her prayers might be just as efficacious—if they came from the heart.

So little Miss Bracegirdle curved her body and placed her hands in a devout attitude in front of her face, and quite inaudibly murmured her prayers under the strange man's bed.

At the end she added, fervently:

"Please God protect me from the dangers and perils of this night."

Then she lay silent and inert, strangely soothed by the effort of praying.

It began to get very uncomfortable, stuffy, but at the same time draughty, and the floor was getting harder every minute. She changed her position stealthily and controlled her desire to cough. Her heart was beating rapidly. Over and over again recurred the vivid impression of every little incident and argument that had occurred to her from the moment she left the bathroom. This must, of course, be the room next to her own. So confusing, with perhaps twenty bedrooms all exactly alike on one side of a passage—how was one to remember whether one's number was one hundred and fifteen or one hundred and sixteen? Her mind began to wander idly off into her schooldays. She was always very bad at figures. She disliked Euclid and all those subjects about angles and equations—so unimportant, not leading anywhere. History she liked, and botany, and reading abut strange foreign lands, although she had always been too timid to visit them. And the lives of great people, *most* fascinating—Oliver Cromwell, Lord Beaconsfield, Lincoln, Grace Darling—*there* was a heroine for you—General Booth, a great, good man, even if a little vulgar. She remembered dear old Miss Trimmings talking about him one afternoon at the vicar of St. Bride's garden party. She was *so* amusing. She——*Good heavens!*

Almost unwittingly Millicent Bracegirdle had emitted a violent sneeze!

It was finished! For the second time that night she was conscious of her heart nearly stopping. For the second time that night she was so paralysed with fear that her mentality went to pieces. Now she would hear the man get out of bed. He would walk across to the door, switch on the light, and then lift up the frill. She could almost see that fierce moustachioed face glaring at her and growling something in French. Then he would thrust out an arm and drag her out. And then? O God in Heaven! What then?

"I shall scream before he does it. Perhaps I had better scream now. If he drags me out he will clap his hand over my mouth. Perhaps chloroform——"

But somehow she could not scream. She was too frightened even for that. She lifted the frill and listened. Was he moving stealthily across the carpet? She thought—no, she couldn't be sure. Anything might be happening. He might strike her from above—with one of those heavy boots, perhaps. Nothing seemed to be happening, but the suspense was intolerable. She realised now that she hadn't the power to endure a night of it. Anything would be better than this—disgrace, imprisonment, even death. She would crawl out, wake the man and try to explain as best she could.

She would switch on the light, cough, and say: "Monsieur!"

Then he would start up and stare at her.

Then she would say—what should she say?

"*Pardon, monsieur, mais je*—— What on earth was the French for 'I have made a mistake'?

"*F'ai tort. C'est la chambre*—er—incorrect. *Voulez-vous*—er——?"

What was the French for "door-knob," "let me go"?

It didn't matter. She would turn on the light, cough, and trust to luck. If he got out of bed and came towards her, she would scream the hotel down.

The resolution formed, she crawled deliberately out at the foot of the bed. She scrambled hastily towards the door—a perilous journey. In a few seconds the room was flooded with light. She turned towards the bed, coughed, and cried out boldly:

"Monsieur!"

Then for the third time that night little Miss Bracegirdle's heart all but stopped. In this case the climax of the horror took longer to develop, but when it was reached it clouded the other two experiences into insignificance.

The man on the bed was dead!

She had never beheld death before, but one does not mistake death.

She stared at him, bewildered, and repeated almost in a whisper:

"Monsieur! Monsieur!"

Then she tip-toed towards the bed. The hair and moustache looked extraordinarily black in that grey, wax-like, setting. The mouth was slightly open, and the face, which in life might have been vicious and sensual, looked incredibly peaceful and far away. It was as though she were regarding the features of a man across some fast passage of time, a being who had always been completely remote from mundane preoccupations.

When the full truth came home to her, little Miss Bracegirdle buried her face in her hands and murmured:

"Poor fellow—poor fellow!"

For the moment her own position seemed an affair of small consequence. She was in the presence of something greater and more all-pervading. Almost instinctively she knelt by the bed and prayed.

For a few moments she seemed to be possessed by an extraordinary calmness and detachment. The burden of her hotel predicament was a gossamer trouble—a silly, trivial, almost comic episode, something that could be explained away.

But this man—he had lived his life, whatever it was like, and now he was in the presence of his Maker. What kind of man had he been?

Her meditations were broken by an abrupt sound. It was that of a pair of heavy boots being thrown down by the door outside. She started, thinking at first it was someone knocking or trying to get in. She heard the "boots," however, stumping away down the corridor, and the realisation stabbed her with the truth of her own position. She mustn't stop there. The necessity to get out was even more urgent.

To be found in a strange man's bedroom in the night is bad enough, but to be found in a dead man's bedroom was even worse. They would accuse her of murder, perhaps. Yes, that would be it—how could she possibly explain to these foreigners? Good God! they would hang her. No, guillotine her—that's what they do in France. They would chop her head off with a great steel knife. Merciful heavens! She envisaged herself standing blindfold, by a priest and an executioner in a red cap, like that man in the Dickens story. What was his name?—Sydney Carton, that was it. And before he went on the scaffold he said:

"It is a far, far better thing that I do than I have ever done——"

But no, she couldn't say that. It would be a far, far worse thing that she did. What about the dear dean; her sister-in-law arriving alone from Paraguay to-morrow; all her dear people and friends in Easingstoke; her darling Tony, the large grey tabby-cat? It was her duty not to have her head chopped off if it could possible be avoided. She could do no good in the room. She could not recall the dead to life. Her only mission was to escape. Any minute people might arrive. The chambermaid, the boots, the manager, the gendarmes. Visions of gendarmes arriving armed with swords and notebooks vitalised her almost exhausted energies. She was a desperate woman. Fortunately now she had not to worry about the light. She sprang once more at the door and tried to force it open with her fingers. The result hurt her and gave her pause. If she was to escape she must *think*, and think intensely. She mustn't do anything rash and silly; she must just think and plan calmly.

She examined the lock carefully. There was no keyhole, but there was a slip-bolt, so that the hotel guest could lock the door on the inside, but it couldn't be locked on the outside. Oh, why didn't this poor dear dead man lock his door last night? Then this trouble could not have happened. She could see the end of the steel pin. It was about half an inch down the hole. If anyone was passing they must surely notice the handle sticking out too far the other side! She drew a hairpin out of her hair and tried to coax the pin back, but she only succeeded in pushing it a little farther in. She felt the colour leaving her face, and a strange feeling of faintness came over her.

She was fighting for her life; she mustn't give way. She darted round the room like an animal in a trap, her mind alert for the slightest crevice of escape. The window had no balcony, and there was a drop of five storeys to the street below. Dawn was breaking. Soon the activities of the hotel and the city would begin. The thing must be accomplished before then.

She went back once more and stared hard at the lock. She stared at the dead man's property, his razors and brushes and writing materials. He appeared to have a lot of writing materials, pens and pencils and rubber and sealing-wax. Sealing-wax!

Necessity is truly the mother of invention. It is in any case quite certain that Millicent Bracegirdle, who had never invented a thing in her life, would never have evolved the ingenious little device she did, had she not believed that her position was utterly desperate. For in the end this is what she did. She got together a box of matches, a candle, a bar of sealing-wax, and a hairpin. She made a little pool of hot sealing-wax, into which she dipped the end of the hairpin. Collecting a small blob on the end of it, she thrust in into the hole, and let it adhere to the end of the steel pin. At the seventh attempt she got the thing to move.

It took her just an hour and ten minutes to get that steel pin back into the room, and when at length it came far enough through for her to grip it with her finger-nails, she burst into tears through the sheer physical tenseness of the strain. Very, very carefully she pulled it through, and holding it firmly with her left hand she fixed the knob with her right, then slowly turned it.

The door opened!

The temptation to dash out into the corridor and scream with relief was almost irresistible, but she forebore. She listened. She peeped out. No one was about. With beating heart she went out, closing the door inaudibly; she crept like a little mouse to the room next door, stole in, and flung herself on the bed. Immediately she did so, it flashed through her mind that *she had left her sponge-bag and towel in the dead man's room!*

In looking back upon her experience she always considered that that second expedition was the worst of all. She might have let the sponge-bag and towel remain there, only that the towel— she never used hotel towels—had neatly inscribed in the corner "M.B."

With furtive caution she managed to retrace her steps. She re-entered the dead man's room, reclaimed her property, and returned to her own. When the mission was accomplished she was indeed well-nigh spent. She lay on her bed and groaned feebly. At last she fell into a fevered sleep.

It was eleven o'clock when she awoke, and no one had been

to disturb her. The sun was shining, and the experiences of the night appeared a dubious nightmare. Surely she had dreamt it all?

With dread still burning in her heart she rang the bell. After a short interval of time the chambermaid appeared. The girl's eyes were bright with some uncontrollable excitement. No, she had not been dreaming. This girl had heard something.

"Will you bring me some tea, please?"

"Certainly, madame."

The maid drew back the curtains and fussed about the room. She was under a pledge of secrecy, but she could contain herself no longer. Suddenly she approached the bed and whispered, excitedly:

"Oh, madame, I am promised not to tell—but a terrible thing had happened! A man, a dead man, has been found in room one hundred and seventeen—a guest! Please not to say I tell you. But they have all been here—the gendarmes, the doctors, the inspectors. Oh, it is terrible—terrible!"

The little lady in the bed said nothing. There was indeed nothing to say. But Marie Louise Lancret was too full of emotional excitement to spare her.

"But the terrible thing is——Do you know who he was, madame? They say it is Boldhu, the man wanted for the murder of Jeanne Carreton in the barn at Vincennes. They say he strangled her, and then cut her up in pieces and hid her in two barrels, which he threw into the river. Oh, but he was a bad man, madame, a terrible bad man—and he died in the room next door. Suicide, they think; or was it an attack of the heart? Remorse; some shock, perhaps. Did you say a *cafè complet*, madame?"

"No, thank you, my dear—just a cup of tea—strong tea,"

"*Parfaitement,* madame."

The girl retired, and a little later a waiter entered the room with a tray of tea. She could never get over her surprise at this. It seemed so—well, indecorous for a man—although only a waiter—to enter a lady's bedroom. There was, no doubt, a great deal in what the dear dean said. They were certainly very peculiar, these French people—they had most peculiar notions. It was not the way they behaved at Easingstoke. She got farther under the sheets, but the waiter appeared quite indifferent to the situation. He put the tray down and retired.

When he had gone, she sat up and sipped her tea, which gradually warmed her. She was glad the sun was shining. She would have to get up soon. They said that her sister-in-law's boat was due to berth at one o'clock. That would give her time to dress comfortably, write to her brother, and then go down to the docks.

Poor man! So he had been a murderer, a man who cut up the bodies of his victims—and she had spent the night in his bedroom! They were certainly a most—how could she describe it?—people. Nevertheless she felt a little glad that at the end she had been there to kneel and pray by his bedside. Probably nobody else had ever done that. It was very difficult to judge people. Something at some time might have gone wrong. He might not have murdered the woman after all. People were often wrongly convicted. She herself. If the police had found her in that room at three o'clock that morning—— It is that which takes place in the heart which counts. One learns and learns. Had she not learnt that one can pray just as effectively lying under a bed as kneeling beside it? Poor man!

She washed and dressed herself and walked calmly down to the writing-room. There was no evidence of excitement among the other hotel guests. Probably none of them knew about the tragedy except herself. She went to a writing-table, and after profound meditation wrote as follows:

"My Dear Brother,—I arrived late last night, after a very pleasant journey. Everyone was very kind and attentive, the manager was sitting up for me. I nearly lost my spectacles in the restaurant-car, but a kind old gentleman found them and returned them to me. There was a most amusing American child on the train. I will tell you about her on my return. The people are very pleasant, but the food is peculiar, nothing plain and wholesome. I am going down to meet Annie at one o'clock. How have you been keeping, my dear? I hope you have not had any further return of the bronchial attacks. Please tell Lizzie that I remembered in the train on the way here that that large stone jar of marmalade that Mrs. Hunt made is behind those empty tins on the top shelf of the cupboard next to the coach-house. I wonder whether Mrs. Buller was able to come to evensong after all? This is a nice hotel, but I think Annie and I will stay at the Grand to-night, as the bedrooms here are rather noisy. Well, my dear, nothing more till I return. Do take care of yourself.

"Your loving sister,
"Millicent."

Yes, she couldn't tell Peter about it, neither in the letter nor when she went back to him. It was her duty not to tell him. It would only distress him: she felt convinced of it. In this curious foreign atmosphere the thing appeared possible, but in Easingstoke the mere recounting of the fantastic situation would be positively indelicate. There was no escaping that broad general fact—she had spent a night in a strange man's bedroom. Whether he was a gentleman or a criminal, even whether he was dead or alive, did not seem to mitigate the jar upon her sensibilities, or, rather, it would not mitigate the jar upon the peculiarly sensitive relationship between her brother and herself. To say that she had been to the bathroom, the knob of the door-handle came off in her hand, she was too frightened to awaken the sleeper or scream, she got under the bed—well, it was all perfectly true. Peter would believe her, but—one simply could not conceive such a situation in Easingstoke deanery. It would create a curious little barrier between them, as though she had been dipped in some mysterious solution which alienated her. It was her duty not to tell.

She put on her hat and went out to post the letter. She distrusted an hotel letter-box. One never knew who handled these letters. It was not a proper official way of treating them. She walked to the head post-office in Bordeaux.

The sun was shining. It was very pleasant walking about amongst these queer, excitable people, so foreign and different looking—and the *cafés* already crowded with chattering men and women; and the flower stalls, and the strange odour of—what was it? salt? brine? charcoal? A military band was playing in the square—very gay and moving. It was all life, and movement, and bustle—thrilling rather.

"I spent a night in a strange man's bedroom."

Little Miss Bracegirdle hunched her shoulders, hummed to herself, and walked faster. She reached the post-office, and found the large metal plate with the slot for letters and R.F. stamped above it. Something official at last! Her face was a little flushed—was it the warmth of the day, or the contact of movement and life?—as she put her letter into the slot. After posting it she put her hand into the slot and flicked it round to see that there were no foreign contraptions to impede its safe delivery. No, the letter had dropped safely in. She sighed contentedly, and walked off in the direction of the docks to meet her sister-in-law from Paraguay.

STACY AUMONIER